A SIERRA THE SEARCH DOG NOVEL

DIGGER

THE CASE OF THE CHIMERA KILLER

Darla –
All The best and
Stay Found!

ROBERT D. CALKINS

Digger
The Case of the Chimera Killer
By Robert D. Calkins

Callout Press

Published by Callout Press, Olalla, Washington, U.S.A.
Copyright © 2016 Robert D. Calkins
All rights reserved.

This is a work of fiction. Names, characters, businesses, places, events and incidents are either the products of the author's imagination or used in a fictitious manner. Any resemblance to actual persons, living or dead, or actual events is purely coincidental.

Copyeditor: Lisa Canfield, www.copycoachlisa.com
Proofreader: Clarisa Marcee, avenuecmedia@gmail.com
Cover and Interior design: Pear Creative, www.PearCreative.com

ISBN: 978-0-9971911-2-7

Library of Congress Control Number: 2016901040

To Mary Ann, without whom I'd be the one who was lost.

ACKNOWLEDGMENTS

The author wishes to acknowledge all those who contributed to the life experiences that make up this book.

To the teachers and staff at Benson Polytechnic High School in Portland, OR for teaching me that anything worth doing is worth doing well.

To the members of the Portland Police Bureau who demonstrated pride and integrity to a young man still finding his way.

To my former co-workers at the Washington State Patrol, who live their motto of "Service with Humility" every day.

And most closely aligned with this book, to all the search and rescue dog handlers who went before me, who so willingly shared their knowledge and experience, and to whom I will be forever thankful for your friendship and trust.

Chimera noun.

1. A mythological, fire-breathing monster with a lion's head, a goat's body, and a serpent's tail.

2. Any similarly grotesque-but-impossible monster with the key element being distinct, disparate parts, especially as depicted in decorative art.

3. Genetics: an individual, organ, or part consisting of tissues of diverse genetic constitution.

CHAPTER ONE
Trust Your Dog

Bryce knew Sierra had nailed it. He couldn't even see her in the thick woods, but knew she was about to find their hidden subject.

"Listen to her bell," he told the evaluator. "The sound has changed. It's more rhythmic. She's more animated, moving faster. She's headed right in on 'em."

Bryce Finn was the youngest dog handler ever certified as "mission ready" for search and rescue (SAR) in the state of Washington. He and his Golden Retriever Sierra earned their first SAR qualification when Bryce was just fifteen, and now were going through their required two-year recertification. Just as before, they'd be expected to find two subjects hidden in forty acres of thick western Washington underbrush in less than two hours.

The evaluator was introduced to Bryce as Lefty, a nickname no one understood because both his left arm and left leg were still attached. To maintain objectivity, Lefty was from a SAR team elsewhere in the state. Bryce's team was based in Kitsap County, directly across Puget Sound from the big city of Seattle.

There had been a rumor going around about Lefty, and Bryce wondered if it was true. He'd reportedly once declined to recertify an icon in the local search and rescue community after she'd found both subjects in record time. He didn't like the way she covered the search area, despite the positive result.

Bryce put the thought out of his mind. His focus had to be on searching, and especially on Sierra. At that moment, his focus was on her bell.

"There! It stopped. She's found one of them."

After a short pause, the bell began ringing again. No special rhythm this time, just ding-ding-ding. Sierra was making a beeline back to Bryce and Lefty. After finding the subject, Sierra had to return to Bryce and give her special signal, the one she only used when she'd found a subject. Sierra had gone so far ahead she couldn't see Bryce, and he wasn't allowed to call her or otherwise cue her behavior. Instead, he casually stepped on a branch. It broke, and Sierra homed in on the noise.

Under a downed tree, through the salal and around the blackberries she came. Sierra skidded to a halt right in front of Bryce and went into a perfect sit—her "trained indication."

"Good girlll! Show me!"

Now it was Bryce's turn to run, trying to keep up with Sierra as she led him back to the first of their two subjects. She glided easily through the woods, as one might expect for a descendant of the wolf.

Conversely, even young and fit humans aren't designed to run through thick Western Washington underbrush. Bryce's pack didn't help. To be safe and effective, a SAR dog handler must carry a triple load: supplies for themselves, supplies for the dog and supplies for the person they find. While searching, handlers generally take the path of least resistance. It's the dog's job to wiggle and squeeze through the brush, looking for scent.

In this case, finding the subject's scent was intended to be tricky. The "missing" subject was in a hole previously occupied by the root ball of a large tree. When the tree blew over in a storm, the roots pulled up out of the ground, leaving a six-foot-deep indentation in the forest floor. Human scent can move in funny ways when the subject is below ground level, but Sierra had no trouble working it out. She now stood next to the man, barking. It was her way of saying "Hurry up! It's payday!"

Bryce did a quick high five with the subject and tossed Sierra her ball. The high five wasn't just celebration—he'd taught Sierra that he needed to touch the subject before she got her reward. That would help assure she'd always bring him all the way back.

Bryce also broke into a falsetto voice that would make any opera singer proud. "Good-girl-oh-you're-the-best-what-a-great-dog-you-found-me-you-found-me!"

"Belly-rubz-butt-scratches…yessss…belly-rubs-and-butt-scratches-for-you, good girl!"

The subject was smiling brightly, happy to have been found. But the job wasn't done. Sierra had done the searching part; it was now Bryce's turn to do the rescue part.

"Hi. My name's Bryce and I'm with Search and Rescue. What's your name?"

"Uhhhhh…Mike."

"How'd you get here, Mike?"

"I don't remember," Mike said, staying right in character.

"Are you hurt?"

"No, I'm just fine. I'm pretty warm though. I feel like taking off my clothes. Can I have a soda?"

Alarm bells. When someone is freezing to death, the brain gets confused and makes the person think they're burning up. They start taking off their clothes. People who've died of hypothermia are frequently found completely undressed in glacial streams.

"Mike, you need to stay right there and keep your clothes on. I think you're so cold that your brain might not be working right. We need to get you warmed up. Can I check you for other injuries?"

"OK…but I'm fine, really. I'm just hot."

Bryce went about a primary and secondary survey. He'd already determined the subject was confused and hypothermic. That would be trouble enough to treat. Now he had to make sure his patient wasn't bleeding from an unseen injury or suffering a broken limb.

"Mike, where's your pack? Do you have a sleeping bag in there?"

Mike pointed silently to his pack, his arm barely moving. Bryce simulated getting the bag out, and gingerly getting Mike into it. Too much movement by a hypothermic patient can trigger a heart attack. He turned to the evaluator.

"The patient is stable and we've started the rewarming process. Time to call base and let them know we've found the first one," he told Lefty as he reached for his two-way radio.

4

"Search base, Dog 44."

"Base, go ahead."

"Search Base, we've located subject M. Initial indications are severe hypothermia but no other injuries. We've got him in a simulated sleeping bag, I've simulated placing chemical hand warmers against his wrists and thighs, and he's drinking from my simulated thermos. I have coordinates when you're ready."

"Ready to copy."

"Coordinates follow: 10-Tango 0518654. Next line: 5270894. This will definitely be a pack-out, but there's no hurry. We have what we need to get him warmed up and, until his temp is closer to normal, we don't want to be jostling him around."

"Good job! Subject M is magically healed and can return to base. You can resume your test. Base out."

Well not quite. There was still the job of trying to pump Mike for info on his still-missing friend. On evaluations it never worked, and usually ended up with threats to use a rubber hose. But Bryce had to show Lefty he'd remembered that step.

"Mike, when did you last see your hiking partner? Which way should we look for her?"

"Uhhh…I don't remember," Mike said, slipping right back into character. "She was here a minute ago."

Bryce smiled at Lefty, and was surprised to see him crack a very small smile in return. They then set off to cover the rest of the forty acres, which would be no easy task. The area was filled with thigh-high salal, chest-high ferns and the occasional blackberry sticker pulling at their sleeves.

Lefty, from eastern Washington, was used to desert and scrub.

5

On that side, K9 tests covered 160 acres instead of forty. But he'd given other tests on the "wet side" of the state and understood the differences. He complimented Bryce on how well he moved through the thick brush.

"That's pretty tough for me. I just hit the big 6-0," Lefty admitted. "In dog years, that makes me 420 years old."

It took Bryce a second to do the math and then he smiled. "You do pretty well, sir. Are we back on the clock?"

Time was starting to be a factor. Bryce and Sierra now had to cover the remaining area with less than an hour left in the test. If they failed, they'd lose their qualification to respond on search missions around the state. Their team was short of qualified handlers, and needed them.

More importantly, he would make his teammates look bad. His team was the only one in the state that permitted handlers under the age of eighteen. If he failed today's recert, the team's decision to allow such a young handler would look very bad. He couldn't let them down.

"Yes. You've treated your subject and rewarded your dog. We're back on the search clock."

A quick look at his GPS device told Bryce which parts of the forty acres they hadn't yet covered. He didn't need to walk the whole area. He just had to get Sierra's nose downwind of it all. The next step was to check the wind direction. A bottle of over-the-counter nasal spray, emptied of medicine and refilled with water, was the perfect tool for checking wind.

A quick spritz into the air and then, "C'mon, Sierra. Let's check this way."

The hardest part of being a search and rescue dog handler is knowing when to depart from your own search plan and follow the dog. In the woods, the dog is in charge. The handler guides it through the general search area, but when the dog decides to go in a specific direction, it's up to the handler to follow. Bryce had a basic search pattern in mind, and was waiting for Sierra to react to scent carried on the wind.

It wasn't happening. Time ticked on. Thirty minutes remaining, then fifteen. Things were getting tight. Bryce resorted to plunging through even difficult brush, just to get Sierra's nose to every possible place that scent could be. Not only was no one there, it didn't appear anyone had ever been there. Sierra was showing no signs of smelling anyone at all, even someone who might have walked through the area the day before. There was just...nothing.

Now Bryce was starting to second-guess himself. Were the two subjects close together? Should they have circled around Mike to make sure the second person wasn't just a tree or two away? Was Mike actually the second subject, and they'd missed the first just as they started? Should they go back and recheck that area? Bryce had to push such thoughts out of his mind, focus on the problem, and trust Sierra.

The sound of the bell changed again. Sierra was moving with purpose now, in a single direction and through very thick brush. That would have been a good sign, except that she was moving out of the assigned search area. Bryce started to call her back, then stopped himself.

"*Sierra has never let me down,*" he thought. "*I have to trust her. Maybe she smells another searcher or a backpacker who picked today to hike here. But I have to follow her.*"

They crossed the designated boundary, a logging road through the remote patch of woods. Sierra never hesitated; she crossed the road quickly and went right into a patch of woods across the way. Bryce followed, but Lefty started to lag behind. Bryce could feel himself tensing up, and had to relax. Dogs can tell when their handlers are upset.

He continued to follow, and then it happened. The bell stopped ringing for a moment and just as quickly Sierra was on her way back. She'd found somebody alright, but outside the search area. With less than five minutes to go in the test, there was probably not enough time left to make up for a mistake. Bryce struggled to be positive when Sierra came screaming up and left skid marks going into a sit position.

"Good girl. Show me!" and off they went. Lefty lagged even further behind, and not because of his age. Bryce took that as a hint that the wheels were indeed coming off this test. Lefty, in turn, made a mental note to praise Bryce for trusting his dog. He expected to offer that as a way of taking the sting out of failure.

Sierra led Bryce back to a young woman sitting under a tree. "My name's Bryce and I'm from Search and Rescue. What's your name?"

"Chris."

"Um, we're supposed to be looking for Chris, but over across the road. Are you part of our test?"

"Yes. See my fake broken leg and fake bloody forehead."

Lefty, who'd set up the test, had heard the voices and recognized Chris's. He was now hurrying to join them. Despite his joke about being more than four centuries old, he suddenly moved pretty well through the underbrush.

"What the hell are you doing over here?" Lefty said to Chris. He caught himself immediately. "Go with it," he whispered to Bryce. "It's her."

Bryce played briefly with Sierra, and asked Lefty to make the belly rubs and butt scratches especially good. He focused on evaluating and treating his patient. Then he got on the radio.

"Search Base, Dog 44. We've found subject C and are treating for a head wound and broken left leg. This will also be a pack-out, and in real life I'd recommend getting her out first. Subject M would still need to be rewarming. Let me know when you're ready for coordinates."

Base replied, *"Good call on the medical, that's the recommendation we were looking for. Go ahead with coordinates."*

Bryce sent the numbers, and the base operator's voice immediately changed for the worse.

"Are you sure you're reading that right? Those coordinates are outside your assigned search area."

"We are indeed out of our search area, but I'm informed by the evaluator that this is the correct subject. We'll clear it all up when we get back to base."

"OK...base copies...I guess. Out."

Sierra had been right all along. It was Chris who'd hidden in the wrong place. A missed setting on her GPS put Chris 200 yards from where she was supposed to be. Lefty had failed to catch the error, and he took what should have been his own embarrassment out on Chris.

"I showed you how to work the GPS, and I described the search area verbally. Do you remember me mentioning that you'd turn right off the road, not left?"

"Yes, I'm sorry...but they found me anyway."

Lefty continued to lay it on Chris. "That's not the point. The

9

point is to demonstrate the dog's skills and if you can't even hide where I tell you, how can we do that? What if they *hadn't* found you because you weren't there to be found? I'd be in quite a pickle trying to decide whether they deserve a passing grade."

"Well, do we?" Bryce interrupted. He wondered if the foul-up would negate the whole test.

"Yesss, you pass," Lefty answered begrudgingly. "You found both subjects and covered your area…acceptably." Lefty was too irritated with Chris to offer a real compliment. He stopped talking, still tight-jawed over a mistake that, in the end, was his own responsibility.

Chris turned and spoke to Bryce, ignoring Lefty but sending him a message nonetheless.

"Bryce, you and Sierra did wonderfully despite my screw-up. You found me all this way outside your assigned search area. I don't really care what Lefty thinks, but if somebody in my family ever goes missing, I want you two looking for them."

CHAPTER TWO
Runaway

Nobody ever looked at her, and especially not cute guys. She was sure he was checking her out, but he seemed totally out of her class. The shoes were Nike, the tight-fitting shirt from Under Armour, and his perfectly flat stomach probably came from that expensive gym down the street.

Was he a cop? Too young, she thought. Close enough to her own age that something might actually develop.

Maybe it was her blouse. She didn't usually wear it that low cut, but it made it easier to put small items down her bra. A set of earrings here, a pendant there, maybe even a ring if the clerk forgot to put one back.

She moved to the next aisle, and a few minutes later he was there again. Even at fifteen, she understood some men had a thing for large chests. But this fellow didn't look like her step-father's friends, who deliberately let her hear their crude remarks. He also didn't look like the boys at school, who were kind enough to at least whisper. He wasn't creepy which was, in its own way, creepier.

She decided to leave, despite only having taken three watches. They were in a coat pocket—even *her* bra didn't have room for three men's watches. She made her way past the customer service desk and out the door.

"Excuse me, miss. Did you forget to pay for something back in the store?"

"*Oh God…he WAS watching me*," she thought. "*I should have known he wasn't interested in ME. I've got to get to the car.*"

"I didn't buy anything. They didn't have what I was looking for," she said, picking up her pace. "What's it to you?"

"I work for the store. You'll need to come back inside with me."

"Get away from me. I'm not going anywhere." She was almost in a run. "I'm going home."

She ratcheted up her attempt to get away, and the guard ratcheted up his attempt to catch her. He reached for her arm, but she was too quick. He managed to brush her with his fingertips, but missed getting a grip.

She looked for the car, but her mom and David were probably too out of it to notice her plight. She'd lost count of the times she'd return from stealing to find them nodding off, having shot up their drugs while waiting for her to arrive with the day's booty.

Her fifteen-year-old mind, not addled by drugs, was working in overdrive. She decided to use the guard's youthful appearance against him. He did indeed appear young enough to be a suitor. Better yet, a rejected suitor.

"You expect me to believe you went out with her but didn't sleep with her!?" she screamed. "Everybody knows she's the school slut. That's the only reason any boy goes out with her! I never want to see you again." She hoped some chivalrous customer would assume she was being harassed by a boyfriend and intervene.

It worked.

"Hey buddy, the girl obviously doesn't want to talk to you…"

"Store security!" the guard shouted. His physical appearance had been crafted to make him appear young, but his voice had an air of adult authority. "Young lady, you're under arrest! And mister, don't butt in."

But the kind man had butted in just enough, initially stepping in front of the security guard. She now had a decent head start. David finally heard the yelling. He started the car and laid a patch of rubber through the parking lot, weaving between shoppers with carts…and kids. He did a creditable slalom and greatly shortened the distance. It wasn't enough. The guard caught up just as she reached for the car door.

"I told you…you're under arrest," he said, grabbing her arm. "Don't make this any harder than it has to be."

The guard was on his way to being a police officer. He'd studied criminal justice in college, and had even taken some private classes in defensive tactics. He knew how to control a resisting suspect and had done so in the past. She, on the other hand, was a panicked teenager who was angry at being expected to steal, and even angrier at the prospect of being arrested.

The fingernails across the eyes came first. His hands instinctively rose to his face, exposing his solar plexus and points further south. Her knee found his zipper, and she didn't stop there. She was no longer trying to get away. She was angry at the whole damned world and taking it out on this poor fellow. She didn't

13

fight like a girl.

The guard was bent over, holding his groin and trying not to puke. She delivered a closed fist to his temple, grabbed his hair and did it again. As he was sagging forward she kneed him again, this time in the face. He fell completely back and hit his head on the pavement. The fight was over.

"JEE-sus. Just get in the car," David yelled. "We gotta go!"

The cantaloupe sound of the guard's head hitting pavement had broken her angry trance. She turned, jumped in, and they sped out. Hopefully the only person trained to get a license number was still hearing birdies and seeing stars.

"What did you get?" David asked.

"What do you mean 'what did I get?' What I almost got was *arrested.* I was sure I was being watched, so I bailed. If I go to jail you get nothing."

David had made it clear on many occasions that if she wanted to live in his home, she'd have to earn her keep. He'd been arrested plenty of times and it was no big deal. At fifteen she'd go to juvie and probably be released before dark.

And, he frequently reminded her, there were worse things than stealing to "earn her keep."

When they got home, the watches came out from her coat. She'd been so scared she wouldn't take them out until they were all safely back in the double-wide trailer off Highway 3.

There were three watches, of the more expensive kind. She had been surprised the store left them out, with no one watching. Well, actually, someone had been watching. She felt terrible for the security guard. He was just doing his job, and she'd probably given him a concussion. Could people die from concussions?

"THREE LOUSY WATCHES?! THAT'S ALL YOU GOT? How are we supposed to feed you and us on three lousy watches?" David started to look wild-eyed, like he needed another fix. She tried to explain.

"The guy was watching me. He kept popping up in every aisle I went to. I started to think he liked me, but I should have known better with these crummy clothes. No cute guy is going to be interested in me."

David wasn't satisfied. They needed money all right, and soon. All three of them knew it wasn't hunger driving his tantrum. He was starting to come off his last high, and needed a fix. The needier he got, the less rational he got. Her mom still had some vestige of material protectiveness left. She told David to cool it, and they'd figure something out.

She knew her mother had done worse than steal to get the drugs they craved. Her own ineptness at thievery probably meant her mother would have to humiliate herself again that night.

She went to her room and thought. She couldn't live like this. She couldn't, *wouldn't*, steal for a living. Not only was it wrong, but it was how David and her mom fed their drug habits. She was enabling their self-destruction.

Something would have to change. She couldn't fix them, but maybe she could fix her own situation. She made the same decision millions of other young people made when they didn't have good role models in their lives. It was a bad decision, but to her it was the only choice she had. She would leave home. Right then.

She began packing things into the only decent backpack she'd managed to steal. That was funny, she thought. Using stolen goods to get out of a life of crime.

Her mom and David were arguing when she came out of the bedroom. At least she didn't have to worry about them pursuing her. They were too busy figuring out how to get some money and where to score their drugs. She heard her mother whisper, "I'm not doing that again…ever."

"I'm leaving! You two have a wonderful life together…without me." They stopped, looked at her, and went back to their discussion. Apparently maternal protectiveness only went so far. The door slammed and she was gone.

She was hardly off the porch before she discovered her first problem. She knew with great certainty what she was running from. She hadn't yet figured out what, or where, she was running *to*. She didn't have many friends, and none close enough that she could crash at their house.

Despite her one attribute, boys weren't attracted to her. Girls didn't like her either. In the school lunchroom she'd hear them talking about BFFs and sleepovers, about getting pedis before the prom. The closest she ever got to a pedicure was stealing nail polish. The same horrible life she was running from also meant she had no friends to ask for help.

But anything had to be better than what she'd called home. With no bus ticket, her transportation would be her thumb. She used a different digit in a final goodbye wave to David and her mom.

It was cold and raining as she tried to catch a ride. She'd heard there was a shelter in Belfair, and maybe a real counseling program in Shelton. She stood along Highway 3, bathed in the lights from Bremerton Airport, hoping for a ride to anyplace.

The pickup pulled over just beyond her and she ran to catch up. It was one of those four-door models with the long bed. It was old, beat-up and very dirty. A decal on the fender said "four-wheel drive," and this truck looked like it had indeed gone off-road a lot. This rig was no "grocery-getter," the kind that only go to Costco on the weekends.

The driver seemed old and harmless, though the passenger compartment smelled funny. But it wasn't raining inside and there was room for her pack right next to a wet dog in the back seat. Apparently wet dogs really do stink, she thought. She had heard the expression, but had no experience with animals. The only time she had a pet was when David stole a dog from someone's yard, and only for a few hours until he could sell it online.

The driver asked where she was headed.

"I don't know. I just have to get away from my parents. I guess I'm sort of a runaway, I hope you don't mind."

The driver didn't react at all. Not a turn of the head, nor a blink of the eye. "I split from my parents when I was thirteen. Just because someone is older doesn't make them better," the driver said.

"Wow! Really? What a coincidence! What did you do when you first left? Where did you go? Where did you spend that first night? How did you eat? Did you get robbed?"

"Whoa, slow down. I'm here, aren't I? This isn't a Cadillac and my shirt isn't from Nordstrom's, but I came out OK. You will too. I'm headed out towards Belfair."

"There's supposed to be a shelter in Belfair. Have you heard of it?"

"It's not really in Belfair itself. It's outside of town at a remote spot in the woods. Keeps the kids from being tempted by street stuff and all. Yeah, I know where it is," the driver said, looking at

17

his watch. "I suppose I can drop you off."

The traffic was light, and they were in Belfair quickly. She became confused when the driver made two quick rights, and headed out of town on a county road.

"Like I said, the shelter isn't really in Belfair," the driver offered without prompting. "It's off Old Belfair Road by the golf course, about halfway to Gorst."

After a left up the hill and a turn onto an unpaved road, she wondered if there could really be a shelter in such a remote spot. Wonder turned to panic when the truck turned onto an even rougher road with Scotch broom brushing up against both sides of the truck. They couldn't possibly be headed to any kind of real shelter. She started looking for a place to jump out.

"The door's locked. You can't get out," the driver said in the calmest of voices.

"Why? Where are you taking me? There can't be a shelter up here. I don't have any money to give you and...and..."

"Don't make such a fuss. It's unseemly and I don't want your money. We'll be there shortly."

"There? Where is 'there?' I don't want to be *there*. You said we were going to a shelter in Belfair."

She remembered the folding knife in her purse. She didn't carry it regularly, because they weren't allowed at school. She was glad now that she'd remembered to grab it before leaving. Her purse was on the floorboard, right between her feet.

"Ah ah ah...there's nothing in there you need right now. Put the purse down and keep your hands in your lap." It would have made more sense had the driver been yelling, but he was scary-calm. The kind of scary-calm that made her do as told.

"See, we're here. You'll like this place."

He'd pulled into what was little more than a turnaround which would hide the truck. He got out, walked casually around the truck, and unlocked the door with his key. She came out fighting.

She still felt bad for the security guard, but had completely cleaned his clock. By comparison, she thought, this old man should be no trouble.

She was wrong.

First, she pushed him, and tried to knee him between the legs. He dodged left and blocked the blow. For an old man, he was very quick.

She tried the eye gouge that had worked so well at the store. The old man slapped her hand away, and swept his leg under hers. She fell and hit her head on the car's door sill. She was dazed but still functioning, and again tried to punch her way out of trouble.

He continued to block and parry as the security guard had not. None of her blows landed, and the driver's calm response only heightened her fears. No commands, no orders to stop or submit, not even a grunt as he blocked her kicks and punches. It was as if he expected them, and was neither surprised nor angered. He simply turned away every blow, and then a powerful hand smacked the side of her head.

This time she wondered if she'd be the one with the concussion. She was dazed but still thinking. At least when he hit her, he knocked her a few feet away. There was now some space. She decided to run.

The logging road was uneven ground, and being overweight she was not fast. But surely she'd be faster than this old man. She was.

She was not, however, faster than his dog. The old gray-bearded German Shepherd, laying in the back seat for the entire trip to what wasn't Belfair, had yet to make a sound.

She heard some talking, and looked over her shoulder. The man seemed to be whispering in the dog's ear. He had a hold on its collar and it seemed ready to come after her.

Then he turned the dog loose. When he'd closed the gap to a few feet, he jumped, hitting her right in the back. On the ground and with the wind knocked out of her, she expected to be bitten. But just as suddenly as the dog had hit her, it retreated without so much as a growl.

By that time the old man had caught up. He tossed a squeaky toy to the dog, and then pounced on her. The new blows came in earnest. She pleaded, she squirmed, she screamed—all to no avail. There was no one to hear her, late at night, on a logging road, near Belfair, Washington.

Her adrenaline reserve ran out. The strength borne of panic turned to fatigue, and then to exhaustion. Resistance ended. All she had left were sobs. Those too would end in fairly short order.

CHAPTER THREE
Service Day

"What's your dog's name?"

"Sierra," Bryce answered for the fiftieth time that day. "She's a search and rescue dog."

Bryce's school was having Service Day, when students who volunteer in the community get to show their schoolmates what they do. His booth had been set up in the hall right outside the girl's restroom. He originally felt slighted, until he realized the value of that location.

Teenage girls love dogs. Bryce had only recently become interested in girls, having been totally into dogs ever since he could remember. Over the past few months, he'd started feeling the need to expand his horizons.

"She's beautiful," the young lady commented.

Bryce had a standard answer for that question.

"Shhh. Don't let her hear you say that," he whispered. "It'll go to her head." That remark usually got people laughing and asking more questions.

"Yeah, I had a dog once, and she was really the queen. She knew how beautiful she was, alright. Have you found any missing people?"

"A few," was Bryce's understated answer. In fact, Sierra had been very successful in the field. At seventeen, Bryce had already learned that those who brag the most search the least. He was careful to be modest.

"She's a pretty good dog, and makes up for some of my failings," he added.

Bryce had seen the young lady around school before. No, "seen" was not the right word. He'd *noticed* her. She always seemed to have a smile on her face, was dressed a little more neatly than the other girls, and her hair was done. No PJs and flip flops on this girl. He figured she had started mid-term, because he hadn't seen her at orientation.

They weren't in any classes together and hadn't had a reason to talk. That was OK, because Bryce didn't have much practice talking to girls. Now, thanks to Sierra, this particular girl was talking to *him*.

"My name's Bryce. You're new here, aren't you?"

"Couple of months. My folks split up, so Mom and I moved here for her new job. My dad got the dog, and I don't see them… anyway, I really like this school. Everybody's really nice."

"And your name is…?"

"Katie! Katie Lovering. I'm sorry, I was just looking at Sierra and

22

missing my girl."

Katie was stroking Sierra's chest instead of petting her on the head. That told Bryce she knew a little bit about dogs. Most people try to pet the top of the head, which dogs don't really like. Most humans wouldn't like it if a huge oversized hand came down on top of their head.

"She really is beautiful, even if I shouldn't say it. How do you train search and rescue dogs?"

"Actually, the dogs train us," Bryce admitted. "Dogs would have gone extinct long ago if they couldn't use their nose to find food. We just show them what odor we want them to find, and what we want them to do when they find it. The hard part is turning off our brains and letting the dog be in charge."

With that simple sentence, Bryce Finn had just described the essence of K9 search and rescue. People of all ages, all education levels and all walks of life have failed at search and rescue because they couldn't give up the illusion of being smarter than their dog.

Dogs can't do brain surgery. They chew couches, dig up gardens, and bark at themselves in the mirror. Really special dogs greet visitors with a piece of underwear off the bedroom floor—the dirtier or frillier the better.

But in the wilderness, dogs rule. Handlers sometimes have trouble accepting that their dog's nose is a better search tool than the human brain. Letting the dog decide what direction to go is hard for them. Human handlers frequently try to direct the dog according to what they think a missing subject would have done. They're virtually always wrong.

Bryce was convinced his success in SAR had come because he was willing to yield to Sierra. Teenagers are used to taking orders from adults, so taking orders from a dog he loved wasn't a huge leap.

"I'd love to see her search sometime," Katie hinted.

"We're wrapping up in here, and we're going to do a demonstration outside. You'd be welcome to come watch," Bryce replied, completely failing to get Katie's point. Though inexperienced at talking to girls, Bryce had already mastered the manly art of missing hints.

"That would be fun," Katie replied coolly. She was trying to choose between strengthening her hint or being too forward. She decided to go slow.

The light was beginning to flicker on for Bryce. Was she asking to see him again, outside school? No matter, he'd already picked his path and couldn't switch now. "The demo's in about twenty minutes, right outside the front door. We'll do a cadaver problem."

"Eewww, that sounds gross. But I'll be there. I need to run down to the library and return a book, and then I'll see you outside."

As Katie left, Bryce handed her a baseball card with Sierra's picture on it. Katie knew he'd given one to every person who'd walked up to the booth, but not much had gone right in her life recently. The card was like Bryce had offered her flowers. By that night it would be taped to the mirror above her dresser.

Bryce talked to a few more of his fellow students, answered their questions and handed out more trading cards. But he kept thinking about Katie and hoping she really would show up for the cadaver demonstration. He knew that having your dog find dead human tissue wasn't the way to score points with most girls. He was already starting to suspect that Katie wasn't "most girls."

The afternoon was good for searching. It was cool, and it had rained the night before. There was a steady breeze from a single direction, not a swirling wind that could scatter scent in many directions. Bryce had set up a no-fail problem for Sierra. He'd just obtained some fresh bloody gauze from the school nurse. A freshman had cut his hand in shop class, and the school nurse had responded. She was always on the lookout for items contaminated with human blood, and had given the leftover gauze to Bryce.

Although cadaver dogs frequently look for bodies, more often they look for parts of bodies. It's a sad fact that when someone dies alone in a remote area, animals will eventually see their body as food. They scatter the remains, take pieces back to a den, or hide them so that they don't lose them to bigger predators.

For that reason, cadaver dog handlers learn to work their dogs on sources much smaller than entire bodies. Well, that and the fact that it's pretty hard to keep an entire human body in the family freezer.

A small crowd had gathered for the demonstration and Bryce looked to see if Katie was among them. She was, and was smiling when he looked her way. He smiled in return, but needed to stay focused on his demonstration.

The nurse's bloody gauze was in a small Mason jar with holes drilled in the lid. Bryce had worn rubber gloves when placing the item, so his scent wouldn't be on it. The only odor present would be that of the decaying human blood on the gauze.

The jar was in a large flower bed next to the building, underneath a very bushy plant that completely hid the item. Sierra would have to use her nose, not her eyes, to find it.

Now it was time to get the crowd fired up and have a little fun. Bryce had noticed one of the football stars in the back, a huge defensive lineman named Jeff. The young man was known for his booming voice as well as his ability to deliver booming hits on the field.

"Hey Jeff, can you come here for a second? We're going to need your help."

Jeff stepped forward, though somewhat confused. In his mind, this Finn dude had always been a geek. A poindexter. A bit of a wimp for playing with dogs. Jeff had hunted birds with the family Labrador and that was real dog work. He was really only there to kill time and because the crowd was mostly girls.

"One of the most important things we do is reward our dogs properly after a find," Bryce told the crowd. "Would you work for hours on a hot day for no paycheck?"

Jeff didn't respond. The entire crowd picked up on the awkward silence.

Bryce continued. "We give them their favorite toy and heap massive praise on them, but we have to speak in their language. Jeff, can you speak dog?"

"Uh…woof woof?"

"Nice try, but it's not the words. Dogs can learn words, like "car" and "treat" and a few key phrases. But what they really understand is the tone of your voice. Jeff, I picked you because your voice is so deep. Most everything you'd say to a dog would sound like a correction. When dogs growl, they do it in a low voice. When they're happy they're all yippy and high pitched.

"Can you be yippy and high-pitched?" Bryce challenged the jock.

"Uh…weef weef," Jeff managed to cough up. The crowd laughed and it actually hurt Jeff's throat to speak in such a high tone.

"Good start," Bryce said. "Now let's add some praise to the mix.

Can you say 'good dog, you da best, you da best, belly rubs and butt scratches' in your highest voice?"

Jeff tried, and got about halfway through the sentence before coughing up some phlegm and resorting to his normal deep voice. The crowd was getting into it now, watching this huge football player try to talk like a girl. The principal heard the squealing and came over, thinking something was wrong.

"OK, Jeff will lead the effort, but when you hear me say 'reward!' everybody cheers, claps and hollers for Sierra. This is all a big game to her, and to keep her interested the paycheck needs to be huge. Today, you're all part of that paycheck."

"Question?" came a comment from the crowd. "Do you ever reward with food?"

"Some handlers do, but that doesn't work for Sierra," Bryce replied. "I tried giving her food when we first started training and it was hilarious. She wanted the food, but didn't want to spit out her ball to eat it. She's psychotic for her ball, which is what I use to reward her. You could see the wheels turning in her head, trying to figure out how to eat the chunk of hot dog without giving up her ball."

"Does she only find dead people?"

"Oh, no. Her bread and butter is finding live people. We didn't even expose her to deceased remains until she was solid on live finds. Any other questions…anybody?"

Hearing none, Bryce got Sierra out of her crate and took her to the downwind side of the big garden.

"If this goes right, you'll see her weave back and forth in sort of a cone fashion with the point of the cone right at the source I've hidden. It's bloody gauze from somebody who cut themselves in shop class this week. If you're here, by the way, thanks for your sacrifice."

A bandaged hand went up in the back of the crowd. "You're welcome," was the sarcastic response.

It was time for Sierra to work. "Find Digger" was the command, and Bryce didn't need to say it twice. Sierra knew full well what "Digger" was, and that ball time would follow. She immediately set about working the cone of scent. Back and forth she went across the flower bed, smashing a couple of the more delicate plants, much to the principal's dismay.

The crowd stepped forward for a better look, which Bryce took to mean the demonstration was going well. Sierra continued to work the cone of scent, getting to an ever smaller area near the source.

She shot past the item and was suddenly upwind of it. The scent was gone. She quickly hooked a U-turn and came back to it, spending some extra time sniffing the correct bush. She sat, staring at the bush.

"Show me!" was Bryce's response. Sierra's nose went under the bush at which point Bryce tossed Sierra's tennis ball in from the side. The goal was for Sierra to think the ball had come from the source of odor.

"Reward!" Bryce shouted, and continued to praise Sierra. "Good girl…yay…woohoo! Belly-rubz-and-butt-scratches-for-you…da-best-girl-in-the-whole-world! C'mon, Jeff, get in here. Everybody…clap and cheer!"

The fact that speaking in falsetto hurt Jeff's throat was no longer an issue. He had gone from cynic to supporter in the couple of minutes he'd been watching Sierra. He'd seen his Lab work a scent cone to find a bird he'd shot, but hadn't previously understood what his dog had been doing. He'd learned something from this non-athlete wimp, and realized that Sierra was the real deal.

"Good girl, yay, whatta-dog-whatta-dog! Roll over and I'll give you some belly rubs!" Jeff cried, in a voice that seemed three octaves higher than normal.

The crowd was laughing and clapping as well. They were impressed with Sierra, but it was even more fun watching one of the most macho men on the football team rolling around with a dog, tossing her ball and squeaking his praise. Somebody was taking cell phone video and it would be on Facebook by that night. An hour before, Jeff might have cared. Right now, he was just thinking about how to better praise his own dog for retrieving birds.

Katie had stepped to the front of the crowd. "I noticed she overshot and came back to it. Is that normal?"

"Totally. In fact, sometimes she'll do it deliberately if the wind is weird," was Bryce's answer. "I've seen her leave the scent pool, hook around to a completely different side of the search area, and come back in on it from another direction."

Bryce didn't mention that some human handlers had to be taught what Sierra had picked up naturally. When a handler sees their dog struggling and they suspect an odor source is present, the book says to take them out of the area and approach from a different direction.

"Why did you have your hands in your pockets while she searched?" Katie again.

"I'm trying to not give her any hints or any direction. She searches much better when I shut my mouth and put my hands in my pockets. She's the one with the nose and I'm potentially a distraction. When she's getting close and really working, I try to

29

find a tree to casually lean against."

The crowd was starting to thin out. Katie continued to ask questions. Bryce began to focus on that conversation while letting Jeff play with Sierra. Suddenly, he realized things had gone quiet. He looked around, and Sierra was nowhere to be seen. There was a road nearby and although Sierra was not a wanderer, roads always made him nervous. He mentally kicked himself for losing track of his dog.

"Hey, over here." It was the clumsy freshman who'd been the source of the bloody gauze. "Your dog seems to like my hand."

Sierra was in a perfect sit, staring at the young man's bandaged hand. Bryce knew in a flash what was happening, and that it presented a huge training opportunity.

"Stand perfectly still, please," Bryce said in the calmest voice he could muster. "Just let her stare at your hand for a minute."

Bryce slipped Sierra's ball into the freshman's other hand and whispered "when I tell you, slip it to her *with your injured hand,* please."

Bryce waited a few moments and then gave Sierra the "show me" command. She leaned forward slightly, and touched her nose to the bandaged hand.

"Yay...good girl, Sierra. You found Digger you found Digger you found Digger!! Give her the ball!"

Experienced dog handlers know that rewarding "from the source" is an excellent way to improve a dog's alert. If the dog thinks their toy is coming from the source of the odor, they won't leave it for any reason. Having the chance to actually hand Sierra the ball from a bandaged hand would reinforce that training like nothing Bryce had ever tried. He'd remember that in the future.

Bryce hadn't intended for Sierra to get a second find as part of the demonstration. She'd shown great initiative by walking up to the person and doing her trained indication, the perfect sit, without being told to "find Digger."

"Time to head back to class," said the principal. "I wish I could let you take Sierra with you, but she'd be a huge distraction. Do you have someplace you can kennel her up?"

Sierra's kennel was in Bryce's fifteen-year-old Chevy Suburban. The day was cool, and Bryce had parked under a tree. He'd put a bowl of water in the kennel with her, and Sierra would be fine for the couple of class periods left in the day.

The principal had been wrong about the distraction. Sierra wasn't the problem.

CHAPTER FOUR
An Inconvenient Possibility

Elroy Patterson hated county council meetings. As the elected sheriff of Kitsap County, he didn't have to attend, but the council did control his annual budget, so keeping tabs on them was a good idea. He went to as many of their blah blah blah drone-fests as he could, so long as they didn't interfere with important work like sorting his sock drawer.

There had been no choice about attending this meeting, however, and no doubt that he'd hate it more than most.

Patterson would be there with his hand extended, asking for money for a situation no one wanted to admit was even possible.

In the previous two months, three women had been found dead in rural parts of south Kitsap County. The bodies were all thoroughly decomposed, meaning they'd been killed weeks to months before. Once ID'd by the county coroner, all the victims turned out to have similar backgrounds. They were teenage runaways, drug users and prostitutes, all generally acknowledged to be low-hanging fruit for someone who likes killing.

Patterson couldn't say for sure there was a serial killer at work. Crime was rampant in neighboring Pierce County. Could those in the drug trade simply be crossing the Narrows Bridge to dispose of their murder victims in a more rural area? Maybe one particular gang had found a dumping ground they liked. Patterson had to admit it was possible. He also had to make sure he wasn't joining the rest of the elected leadership in Kitsap County by putting his head in the sand.

Patterson had been warned about political ostriches during his time at the FBI National Academy. He'd attended the three-month course along with police executives from around the country. The Academy's main purpose is to take experienced street cops and get them used to seeing the big picture on police leadership. One of the many lessons Patterson heard was that local political officials never want to admit a serial killer might be preying on their community.

They'd deny it until it was undeniable, the FBI had said, and then they'd look around for someone to blame. The pattern, repeated many times in many cities, was to accuse police of not taking the disappearances seriously because most victims of serial killers are not upstanding citizens.

As usual, the politicians wanted to have it both ways. They were in denial now, but positioning themselves to blame police for being slow to act. Sheriff Patterson was going to make sure that didn't happen to him and especially not to those who worked for him. He was the most loyal of bosses, exceptionally so for an elected official. There had been many times when he could have shifted blame from himself onto an employee, but he always refused. When something went awry he took responsibility in public and corrected his people in private.

But there would be nothing private tonight. Just the opposite. Patterson would be going public with his concerns. Best case, he might get a little money for a deeper dive into the cases. At the very least, he'd head off accusations that he didn't take the cases seriously. He'd rather be accused of being Chicken Little than of not caring about young women whose lives had gotten off track.

Council Chairman Wallace Curry had thankfully placed Patterson first on the agenda. That was a concession to their relationship. Even though they would probably disagree on this topic, their long-term relationship was good. Curry's son had a penchant for getting into trouble, and Patterson had handled those cases sensitively. He didn't sweep anything under the rug, but he managed the negative publicity very smartly. As a result, there was little damage to the elder Curry's political career and Curry was smart enough to repay favors.

Council member James Garrison, from the county's wealthier northern end, would be a tougher nut to crack. He was elected on a platform of being friendly to business and serial killers were bad for business. He was exactly the kind of politician the FBI had warned about. He'd worry about the media portraying the area as riddled with crime. He'd worry about tourists staying away. He'd worry that business would suffer.

But for Garrison, the worst part of a serial killing would be admitting they had victims, the low-hanging fruit, in their midst at all. Admitting they had teenage girls in the county who were addicted to drugs and living on the street would run counter to the Camelot image that Garrison tried to portray. When crime did occur, he was the poster child for that ubiquitous TV sound bite, "This isn't supposed to happen here."

He'd routinely voted against funding social services, opting instead to reduce taxes on business. His justification was that troubled youth were not present in significant numbers, and that the best crime prevention tool was a booming economy.

"When good people move in, bad people move out," he'd once said. "We need good businesses with good jobs to attract the right kind of people. We can't arrest our way out of crime, but we can build our way out by attracting major employers and making it easy for them to locate here."

While there was certainly a grain of truth to what he'd said, for the carrot to be effective you also need a stick. The sheriff's office was the stick and Garrison routinely refused to support that side of the equation. His hypocrisy was frustrating to Patterson.

The meeting was called to order and after the usual rituals such as the flag salute and approval of the previous meeting's minutes, it was Patterson's turn to speak.

"Council members, thank you for your time tonight," the sheriff began. "I'm here on a topic none of us likes, but if we have a problem I'd rather get ahead of it. You're well aware that we've had three recent homicides with remains discovered in rural parts of the south county. It's possible these are unrelated to each other, but I doubt it. If there is a serial killer at work here we want to get on that before any more women lose their lives."

He could see the frowns developing, even on the faces of those from whom he'd expected support. He put that out of his mind, and went on with his prepared remarks.

"I'm here to ask you for some money from the county reserve fund to put some extra manpower into these cases."

Like most police departments, the Kitsap County Sheriff's Office was short of staff. It wasn't because the county was short of money. The economy had mostly recovered from the Great Recession, and growth in the populated areas of the county had generated a comfortable tax base. The problem was finding qualified applicants. Millennial kids had little interest in being cops. The sheriff had tried a major recruiting campaign, but avoided the temptation to reduce hiring standards. The message from his deputies was that they'd rather work short-handed than work next to unqualified people.

Patterson was in his first term as sheriff, but had been a law enforcement officer for nearly thirty-five years. He'd been a street cop in Seattle, working his way up to the rank of deputy chief before retiring to Kitsap County. In the words of his wife he "flunked retirement" and soon ran a successful campaign for sheriff.

The good news was that, because he didn't really need the job, he could speak truth to both elected officials and even voters. He dropped a bombshell that hadn't previously been made public.

"This is more than three homicides and we need to figure out if they're related," he explained. "We have a number of other young, troubled women who appear to be missing. With our detectives focusing on the actual homicides, I need to redirect some road deputies to work these potential missing-person cases."

The fact that additional women were possibly missing had been discussed only at the highest levels of the sheriff's office, and always with a worried tone.

"What I need to do is peel off some of our most experienced deputies—the ones who know the streets and know the girls— from routine patrol. I want them to find out what's happened to those we haven't heard from lately. To do that, I need to backfill their patrol shifts with other deputies on overtime."

"They're probably not dead or missing" Garrison interrupted. "They're probably hanging out buying their drugs in Seattle,

Portland or Vancouver. These people don't tell their friends where they're headed. They don't tell their families where they're headed. They go where the drugs are the cheapest and where social services coddle them."

The battle had started. The FBI had been spot-on. Sheriff Patterson was trying to get ahead of a problem, and Councilman Garrison was trying to deny it existed.

"Some probably *are* in Vancouver or Portland, sir," Patterson replied. "My concern is that drug addicts and street kids are talking to my deputies, and *they're* worried. It's unusual for them to show that kind of concern about their friends. As you say, they're usually more worried about where their next fix is coming from. Even more concerning is that they're actively seeking out my deputies to express concern. This is not a culture that normally talks to the cops."

"I'm not asking for a lot," Patterson continued. "I'm mainly putting you on notice that we have the early indicators of a problem. I'd like a little extra padding in my overtime budget to run a few ideas to ground. We don't yet need a task force with its own building and support staff. I saw one of those early in my career and I know what they cost."

"How much are you asking for? We need specifics to craft a motion," Chairman Curry pointed out.

"The county budget is good right now. Sales tax revenue has exceeded forecasts and there's no sign that will change. I'm asking for authority to spend up to an extra $50,000 in overtime to resolve our concerns. That's chump change if there is a serial killer and we have to eventually create a task force."

The sheriff was right. In the 1980s, the sheriff's office in Seattle was slow to recognize that a serial killer was preying on vulnerable women in their community. The Green River Serial Killer case ended up costing millions of dollars, and forty-nine women were known to have been murdered. The prosecution alone cost $12 million.

"The emphasis is on 'up to' $50,000. If I don't need it, I won't spend it" the sheriff added.

"My experience with department heads is that if we give you the money, you'll spend it." Garrison again. "Sheriff, I think you're bored. You've come here from the big city expecting to see crime everywhere and it's just not here. I'm not prepared to drop fifty grand on some chimera of yours."

"My what, sir?"

"Chimera." Garrison was known for being a little puffy in his language, especially when he had the floor in a room of constituents. "A chimera is a mythological fire-breathing monster...with the emphasis on 'mythological.' I think this whole idea of yours is...is...well, it's mythological."

"Sir, I suggest you say that to the families of three young women whose remains we recovered from the woods. There's nothing mythological about their pain and loss. My detectives and I went to the funerals...sir."

A reporter from the Kitsap Sun was careful to get that exchange in his notebook. The media loves controversy and in a county where politicians got along surprisingly well, this was gold. Even better, thanks to Garrison's stuffy demeanor, the killer now had a name. The next morning's Sun would attribute the deaths of three women and the disappearance of several others to the newly named "Chimera Killer."

The sheriff was well known for keeping his cool, and, in a few seconds, his voice had returned to its usual respectful self.

"Council members, I'm aware this isn't good news. But I felt it necessary to bring this up in public session to stop the speculation and rumors. I'd like fifty grand to either debunk the theory or, if there is a serial killer at work, stop that person as quickly as possible."

"So moved," said council member Jenny Arbuthwaite without a moment's hesitation. She represented the south end of the county, and all the bodies had been found in her district. She was getting calls from worried citizens.

"Seconded," came from councilwoman Leslie Griffith. Although not a strong supporter of law enforcement, Griffith had walked her talk by volunteering in the community. She worked with just the kind of girls who were going missing and understood the sheriff's concern better than most. Tonight, she was supporting the sheriff when the more conservative Garrison was not.

It was not lost on Patterson that his initial supporters were women. Were they relating to the victims better than the men on the council?

"All in favor?" asked the chair. There were two "ayes" among the five council members.

"Opposed?" Garrison voted no, along with a protégé that he'd helped to elect. That made it a tie, leaving it to the council chair to cast the deciding vote.

"I don't like this one bit," Curry said. "I hope we're not throwing away $50,000 and you can bet you'll be expected to explain how you spent every penny. But sheriff, you've earned my respect. You've been right about a lot of things since you were elected, so I'm going to defer to your judgement on this one. The chair votes 'aye,' with the expectation that you'll be back every month to keep us posted on how this is progressing. And I do hope we'll see some of that $50,000 returned unspent."

"That's my hope too, sir. And I have no trouble keeping you posted. If something develops between meetings, I'll let you know personally." The sheriff was a man of his word and he'd do exactly that. What he didn't know was just how soon he'd be doing it.

Undersheriff Bill Burns was in the back of the room and, when Patterson turned around, Burns was wearing a frown. He did not look like someone whose boss had just won a significant political victory.

"Hey, Bill, why the long face?" Patterson whispered as they walked out. "You look like you did the night you lost the election to me."

"Boss, you should have asked for seventy grand," Burns whispered as they left the council chambers. "This 'chimera killer' that Garrison doesn't think exists…we might just have another mythological victim."

———————————

The ride out of town was a quick one, and it was once again to the southern part of the county. The power line road was dusty, but Patterson refused to roll up his window. That was a carryover from his days patrolling the north end of Seattle. He wanted to hear what was going on outside his police car. Even on one of those famous Seattle rainy days, he kept the window cracked so he could patrol with his ears as well as his eyes.

They weren't on-scene yet, and the information was sketchy. A security guard patrolling the power line for the utility had spotted a purse by the road. Thinking it had to either be lost or dumped by a thief, he'd brought it all the way back to the sheriff's office without noticing the blood on one side. When he turned it into the front desk clerk, she ran the name on the wallet inside and quickly became concerned.

The purse contained more than ID. It had a few rocks of meth, needles, a wallet and money. That was ominous. Had the purse merely been purloined from someone's car, the thief would not have left drugs and money in the wallet.

Deputies took the security guard back to where he *thought* he'd found the purse.

"What we don't know is whether the body is nearby, in the next county, or if there's a body at all," Burns said. "Patrol ran one of their dogs around the immediate area and didn't find anything, but it wasn't a cadaver dog."

Police K9s are trained very differently than search and rescue dogs. Although some of the principles, such as how scent moves through the air, are similar, there are also many differences. Police K9s are virtually always looking for a fresh trail from a recent crime scene.

The sheriff's cell phone rang and he recognized the caller ID as dispatch. He took the call, and put it on speaker so both he and Burns could hear.

"Jones just looked at the ID, and thinks it's a girl that some of his street contacts were asking about last week," the dispatcher said. David "Davy" Jones was a deputy destined for stardom in the department. In particular, he'd built a bridge to street youth and they'd begun confiding in him. He had impressed his bosses by knowing when to handle things himself and when to push information up to the boss. This was one of those times to push things up.

"He's going to take the DMV picture and show it to some of the girls over on the highway. None of them knew the real name of the girl they were worried about, so he'll work with the picture. She just stopped showing up about two weeks ago. I'll call you back if he comes up with anything."

"OK, thanks," the sheriff said. "And thank Jones. This makes me think we're not wasting our time out here. Stand by for a SAR callout in a few minutes."

It didn't take much discussion for the sheriff and undersheriff to confirm that they were thinking the same thing. If there was even a hint that this girl was a fourth victim, they needed to scour the power line road and neighboring woods. Quickly.

"Call 'em out tonight?" Burns asked.

"Let's do the callout tonight, but ask them to report at first light tomorrow. If she's been out here for two weeks, she's not getting any deader," the sheriff sighed. "Let's make this a big one. Call the state EOC and let's get teams from the neighboring counties. We've got lots of woods to cover. Right now, I've got a phone call to make."

The county council members were still droning on. Curry's cell phone was on silent, but he noticed the caller ID was from the sheriff. He'd check voice mail as soon as the meeting adjourned.

———————————

Aretha Franklin's "Rescue Me!" ringtone interrupted Bryce's math homework. His first thought upon hearing the special ringtone was that he'd be going on a search immediately and would need a note from his folks to get his schoolwork turned in late. His parents had done a deal with the school principal and Bryce was careful not to abuse it. When there weren't searches, he got his work in on time and made sure to keep his grades up.

Listening to the recorded message, he learned this would be a planned evidence search in the morning. He'd still miss some school, but that was OK. Bryce's teachers each had a different take on his extra-curricular activities. One teacher who particularly loved dogs would let him off the hook if he'd tell her how Sierra had searched. Bryce always made sure to honor her request, at least for details that weren't confidential. His cat-loving teachers didn't like anyone missing their classes, but were forced to admit that Bryce's schoolwork was better than most of their other students'.

The search would start early and hopefully be done before the heat of the day. A little morning heat can be helpful, making scent rise predictably up a hillside. Beyond that one benefit, heat was hard on the dogs. Bryce and Sierra would start out working any ridgelines and probably be out of the field by noon.

Bryce finished up his homework, set his alarm for 4:00 a.m. and let his folks know they'd be writing another excuse for school. Despite the potential excitement of a morning search, Bryce slept like a baby that night. The only time he woke up was because Sierra was snoring loudly in her crate. He fell back to sleep being thankful that Sierra merely snored. The family's last dog made noises from the other end and it didn't take the nose of a search dog to detect that odor.

Briefing was at five in the morning, and everybody was in the field by six. Bryce and Sierra were assigned a long stretch of woods adjacent to the power line road. He knew they were looking for a body or other evidence, and the detective running the search had acknowledged that this could be related to the other three murders. He stopped short of saying "serial killer," but from the size of the response, that was a given.

Search and rescue is not a footrace. Handlers and dogs don't all run at top speed from the command post, with the strongest runner or the best dog making the find. Searchers are assigned areas. If a handler's assigned area holds no one, the handler finds nothing regardless of how much they've trained or how diligently they've searched. If the area holds a subject, living or dead, they get to make the find.

Most handlers don't care where they're assigned. Oh, they gripe about steep terrain or thick brush, but one area is as good as the next. They know deputies will put resources in the most probable areas, so no one gets too worked up about where they were assigned to work.

The exception was Alan Granger, a handler from nearby Mason County. He believed that handlers should pick their areas, on the grounds that one would search more diligently if they really believed the subject was in their area. He'd been successful, and deputies had begun deferring to him. They'd seek him out when he arrived at base, let him pick his area, and then make the rest of the assignments.

As a testament to Granger's success, he'd found two of the three women missing in the current series of cases. It was generally conceded that he'd probably have found the third had he not been out of town on business when the search was conducted.

Today, Bryce had been assigned the area next to Granger's and downwind of him. The area was long and relatively narrow, and Bryce had decided to grid it by bouncing from side to side. After each pass, they'd move into the wind a little bit and make another pass. The terrain wasn't bad and Sierra was able to move easily through the brush. There were a few places where she and Bryce struggled with the brush, and Bryce made sure to spend extra time at those places. But so far, Sierra had come up with nothing.

They were about three-quarters of the way through their assignment when Sierra began moving with purpose. Her bell took on the rhythmic ring of "I've got something" and she was off to check it out.

Bryce realized she was headed out of their assigned area and into Granger's.

Granger was also different than most other handlers in that he didn't like interlopers in his assigned area. The vast majority of SAR dog handlers understand that a handler needs to follow their dog. If an interesting odor takes them out of their assigned area, OK. Everyone works together and the dogs all get along. So long as a radio call is made there's never a problem.

With Granger, it was a problem. Bryce followed protocol and got on the radio, knowing exactly what the response would be.

"Base, Dog 44. My dog is in scent, and is moving east into Mason 20's area. We'll resolve whatever this is and get back to our area as soon as possible."

"Dog 44, Base. Understood. Break—Mason 20 did you copy?"

"Mason 20 I did copy. Please have them leave our area immediately."

The second-to-last thing Bryce wanted was an argument over the radio. But the absolute last thing he wanted was to pull his dog off scent and return her to an empty area. It potentially confused the dog, and might leave a subject in the field, unfound.

Bryce put on his least confrontational voice, but spoke with clarity. "Dog 44, I understand. We'll make it quick, but I'm going to let Sierra resolve whatever she smells. As soon as she's satisfied, I'll take her back to our area."

His answer didn't come over the radio.

"Leave! Now! I will not have freelancers wandering through my area." Granger had stepped out from behind a tree, and the look on his face matched the anger in his voice. His dog, a Belgian Malinois, was at his side. Although this dog was well-socialized and not a threat, Mals just generally look mean. They aren't called "Malligators" for no reason.

"Alan, I'm not trying to poach or anything, but I have to trust that Sierra is bringing me here for a reason. Her nose doesn't know that a deputy drew a line on a map and put your number on the other side of it." Bryce wasn't backing down.

"Get your dog and get out of my area. I'm not going to tell you again," Granger shouted. By that time, it was useless to argue. Sierra could tell when there was tension in the air, and she'd stopped searching. She went back to Bryce's side and waited for his next command.

Bryce was determined to be the adult in the room.

"Base, Dog 44. We've resolved our concern and are returning to our area."

"Dog 44, Base. Understood." The tone in the deputy's voice made it clear he really did understand. Bryce relaxed, played a little with Sierra and gave her some water, and got her back to searching their assigned area.

It didn't take long for the other shoe to drop. About ten minutes, to be exact.

"Base, Mason 20. We'd like to meet law enforcement at the west end of our area."

That was the code-of-the-day. Asking to meet law enforcement was the way to tell Base that a body had been found. *"That bastard,"* Bryce couldn't help thinking. For Granger to have

47

found the body so soon after their argument, Sierra must have been on the right track. The remains had to have been nearby. Granger had probably interrupted them just as Sierra was about to make the find.

Probably Granger's dog had been in scent also. It explained why they both were in that portion of Granger's assigned area. His Mal was likely still trying to work out the scent cone, and he didn't want to risk being shown up by a seventeen-year-old assigned to the next area.

Bryce didn't mind not getting the find. He'd found plenty of people, living and dead, and was happy to share, especially with inexperienced handlers who needed to build their confidence. But it stuck in his craw that an arrogant jerk like Alan Granger had been the one to ace him out.

He'd make one concession to ego. He got on the radio.

"Base, Dog 44. Can you have someone hide in the bushes just outside base? Sierra worked really well today and I'd like to end it on a positive note before she goes back in the truck. Just a quickie search problem…something small and easy."

The deputy at base, himself a police K9 handler, knew exactly what Bryce was doing. First, he was politely sticking his finger in Granger's eye via radio. He and everybody listening to the radio knew that Sierra had been pulled off a find. But more importantly it was good protocol to end a dog's day with something positive.

"Dog 44, Base. Understand completely. We'll have somebody hidden by the time you return. Other teams will be welcome to run on them after you. Base clear."

It would be a live find, not cadaver. But it would be a find, nonetheless. Bryce would be able to praise the daylights out of Sierra and let her play to her heart's content. She deserved that.

The not-so-positive part would come after Sierra was in the car, confronting Granger about his possessiveness. With the discovery of the fourth body it was clear there was major dirty work afoot. The victims, the sheriff's office, and the people of Kitsap County didn't need two dog handlers competing to find the most bodies. They had to leave their egos aside.

CHAPTER FIVE
First Date

"He's seventeen and he's never been on a date?" Katie's mom asked quietly as she put water in the vase.

"I asked a few of the girls and they didn't think so," Katie whispered back. "They just know him as 'the dog guy.' They all said he's really sweet…just totally into dogs."

"That fits," Katie's mom replied. "He's so keyed up, he'd make coffee nervous."

Bryce had showed up at their door in a shirt that had obviously been starched and ironed, and slacks with a crease that could cut your finger. He had flowers for Katie's mom, but had forgotten to remove the grocery store price tag. He'd also left dessert in his truck, giving mother and daughter a chance for a quick consult while he retrieved it.

Bryce returned, offered the chocolate cheesecake to his date's mother, and promptly committed the worst sin of the evening.

He called her "ma'am."

"I'm Pam, not ma'am, even if I am old enough to have a teenage daughter."

"Yes mmmm…Pam. Thank you."

Pam had actually begun to accept that some might call her "ma'am." There was a bit of gray hair around her temples and laugh lines around her eyes. But she would put that day off as long as possible, and certainly wouldn't tolerate it from her daughter's date.

When it came to dating her daughter, Pam Lovering had one rule: The first date would start at home. There would be no quick, awkward two-minute meeting on the front porch. Any guy could pretend to be a gentleman for that long. She'd get to know her daughter's suitors over a home cooked dinner and then decide if a movie or trip to town would follow. She was already fairly sure Katie was safe with Bryce. If anything, this boy needed to loosen up.

Bryce had picked entirely the wrong consultant to help get ready for what was indeed the first date of his life. The older sheriff's deputy had befriended him at searches, cornered him actually, and regaled him with stories of his winning ways with women. The man knew everything about how to woo the lovelies. After all, he'd been married to four of them.

"You need to go in looking sharp. Do you own an iron?" the deputy asked. "Even if you're wearing jeans, iron them. A creased pair of pants says 'attention to detail' and women love that. Iron your shirt, too."

"Oh, and if anything starts to go wrong," he added, "just say 'yes, dear.' You'll never win the argument so just suck it up, concede defeat and say 'yes, dear.'"

"I'm not sure kids my age…"

"Stop. It's universal. Women hand it down from generation to generation like some kind of secret handshake. Now, repeat after me: yes, dear."

"Yes, dear," Bryce responded weakly.

"Good. Practice that," the deputy had said before pronouncing him ready to, in his words, "officially chase skirts."

From her perspective, Pam figured Bryce would be good practice for Katie. He indeed seemed really sweet, but needed some guidance on how to dress appropriately for modern times. Nobody ironed anything anymore. Katie could work with him, and at least he'd missed on the high side.

Pam placed the vase of flowers on an end table, minus the store wrapping and price tag. "Goodness, where are my manners? Bryce, sit down…sit down."

"Thank you, ma'am…Pam. What's your favorite chair? I wouldn't want to sit in that." The nervousness came rushing back over something as simple as where to sit.

"Anywhere's fine…we're not like men who have their designated recliners. With only women in the house, we furnish it so we can sit wherever the mood strikes us," Pam answered. "Some days I sit in front of the window, some days by the fireplace. You're the guest, so you get first choice."

Bryce picked a straight-backed wooden chair with a quilted pad on the seat. It wasn't comfortable, but neither was he.

"I've just pulled dinner out of the oven, and it needs to rest a bit before we serve," Pam said. "Bryce, would you like something to drink?"

"Water's fine, if that's no trouble."

Pam had been careful to buy Coke, Pepsi *and* 7-Up when she went to the store. She'd wanted the evening to be perfect for her daughter, right down to her date's choice of soda. This young man was worried about troubling her over a glass of water.

"OK, but if you want something else, just say so. We've got pretty much everything in the way of soft drinks. Oh, there's been something I wanted to ask you. Ever since Katie told me about you I've been wondering…right after we moved here I saw something in the news about a girl getting shot up near Lost Creek. They said she was found by a search dog just before she bled to death. Were you in on that?"

Bryce and Sierra had been more than "in on that." Sierra had indeed found the girl who'd been accidentally shot by a playmate. The two had gone to play in the woods, and the little boy had taken his father's gun "in case of bears." Despite the accolades for saving the young lady, it was one of the saddest searches of Bryce's career.

"Yes, but we're really not supposed to talk about cases like that," Bryce replied, looking at the floor.

"Well I think what you do is just wonderful," Pam gushed. "And I'm glad you're making some time to do other things. Katie thinks you're pretty nice and it's an honor to have you in our home."

Katie just beamed. She loved her estranged father because daughters are supposed to love their dads. But she was old enough to understand that her mom hadn't picked so well in the husband department. Katie was feeling like she'd already outdone her mom with this fellow. She was also starting to get irritated. She couldn't get a word in edgewise, even though she, not her mother, was supposed to be Bryce's date.

A timer went off telling them all that dinner was ready to serve. Pam had made meat loaf for two reasons. One, she made the best meat loaf ever. Two, she would gauge a young man's kindness by his reaction to learning that dinner would be…meat loaf. The last young man Katie had brought home couldn't conceal his disappointment. He ended up agreeing it was the best meat loaf ever, but was not invited back.

Bryce, on the other hand, was grateful for anything that wasn't "search food."

"Some people wince when I tell them we're having meat loaf," Pam told Bryce with a bit of a stern look.

"Ma'am…*Pam*…I've eaten so many freeze-dried meals on searches that I love anything not out of a pouch. Well, almost anything. I'm also a little tired of chili dogs. There's one county that always serves chili dogs when we search there, and we search there a lot."

"Well, OK then. I guess chili dogs are off the list for next time."

Bryce's mind flashed at the casual reference to "next time." He sneaked a glance at Katie and she was smiling, so that was good.

"So we've talked about me since I got here," Bryce said, trying to take a little control of the conversation. He looked at Katie. "I don't know anything about you."

It was Pam who jumped in to answer.

"Katie's father and I split up about nine months ago. He'd cheated on me and I decided I couldn't stay in that town…"

Bryce could see Katie lower her head and shrink down in her chair. Her mother was over-sharing.

"It worked out that I got a really great job at the shipyard in

Bremerton, so here we are. Katie had to switch schools in mid-year, which I didn't like. But I wouldn't let her stay with her father for even a few more months. He set a really bad example."

SAR had exposed Bryce's young mind to more family drama than most seventeen-year-olds. He pretty quickly sized up Katie's mom as the angry ex, and thus over-protective of her daughter. The understanding didn't calm his first-date nervousness. If anything, he was now more on edge.

"Um…Katie, what classes are you taking? I don't see you in any of mine."

Before Katie could answer, Pam jumped in again. "She's taking a heavy math and science load. Next year she'll do Running Start over at Olympic College. She's going to be an engineer, just like me.

Bryce struggled with math and science. His mind went more to the arts and working with intangibles like search dogs. He let the topic go.

"What do you do after school?" Bryce asked, looking directly at Katie.

"Video games, I guess. My Dad and I used to hike a lot, but I don't know any of the trails around here."

"Well I know them all! Green Mountain is awesome and there's both day hikes and…um…day hikes."

Pam laughed, but took over the conversation again. "Don't get ahead of yourself, Junior. There'll be no overnight hikes for you two unless it's a chaperoned group."

Bryce's face turned unbelievably red. He was incredibly attracted to Katie, and that included her physical appearance. But he sensed she was a lady, and wanted to treat her that way. He had picked up on Pam's anger at her ex and didn't want to get lumped in with him.

Pam sensed Bryce's discomfort, and backed off from the teasing. "I know what you meant, and I note that you caught yourself. Nice save," She reached around the corner of the table and patted his knee. "I just couldn't resist a little dig."

The small talk continued over meat loaf that really was exceptional. After Bryce's chocolate cheesecake, it was time for the rest of the date to begin. Again, it was Pam who took the lead.

"So, what do you kids think you're going to do? A movie?"

"I'm up for anything, but I figured probably a movie," Bryce answered, looking at Katie not Pam.

"Sure, there's twelve screens down at the Mile Hill Cinema," Katie answered somewhat coolly. "I'm sure there's something we'd both like."

"Text me with where you end up. I'll wait up," Pam added.

"Here, let me help you pick up dishes," Bryce offered.

"No, you kids get going. I'll clean up the kitchen. It really is Katie's date but I've enjoyed talking with you, Bryce. It's been a long time since I've had a gentleman in my home, and it was very refreshing. Now go…go!"

At least Pam stayed on the porch as they walked to Bryce's truck. He'd scrubbed the old Suburban within an inch of its life. At the suggestion of the womanizing deputy, he'd even hand-waxed it. He also vacuumed and dusted the inside, removed the dog kennel, and sprayed the upholstery with deodorizer.

He helped Katie step up into the passenger seat. She was dressed for a date, but casually. She had on a white blouse with mid-length sleeves, and gray slacks. Her shoes were also gray leather, with just a bit of heel.

As he got ready to close the door, Bryce couldn't help looking at Katie a little longer than necessary. He hoped Pam wouldn't notice. He was officially what his grandparents would call "smitten," and having trouble concealing it.

He didn't need to conceal it from Katie. Her eyes lingered back, even though he'd only be gone long enough to walk around to the driver's side. When he got in, Katie asked the question they'd both been thinking.

"OK, where are we REALLY going?"

"I don't know, but not to a movie," Bryce replied. "I don't want to sit next to you and not talk for the next two hours."

"You're going to think I'm weird…"

"What…?"

"Can we go to your place and play with Sierra? I really miss my dog. I almost cried the other day petting her."

Although Bryce had decided to expand his horizons to include girls, he was still a dog guy at heart. To find a girl who also loved dogs was like winning the lottery. He'd started out "noticing" Kate, moved up to "smitten," and now the needle on the gauge was leaning toward "serious."

Bryce's parents were surprised to see his Suburban pull into the driveway. His mom's first thought was that the date had gone badly and was over already. She steeled herself to console her son when a pretty young woman got out of the passenger side. She was even more surprised to see them both heading for Sierra's kennel.

Now Bryce's dad also looked out the window. "Wow, she's a cutie," he opined, receiving a faux slap from his mother. "And it looks like they're going to spend the evening playing with the dog. Where did I go wrong?"

"You shush. Look at that young lady scratching Sierra's ears. Bryce is just standing there. She's obviously as much of a dog lover as he is." Mothers could read their sons, and their son's girlfriends, like books. His father had learned long ago to just go with it.

The parents went outside to meet the young lady, and it was her turn to be nervous. Katie even slipped and called his father "sir." Bryce jumped all over that.

"If I have to call your mom Pam, then you can call my Dad by his first name. He's Brian and my mom is Diane."

"Nice to meet you, Katie," Diane said. "I hope Bryce didn't drag you over here kicking and screaming instead of taking you to a nice show or something."

"Oh, no. This was my idea. I had a dog before my parents split up and Sierra is such a sweetheart. I love that she goes out and saves people. I can't imagine training a dog to do that."

"Bryce does work hard at it…a little too hard sometimes," Diane said. She turned to Brian. "Oh honey, it's time for our show. Let's get back inside and see who gets voted out this week."

Brian had absolutely no idea what his wife was talking about. Yes, they liked the talent show that was about to come on, but they'd never referred to it as "our show." It wasn't THAT big a deal. He finally got the hint as Diane took his hand and squeezed like a vise.

"Yes, dear," he said. Bryce had heard his dad say that before, but hadn't ever given it much thought. After his coaching session with the womanizing deputy he was now more attuned to the phrase. He stared at his dad, which only served to further confuse the elder Finn.

Bryce's mom spoke next. "OK, you kids have fun and if you need anything from the kitchen, just come on in." She realized the kids needed to be left alone.

Katie was playing with Sierra and tossing a squeaky toy. Unlike the tennis ball she got for finding a missing subject, Sierra would bring the squeaky bone back and drop it to be tossed again and again. Katie seemed to like the game as much as Sierra, and continued tossing it.

Finally, Katie sat down in the grass, risking green stains on her nice pants. She didn't care. She liked Bryce and loved Sierra. "You're a big lovey lovey lovey," she said while scratching Sierra on the chin.

She turned and looked Bryce in the eye. "You're not too shabby yourself."

Bryce choked on the comment, and didn't really know how to respond.

"I'm really enjoying our time together," was the best he could muster.

Like women through the ages, Katie knew instinctively what her man meant. Guys were terrible at saying nice stuff, but women were good at catching the drift—and knowing when it was sincere.

"Hey, want to see a runaway?" Bryce wasn't overtly trying to change the subject. But when he got nervous, he always shifted to talking about what he knew.

"What's a runaway?"

"It's the basic drill that search dogs do. It's like Cal Ripken taking soft ground balls and throwing them to first even though he's done it a million times."

"Riiight. Al Whipken...sure." The baseball analogy was lost on Katie.

"C'mon, I'll show you."

The two walked out behind the kennel to find a trail leading to the rear of the property. The Finns owned ten wooded acres, and Bryce had cut trails all through it. He would walk Sierra, hide cadaver "source" or do small but useful practice searches.

Bryce took Katie to a straight stretch of trail that ended in a couple of sweeping curves. He began the explanation of a runaway.

"You'll have to be the subject, but you'll get to see what she does. I'll hold Sierra so she can't go after you. You'll talk to her a bit— tease her—and then run off. Go just beyond the bend out of sight and then duck right or left into the bushes."

"What do I do when she finds me?"

"Absolutely nothing. It's critical that you give her no reaction until she comes and gets me. It's not enough for the dog to find the subject. The dog's job is to arrange an introduction. We'll do a high five so she sees me actually touch you. Then...massive play. Like you saw the other day."

Bryce grabbed Sierra's collar and held her between his legs. Katie tentatively turned around to face Sierra and started backing up.

"Sierrrrrra...I'm getting losssst. Can you come help me? We

humans keep getting lossssst and need Sierraaa to finnnnd us." Katie was proving to be a natural at this.

Bryce was having trouble holding onto Sierra. After more than three years of runaways, Sierra was like a pro wrestler. She knew how to get out of pretty much every hold. Bryce held her collar, and had one calf against her hip to keep her from backing out of it. Despite restraining her, Bryce praised Sierra and kept it positive.

"Oh, she's getting lost, she's getting lost. You'll have to go find her."

At about forty feet away, the perfect distance, Katie turned and ran down the trail. She went around the corner and found a spot between the bushes to duck into. She heard Bryce say, "Go find!" and was surprised that a dog could create such a sound of thundering hooves. It sounded like a horse was after her.

Sierra rounded the bend at a dead run and shot past Katie. She couldn't see Katie behind the bush, but somehow put on the brakes and stopped, leaving skid marks in the dirt. She turned, sniffed the far side of the trail and then came back to where Katie had turned in. She peeked through the bushes, tagged Katie with her paw, and then was gone.

"Good girl…c'mon back…right here," Bryce cued. In training, it was beneficial to cue the dog for the desired behavior. Even an experienced dog like Sierra needed reinforcement. In the woods, on a search, Bryce might not know for sure that she'd found the subject. Reinforcing the behavior now would keep Sierra sharp when he couldn't remind her what to do.

"Annnnd…sit!" Bryce added, just as Sierra got to him.

She touched her butt to the ground but jumped back up and was gone again before Bryce could completely speak the words,

"Show me." Sierra ran directly back to Katie, adding a bark to the mix.

When Bryce arrived, he high five'd Katie and tossed Sierra her ball. The two of them started the kind of loud, excited play Katie had seen at the school demonstration. They both focused on Sierra, with belly rubs, butt scratches and squeaky talk. After a minute or so, Katie turned to Bryce.

"That was awesome! I heard her run by me at top speed, then suddenly stop. She couldn't see me. Can she use her nose when running like that?"

"Apparently," Bryce explained. "I wouldn't have thought so either, but she's done it since her very first runaway. She was at a dead run and then just slammed on the brakes when the person's scent disappeared from the trail."

"I peeked up over the bushes so I could see her come back to you. I hope that was OK...?"

"It's fine," Bryce said. "If we'd had a third person here, I'd have had them hide so you could follow and watch."

Katie looked Bryce directly in the eye. The look was serious, but her voice was soft. "I'm glad there's not a third person here."

"Me too." And then Bryce resorted to what he always did when he didn't know what to say.

"Wanna do that again? We usually do two or three at a time."

Katie was in for the full meal deal, and got lined up to go. She didn't know the trail got a little rougher down the way.

"Sierrrra...I'm getting lost agaaaain! You'll need to come finnnnnd me!"

Sierra was now completely jacked up. She'd gone from pro wrestler to bucking like a rodeo horse, and Bryce wasn't sure he could stay on for the full eight seconds. Thankfully, unlike a rodeo, Bryce could use more than one hand to keep her under control. He watched Katie disappear around the corner and knew she was going to go just a bit further before diving off the trail.

Sierra went out, came back and sat, and was headed back to Katie at warp speed. Bryce rounded the corner to find Katie not in the bushes, but laying on the trail. She had dirt on her face, her pants were torn, and she was holding her ankle.

"Are you OK?" Bryce tossed Sierra's ball well down the trail to get her away from Katie. He wanted to check her out without Sierra jumping all over her.

"I just twisted my ankle," Katie replied, sounding more annoyed than injured. "These probably weren't the best shoes for running in the woods. Don't we need to play with Sierra? She found me."

"She's got her ball, and one time with no belly rubs won't ruin her as a search dog. Let's worry about you."

Bryce avoided the inclination to do a full survey, which would mean putting his hands all over Katie. He simply looked her up and down, and asked her what hurt. Under the tear in her pants, Katie's knee was a bit skinned. She was otherwise fine, but the ankle was already starting to swell up.

Bryce reached down to help Katie up, putting his arm under hers and around her back. Putting her weight on her other foot, Katie came up easily and slipped her arm likewise around Bryce's waist. But instead of remaining side-to-side, she turned to face him, her body against his.

As usual, Bryce vapor-locked. And once again, Katie took the lead. She put her other arm around Bryce and pulled him close.

"I guess you've rescued me for real," she laughed. "Doesn't the damsel in distress need to thank her hero?"

Just as she lifted her face toward Bryce's and closed her eyes, something hit both of them like a sack of flour. They both nearly fell again. It was Sierra, jumping up and trying to get between them.

"She does that when mom and dad hug, too," Bryce explained, simultaneously grateful and not grateful for the interruption. "We can't tell if she's trying to be a chaperone, or just wants in on the group hug."

Bryce got to hear a tone from Katie that he'd not heard before.

"Throw her ball down the trail again. Waaay down the trail."

Bryce was trying hard to be a gentleman. He really liked Katie and didn't want to scare her off by being too forward. But he was also figuring out when a man should take orders.

"Is this where I say 'yes, dear?'"

"Just like your father…."

Bryce threw the ball as far as he could, into the deepest brush on the property. He knew it would take Sierra some time to dig it out.

They used every second of it.

CHAPTER SIX
The Hill

Sitting with her glass of local red wine, Jenny Arbuthwaite couldn't have been more pleased. Despite being a recent widow and knowing nothing about construction, she'd turned an $800,000 dump into a million-dollar fixer-upper.

Oh, it was still a money pit to be sure. More than ninety years old, the home in Fragaria had constant needs, just fewer than before. When Jenny and her husband bought the home the foundation had sagged, the plumbing leaked, and the floor bounced as even her slight ninety-eight-pound frame walked across it. Every single one of the door frames was askew. Some doors wouldn't shut, the rest wouldn't *stay* shut.

But they loved the little home. They'd expected to sit on the porch every evening, sipping wine, and watching boats plying the waters of Puget Sound. They'd done that, for a few months anyway, until Peter dropped dead of a previously undiagnosed heart condition.

With Peter gone, Jenny didn't know whether to consider their new house a blessing or a curse. The real estate market in Kitsap was recovering nicely from the Great Recession of five years earlier. However, it hadn't recovered nearly enough that one could flip a house after just a few months of ownership. Peter had left her comfortable, but selling the home would mean taking a financial bath she couldn't afford.

Staying in the home also meant Jenny could continue doing the one thing left that gave meaning to her life: representing the citizens of south Kitsap County on the county council. In her third term, she'd always found the role rewarding. With a residency requirement, if she was to move to another part of the county she would lose her council position. She didn't want to give that up, because the part-time job was also a valued distraction.

Given that both her heart and her bank account were in agreement, Jenny's decision was easy. She could afford to fix up the house, a little bit at least, and maybe hold on to it long enough to recover her investment. In a few years she'd think about trying to sell, and move to someplace nearby that didn't hold memories of Peter.

When Jenny and Peter first saw the house, it had been love at first sight. The only thing they didn't like was the hill behind it.

The hill rose precipitously behind the home and had caused Jenny some concern when they were considering the purchase. The real estate agent assured them it had been checked by an engineer and was not a threat. The agent had otherwise been very professional to work with. She'd kept every promise and made things happen almost magically. Jenny had come to trust the agent's word, and quickly put the hill out of her mind.

She shouldn't have.

On this night, Jenny noticed her wine glass shaking a bit on the table. Not much, really, but something she'd never noticed before. Fragaria was too far from any major roads for a truck or bus to make the house shake. Low flying helicopters had occasionally rattled the old structure, but she could hear nothing overhead.

Then what was it? The shaking got worse, but seemed to be coming now in rhythmic bumps. Bump. Shudder. Bump. Shudder. Jenny started to have the sensation of going down in a jittery elevator.

No! It wasn't a sensation. It was real. Her house on the hill above Fragaria Road was headed for the waterfront side. The noise was louder now, and had gone from steady bumps to the roar of a thousand freight trains. Jenny looked up from her crumbling front porch to see the house's picture window over her head. That confused her, and she literally didn't know which way was up.

The house tumbled across the street, and into the neighbor's home. They were such nice people, Jenny thought. Through all the confusion and noise and horror, her brain calmly wondered if her neighbors were at home. Their two children were darling.

Squeezed by the mud and rocks piling up behind, both houses finally exploded as if they'd been put in a blender. Jenny knew the debris was headed out into Puget Sound, and her initial fear was of being trapped and drowning. Her fears went away, however, when she was knocked unconscious by the end table that formerly held her wine glass.

It was generally assumed in Kitsap County that the Federal Emergency Management Agency would never be of much use there.

It wasn't personal. Kitsap hadn't somehow been blacklisted by

FEMA. But if a major earthquake were to hit western Washington the need in more densely populated Seattle would make Kitsap's problems seem small.

There was no argument that a major earthquake was coming. Most people think California is earthquake country, and the Golden State does have lots of them. Washington has far fewer, but when they happen they're far bigger.

FEMA, the military and any other groups responding from outside the area would naturally focus on the big cities, where most victims would be. Seattle would have scores of victims trapped in turn-of-the-century warehouses that had been converted into condos. Three people in a farmhouse in Kitsap County would not be a priority.

The result was that virtually every politician in Kitsap County agreed that they'd be on their own for much longer than the three days promised by the federal government. Among the actions they'd considered was creating a team of dogs to search collapsed buildings, believing that FEMA's vaunted Urban Search and Rescue teams would all be deployed in Seattle.

It seemed like a good idea until they figured out the cost, and the training requirements, and all for something that might not happen for another 250 years. But the county did have its team of wilderness SAR dogs, used to finding lost hikers or Alzheimer's patients. Could they be cross-trained to search rubble? They set up a training event with Bryce's team at a rubble pile built for training firefighters. They were astonished at how quickly the dogs adapted to this new environment.

At first, most of the dogs on Bryce's team hopped off the pile and went to the nearby brush. That's where they were used to finding people. Bryce's team quickly learned that all they needed to do was call them back. After a couple of "gimme" training finds the dogs would start to understand that subjects can be in rubble, too.

The night of the Fragaria slide Bryce wasn't thinking about the rubble pile. His attention was focused on getting his forearms to stop tingling. He'd been on a search with Sierra, and had gotten into a patch of stinging nettles. The cure for the tingling is almost worse than the disease: rubbing the affected area with ammonia. After that, it's into the shower to get both the acid and the ammonia off one's arms.

Bryce shut off the water just in time to hear the "Rescue Me" of his cellphone ring tone. The recorded message said there had been a mudslide in the waterfront community of Fragaria with occupied homes buried or partially buried.

Bryce hurriedly got Sierra crated in his truck, and made sure to take the bag that held helmet, goggles, kneepads and heavy leather gloves. He knew he'd need them this night. The drive was a short one, and he arrived to find immense destruction. He could see the remains of four, maybe six, houses in the debris field. He arrived to see the fire chief urgently calling him over before the Suburban was even in "park."

"Really glad you're here, Bryce," said the fire chief. "I've got a couple of other Kitsap dogs, and Alan Granger from Mason County, on the way out. You're the first one here and I want to get you started."

Bryce would take the area closest to the command post. As the others arrived they would leapfrog over him to more distant portions of the debris field. In particular, there was a big pile of debris on what looked like a new point of land the slide had created.

Given the go-ahead, Bryce leaned down to Sierra and removed her collar. Rubble dogs search naked, so there's nothing to catch on a piece of debris. They don't even wear booties. Dogs have a marvelous ability to pick up a foot, quickly, if they step on something sharp.

Sierra's leash and collar went in the cargo pocket on his left pants leg and Bryce stepped off onto what looked like a piece of fencepost in the rubble. He tested it with his weight, and it held.

Sierra was watching Bryce intently, waiting for the command to search. Bryce spoke the words, and watched Sierra leap unhesitatingly onto the debris field.

As had happened when she was first introduced to the rubble pile, Sierra quickly adapted to the watery slurry that had once been much of Fragaria. After freeing herself from the muck, she started hopping from brick to board to bed to bookshelf. It didn't take long before Bryce saw her trademark snap-of-the-head. She'd smelled something.

Sierra's nose was down, right at a seam between two pieces of debris. If someone was in the rubble below, it would make sense for scent to be coming from there.

Sierra moved away from the seam and sniffed the air. She snorted, to clear her nose. That was another sign that meant Sierra had smelled something. Sierra returned, put her nose to the seam one more time, and sat. Her trained indication. Bryce responded with "show me," and Sierra put her nose to the seam Bryce had expected.

"Good girl," Bryce responded, but not with his usual enthusiasm. He didn't offer Sierra her ball.

In training, Bryce or someone present always knew where the subjects were hidden. There was no chance of rewarding a false alert. In the real world, the handler has tough choice. They can risk disappointing (and demotivating) a dog by failing to reward an actual find, or they can reward a false alert and reinforce bad behavior.

Bryce trusted Sierra, but this was a new situation. He didn't want to risk confusing her during probably the most important mission they'd ever been on. He trusted her enough to call in one of the fire department's Rapid Intervention Teams, but the ball and belly rubs would have to wait.

"Sierra hit on that seam right there," he told the team leader. "You might want to peel this back in layers and follow any openings where scent could have moved through the rubble."

As the RIT worked, Bryce looked around and noticed two of the later-arriving dog teams moving through the area. Mattie and Sam, "Dog 5," were headed to the far side of the debris field. Alan, from Mason County, was headed onto the new point of land created by the slide. Mattie waved to Bryce. Alan seemed focused, like he was going into battle.

Suddenly things around Bryce got quiet. The digging had stopped.

"Looks like they've found something," the team leader commented. Just as Bryce could read Sierra's body language, the RIT team leader knew his people.

"It's a body, appears male" one of the team members called. "OK, let's get him out."

Bryce moved back toward the opening. He didn't want Sierra to get bored with searching, and if she never got rewarded for her finds that was a possibility. "Hey guys, can I get the dog up close to the body for a reward?"

"Bring the dog over, but nothing disrespectful, OK?"

Sierra peered over the edge and sat again. This time Bryce handed her the ball.

"Good girl," Bryce almost whispered. He didn't want anyone seeing him celebrate a person's death. "What-a-dog-what-a-dog-yaaaaayy," he continued. They played for a few minutes and then Bryce picked up the ball and put it back in his pocket.

Bryce worked another four hours, and found two more bodies. He'd considered himself just about done for the night when Sierra started moving out of their assigned search area.

Oh great, Bryce thought, she'd headed into Mason 20's area. At least with all these other people out here Alan can't yell like last time.

Just as they passed the boundary for their search area they met Granger coming the other way.

"Sorry, Alan. Sierra got a whiff of something over here and wants to check it out. Hope that's OK."

"No problem, kid. We've finished the area and there's nothing here. Knock yourself out. Watch that one spot over on the east edge. There's some water dammed up or something, it's really soupy."

Bryce was stunned. Alan Granger had never given him the time of day, and definitely not a warning of difficult conditions. He hardly spoke at all. This was like writing him a love letter.

"Thanks, will do. You're sure you're clear here…don't mind us coming in?"

"I'm telling you there's nothing over there but if your dog wants to drag you through that mess go ahead. Be my guest. I'm headed over to get us both hosed down and we're outa here."

As soon as Bryce took a step in the right direction, Sierra resumed slogging through the muck. Bryce noticed she had picked up speed and seemed to be looking over at one particular pile of debris. There was siding on top, but clearly it was siding from two different homes. Maybe one had been pushed into the other?

As Sierra got to the pile she became even more animated. She'd now had three finds in which she was very businesslike. She had always located the spot that was the strongest source of odor and sat down. When Bryce said "show me," she'd calmly put her nose to whatever crack or crevice smelled the strongest.

Now, she was walking on tip-toe with her nose in the air. Her tail was up and wagging, her mouth slightly open with her tongue extended. She almost dove into a small opening, and when she came back up she sat without hesitation.

Then, she started barking.

Sierra had never done that in cadaver work. She only barked when there was a live person there...someone who could toss her ball and scratch her belly once Bryce arrived. So why was she barking now?

"Good girl," Bryce cooed, giving Sierra the soft reward. He praised her, but the full meal deal with her ball would have to wait until there was a confirmed body. Sierra continued to bark and then did something she'd never done before—she jumped up and put both paws on his waist.

It couldn't be, Bryce thought. Sierra was acting like there was a live person under the rubble. Bryce had felt strongly that somebody could be alive, but knew that was his heart talking. His head knew better, he thought.

Still, he had been very successful in the past by trusting Sierra. He knelt down to what looked like an opening in the debris.

"Hellooooo…anybody in there?" He knew if anyone else saw him do that they'd think he was nuts. But he tried again.

"Hellooooo…search and rescue! Anybody there?"

The voice that came back was that of a woman, but frail and shaky. If one could sound like they were at death's door, this was that voice.

"Yes…help…please. I'm stuck."

Initially Bryce's mind wouldn't let him believe he'd gotten a response. As much as he'd wanted to find a survivor, as much as he'd *willed* himself to find a survivor, he now had trouble comprehending that it was happening.

His mind went to a very weird place. Bryce now thought this was another rescuer, who'd perhaps fallen into some debris and been trapped.

"Are you one of us?" He yelled back. "Are you a searcher?"

"No…I live here. I think the hillside came down on my house."

Now it was undeniable, even to a brain that was in complete denial. Sierra had led him to someone who wasn't dead. Bryce had no idea what to do, but his training kicked in. He spoke the phrase that every searcher is taught to use when coming upon a missing subject.

"My name's Bryce, and I'm with search and rescue. What's your name?"

"Jenny. I'm Jenny. Can you get me out of here?"

"Jenny, are you hurt? Can you tell me if anything hurts?"

"My legs are pinned but I don't think they're broken. I'm freezing cold. I don't want to answer questions, I just want out of here."

Bryce's heart was beating so hard he could hear it in his head. He had to force himself to stop breathing so hard or he'd hyperventilate and pass out. He remembered the words of his first SAR instructor, an older man who, by age sixty, had climbed Mt. Rainer more than a dozen times.

"You are the professional. You are the rescuer. You've got to convey that you're calm and in charge, even if you're panicked and confused."

The words ran through Bryce's head, and he stopped long enough to take one deep breath and go back to work.

"Jenny you bet we're going to get you out of here. In about one minute I'm going to have more help here than you can imagine and we're going to get you taken care of."

"How bad was it…how many homes?" the voice asked.

"Right now we need to worry about you, Jenny. We'll fill you in when we get you out of this rubble."

Bryce keyed the microphone on his radio. "Operations, Dog 44."

"Dog 44, Ops. Go ahead."

"This is Dog 44. My K9 has given me a live-find indication, and I have positive voice contact with an entrapped survivor. I need pretty much everybody you've got, with every hand tool you've got. I'm over here near the water. I'll be the one waving my arms like a madman."

Just like Bryce, the Ops Chief was having trouble comprehending that there was a real, live survivor out there. His heart started pounding, and also had to force himself to remain calm on the radio.

"Dog 44 outstanding. That's great news. We have two RITs headed out of base now. They'll be there shortly."

The RITs were literally running across the debris field. They mostly followed the paths that had been created earlier, but occasionally would end up in the mud. They barely slowed down even when knee deep. They just kept their legs pumping and eventually got back to solid ground. They were there in less than five minutes.

"Great job, son," the team leader said. "Have you been talking to her?"

"Yes, her name's Jenny. She keeps asking about the other homes, and I've tried to dodge the subject. She doesn't need any more sadness right now."

"Good call. Here's what we're going to do. You've got an established rapport with her so you'll be the one who keeps talking to her. Eventually the paramedics will take over but until then I want you keeping her calm. Can you do that?"

"My pleasure," Bryce responded. He leaned down to the gap in the debris and resumed contact with Jenny.

"Jenny, I've got some firefighters here now. But Sierra and I are going to stay right here with you. It might get a little noisy, but they're going to get all this stuff moved and get you out."

The weak voice had asked only questions since Bryce first contacted her. She'd spoken nothing about herself except to answer Bryce's first questions about her condition.

"Is Sierra the dog that found me? Is she a search dog?"

"Sierra's my dog, and yes, she's a search dog. We'll both be with you while the others dig. Once we get you out, things will start to happen pretty fast. I might need to move away to give the paramedics some room, but we're here with you until then."

"Thank you…please don't leave me. Her bark was the first noise I've heard in hours, and it was like music. Your voice, too…."

They don't teach this in SAR training. Bryce had no idea what to say to a woman who was in danger of dying and was instead paying compliments to others.

"We're glad to be here, ma'am. It looks like they're going to be starting a chain saw. You won't be able to hear me for a while, but we'll be right here."

The firefighter pulled the rope on the saw and set about to cutting the beams that seemed to block their way. The hope was that once the beams were moved, the other material could be pulled away from Jenny by hand. They'd get down to her, and then try to figure out what was pinning her legs.

After four of the crossed beams were cut and pulled from the hole, they shut down the chain saw and Bryce called down to Jenny.

"You OK down there?"

"Yes, but that was very loud. The last beam you cut on, I could feel it against my legs. I think that's the one that has me pinned in."

"Perfect," was the reply from team leader. He told one of the firefighters to push on the last beam they'd been cutting.

"Ow, stop!" yelled Jenny. "That really hurt."

"OK, we'll stop. I'm sorry, Jenny, but it's really good news," Bryce replied. "The firefighters will follow that beam right through the rubble to you."

If you've ever watched a dog digging on a beach, you've seen the sand come flying out from between their back legs. No dog has anything on the team that was now trying to extract Jenny Arbuthwaite from the rubble of her home. Bricks and boards and beams and blenders all came flying up out of the hole, as they worked their way toward Jenny.

"Ow, let go of me!" Jenny cried.

A firefighter had grabbed at what looked like the railing from a staircase. He pulled, trying to get the piece of wood out of the hole. But Jenny weighed less than one hundred pounds, and the firefighter had grabbed her mud-caked calf.

"I've got her," the firefighter realized, and cried out. Immediately two others went to his side and carefully began pulling debris from around her. Jenny had been trapped face down in a void space just big enough for her. Her frailty had saved her life. Anyone larger would either have been crushed outright, or would not have been able to expand their chest enough to breathe.

The firefighters worked their way into the debris surrounding Jenny, slipped a backboard in to stabilize her spine and then pulled her, feet first, out of the rubble.

"Where's that dog?" Jenny managed to whisper as they brought her out of the hole. "I want to see the dog that saved me."

Medically, meeting the dog was a distraction. But the firefighters knew that happy patients do better, so they set her down long enough to let Sierra approach.

With her one free hand Jenny touched Sierra on the shoulder and scratched her ear. "What a wonderful dog. Thank you for finding me."

And then she looked at Bryce.

"My God, so young, and you're out with your dog rescuing old women from their houses?"

"Yes, ma'am. We're a search team. We normally search in the woods."

"I can't see much, but it looks like everything's gone," Jenny asked. Bryce still didn't want to burden her with the horrible details, but he also couldn't deny the obvious.

"Was anybody killed?" Jenny asked, her voice actually becoming louder as she saw the devastation.

"Yes, ma'am."

"How many?"

"We don't know yet. We think about six houses were hit," Bryce said, trying to put a good spin on bad news.

"Who else made it out?"

"No one else, ma'am," Bryce whispered back. "You're the only one so far."

"Oh my God, oh my God, oh my God. Why me? I'm an old woman who's lived a good life. If I died tomorrow I'd have nothing to gripe about. I don't understand...."

"None of us understands, ma'am, but we're going to keep looking for survivors. Finding you means there's a chance others could be out here."

They arrived at the makeshift landing zone and paramedics were getting ready to load Jenny into the aircraft. Bryce and Sierra obviously couldn't ride with her to Harborview so they said their good byes, and the experienced paramedics began asking questions and building their own rapport with Jenny.

Just before they put her in the machine, she raised her head up as high as the straps and neck brace would allow and called to Bryce. "You come visit me when this is all over, will you? And please bring your dog. She's beautiful."

"I will ma'am I will."

Bryce and Sierra made their way back to the command post. The find had been emotional and they both needed a break.

"Hey kid...nice job." It was Granger, he'd walked up behind Bryce. "I don't mind tossing less experienced handlers a find now and then. I've had plenty in my life."

What an ass, Bryce thought. But this was not the place for an argument. "I appreciate it, sir. I'd be happy to return the favor if it meant finding a second person alive."

Granger didn't make a long conversation of it. He turned and began walking up the road to his truck.

Bryce turned and headed back out on the pile. Since Granger had missed one survivor, he might have missed others. It would be a long night.

CHAPTER SEVEN
Bonus Points

"911, what are you reporting?"

It had been a busy night at WestCom, the center that handled all 911 calls in Kitsap County. The weather was hot, it was the first of the month and a Friday to boot. Much more importantly. it was a full moon.

Every emergency responder, every police officer, every firefighter, every paramedic will all tell you the same thing: The effects of the full moon are very real. Yes, people drink when they get paid and everybody likes to blow off a little steam at the end of the workweek. But a full moon adds a whole new dimension of crazy to a Friday night.

So far, WestCom had sent officers to four cases of domestic violence, one major car crash and an armed robbery at a convenience market. Add in the routine burglaries and shoplifts, and the sheriff's office was starting to get backed up. There were more calls coming into 911 than there were deputies to respond.

An overdue husband would not have been a priority, except that Betty Robinson asked all the right questions. She'd been a dispatcher for nearly a decade, and had a sixth sense about who was sane and sober and who wasn't.

This caller seemed as normal as they come.

"My husband didn't come back from a bike ride in Banner Forest. It's been dark for a couple of hours, so my daughter and I came down to check. His car is here at the trailhead, but he's not here."

Banner Forest is a 600-acre wooded site in the middle of suburban south Kitsap. It's been heavily trailed for hikers and mountain bikers and on most weekends and evenings the parking lot is full.

But there is also the opportunity for solitude. There are so many trails, so well laid out, that it's possible to spend hours in the forest and run into only one or two other parties. Conversely, that means if someone crashed their bike and went into a ravine, they wouldn't necessarily be noticed by other riders or hikers.

"Does he have an iPhone?" Betty asked the caller. An official law enforcement "ping" of a cell phone location could take a while. But if the family had set up the Find My iPhone feature, the ladies could quickly locate their missing husband and father. Betty had solved more than one missing person case that way, without ever having to dispatch a deputy.

"His cell phone is in the center console of the car. He must have forgotten to take it with him."

Betty was quickly becoming convinced this wife's intuition was good. She didn't feel it necessary to mention that about three years prior, a man had been attacked by a bear in Banner Forest. She simply entered the call into the Computer Assisted Dispatch (CAD) system, with instructions for a deputy to meet wife and daughter at the trailhead.

Betty was working the phones that night but checked in several times to see if her colleague working the radio had dispatched it yet. After about an hour and several other high-priority calls, Betty noticed the call had been given to Deputy Davy Jones. *"At least we've sent him our best deputy,"* she thought. *"He'll ferret out whether this guy is really missing or off with a mistress at some motel."*

It didn't take much conversation with the wife for Jones to agree with Betty's assessment. It all added up to the husband having crashed his bike and being stuck in the forest. If one could walk, limp or crawl, there is really no way to stay lost in Banner Forest. All the trails eventually lead either to a paved road on the perimeter of the forest, or a wide gravel road that runs down the middle.

Jones also knew that there was no way he, the wife, and daughter could search the 600 acres themselves. There were too many trails for three people to cover. Given that darkness had fallen three hours before, he had to assume the missing man had been down for at least that long.

He got on the radio. "David-4, WestCom. Please have one of the SAR deputies call my cell. We'll be doing a call-out."

The call was quick in coming, and Jones explained his reasons for wanting SAR. Overdue husband calls were usually met with some skepticism, but, with the car still at the trailhead, the SAR deputy agreed and began the process of getting searchers called out.

The call at Banner Forest was one that Bryce had expected for some time. He knew how heavily the area was used, and had gone jogging there a time or two. It stood to reason that somebody would eventually get hurt or get lost, and need help.

Davy Jones was at base, handling the investigative side of the search. Even with SAR in the field, he'd be checking to see if the man's credit cards had been used—or if there was any other sign that he wasn't dead. In the internet age, a motel charge would appear on someone's account almost instantly. The banks were usually helpful when deputies could document an emergency need. So far, everything seemed to point back to Banner Forest.

Meantime, Deputy Jason Link had been tasked with running the field search. Link was assigned as a SAR deputy, meaning he'd received special training in how to run searches. He still worked the road and took regular calls, but when a search was necessary, Link or one of his fellow SAR deputies would take the lead.

Link had Bryce go to the most likely area where someone could be missing. The southwest corner of the forest was the least used, partially because it had the most difficult trails. There were many places there where someone could crash, go down a brushy hill, and be invisible to subsequent passersby. It would take a dog's nose to know they were there.

This would be a challenging search for Sierra. Because so many people had walked the trails, this would be what handlers call a "dirty" area. There would be lots of scent for her to check out, and at least a couple places where people had stepped behind bushes to relieve themselves.

The saving grace was that if someone was down and stationary for an extended period, their scent would grow into a pool that would be much stronger than the transient smells of those just passing through. The wind would turn the subject's odor plume into a cone moving downwind. A trained air scent dog would react to that stronger scent, and work the cone back to its source. Sierra had done it many times before.

Another bit of good news was that Bryce didn't need to go cross country. Banner Forest had so many trails that he could get Sierra's nose downwind of almost any part without the need to crush brush. There was a steady wind from the south, so Bryce went to nearly the exact middle of the park. He planned to move generally southwest along the various trails, making sure to cover each completely. They'd follow trails until Sierra's nose told him otherwise.

They started out the Fusion Loop Trail, but would be sure to check Rocky Road and Stinky Seat. Sierra had some interest along all three, and checked a couple of spots where people had obviously gone behind a tree for a moment. But she didn't go into real alert mode, and certainly never came back to Bryce to give her trained indication.

"C'mon, Sierra. Let's go check out Donald Duck, and then we'll spend some quality time on Wired Brain." He wondered where the riding club that had revitalized the park came up with such weird names. Regardless, Wired Brain would be a nice wrap up, and would take them out the south end of the park.

After a few minutes on Donald Duck, Bryce noticed Sierra start to pick up speed. She ran down the trail away from Bryce and around a corner. She came back, peeked around a bush, and looked at him. That was her sign that she smelled something interesting, but hadn't yet found the source. She then plunged off the trail to the south.

"*Why does my dog always pick up scent where the brush is the thickest?*" Bryce thought as he moved to follow the sound of her bell. Even Sierra was struggling to get through the thick brush, but her search drive was so strong she never considered going another way. She moved directly south off the Donald Duck trail, making a cross-country beeline for Wired Brain.

Wired Brain moves from the Forest's south entrance in a northwesterly direction, with lots of twisting turns and exciting climbs and descents. Eventually Wired Brain finds its way to a T intersection. Turning right took you back to the main road through the Forest, turning left goes down to a loop that turns you back the way you came.

The brush was so thick that Bryce couldn't take time to look at his GPS or map. He had to simply follow the sound of Sierra's bell. She was heading right for where Bryce figured the T intersection ought to be.

The bell stopped for a second and Bryce wondered if Sierra had finally hit impenetrable brush. He'd hit rough stuff long ago, but found a way to get through. It was up to him to follow Sierra or risk signaling that he wasn't interested in what she was doing.

If Sierra really was stuck, Bryce figured he'd take her back to Donald Duck, walk out to the forest road, and then try to get to the source of odor off of Wired Brain. But Sierra's bell was ringing again, heading back for him.

When Sierra arrived, they were both in a place where the brush was too thick for her to sit. But she dropped her butt a little bit and looked Bryce in the eye. "Show me!"

Without missing a beat, Sierra turned and headed back toward Wired Brain. When her bell stopped and the barking began, Bryce knew she'd found the subject.

It took Bryce almost two full minutes to get through the brush and catch up with Sierra. She never stopped barking the entire time. When he got there, Bryce wasn't sure if the biker was dead or just unconscious. In fact, Sierra's barking was just waking him up. He was groggy and Bryce could see that his helmet was cracked. As Bryce suspected, the man had gone off the trail and down a small hill. He'd obviously hit his head on something and his helmet probably kept him from being killed.

It didn't keep him from being knocked goofy.

"Bootsie, stop that barking. There's nobody out there. Go back to bed."

Bryce tossed Sierra her ball so she'd stop barking, but didn't spend a lot of time playing with her. He needed to focus on his patient.

"Hello...sir? I'm with search and rescue. My name's Bryce. Are you OK?"

"Huh, who are you? What happened?"

"My name's Bryce. I think you crashed your bike and hit your head. Stay right there on the ground and let's get you checked out."

"Man, my head hurts. How did I get here?"

"You were riding your bike. Do you remember being on a bike ride?"

"Not really. Did I crash?"

"It looks that way. How about your neck, any pain there? OK if I touch you?"

"Sure, but it's really just my...ow!"

"Looks like you've tweaked an ankle, too. A doctor will have to tell you whether it's broken, but you won't be walking out on this. Give me a minute to get some help here."

"Wow, until you grabbed it, I hadn't felt a thing. My God, what time is it?" the man said, regaining more consciousness. "My wife will be freaked!"

"She called us, that's why we're here. She's at the trailhead and, when I left her, she was worried but holding up OK. Let me make that radio call and let everybody know your status."

Bryce took a minute to get their GPS coordinates, though the best description would be their location off the T-intersection.

"Search Base, Dog 44."

"Base, go ahead."

"Dog 44, we've located our subject and he is alive and talking, but injured. Let me know when you're ready to copy coordinates and vitals."

"Good job, 44. Go ahead with the info."

"Location is off the trail, in the woods west of the T-intersection on Wired Brain. That's the trail that runs right from the south entrance to the forest. Coordinates are 10-Tango 0533493 5258356. Patient has a head injury and is just regaining consciousness. He is slightly disoriented but making more sense with time. Additionally he has a possible broken left ankle. He'll be a pack out with a backboard and C-spine protection along with splinting the leg."

"OK 44, copy that. We'll have our folks come in with the paramedics. Keep him stable and comfortable and we'll have help there shortly."

"Affirm. I'm not going to splint the ankle at this time. I'll just leave it in a position of comfort and let the medics do it when they get here. They'll have better stuff anyway."

No matter how gently one tries, getting a broken limb splinted is a painful process. The first time Bryce found someone with a broken leg, he'd gone to a lot of trouble and created a marvelous improvised splint from branches on a nearby tree. He'd cut the branches to exactly the right length, shaved them so the ends were rounded, padded them with the subject's fleece jacket, and assembled the whole thing with self-clinging gauze wrap. The paramedics showed up about ten minutes later and cut Bryce's work of art into little pieces, causing more moaning from the patient as they got him into an "official" medical splint.

"44, Base concurs…but check for a pulse in that foot to make sure there's good blood flow. If there's not, get back to us and we'll talk you through repositioning it. The medics should be there pretty quickly."

With night falling, it was getting colder, and shock added to the chill. Bryce got a foam pad under the injured man, to insulate him from the ground. He also got him in a sleeping bag, but left the injured leg out the side zipper for access.

"I'm really hungry. Have you got anything to eat?" rider asked. That was a sign that his mental status was improving, though the head injury prompted Bryce to check with base for the OK. Ronda, a retired ER doc, was handling radio duty, so he knew he'd be getting good advice.

"Base, 44. The patient is thirsty and hungry. OK to give him some water and a granola bar?"

"44, Base. Water's OK. Have him take two bites of the granola bar and see how his stomach does. Be ready to roll him on his side if he gets nauseous. If a couple minutes go by and he doesn't throw up, he can eat the rest of the granola bar. Be sure to mention that in your handoff to the medics. The surgeons will want to know that if they need to do surgery."

"44, understood."

The man drank about half a Nalgene bottle of water to start and Bryce steeled himself for any possible stomach upset that might follow. He was becoming more lucid and understood to only eat a small amount of the granola bar. He took two bites and put the rest aside.

"It sounds like you're starting to get the cobwebs out of your head. Let me ask you a couple questions so I can fill the medics in when they get here. Do you know where you are?"

"Um…I forget the name of the trail…but Banner Forest."

"Close enough…what day is it?"

"Saturday."

"Two for two. The final question…is Mickey Mouse a dog or a cat?"

"He's a…what? I'm sorry, what did you say?"

Bryce just laughed. "That's supposed to confuse you. Somebody who's really messed up will pick one and answer. The fact that you figured out the question is nonsense means your brain is working OK. I do have one more question—who's Bootsie?"

"Bootsie was a dog I had growing up. She was a little dachshund who died when I was in fifth grade. How did you know about her?"

"You called my dog Bootsie when you were waking up. I figured it was something like that."

After twenty more minutes of small talk, the paramedics arrived with about fifteen ground-pounders to handle the pack-out. There were plenty of them, and Bryce didn't want Sierra underfoot while they were carrying the litter. With the team leader's permission, he decided to leave ahead of them. They set out along Wired Brain for the south entrance.

"Base, Dog 44. We're going to get out of the way so Sierra doesn't interfere with those carrying the litter. It's much closer for us to walk out to the south entrance and get transport back to base. Do you have someone in a vehicle able to pick us up?"

"ESAR 47 is already there. She dropped off some folks earlier and she can run you back whenever you make it out."

"Understood…it'll take us about fifteen minutes. 44 clear."

"Base clear."

"47 copies," Patti came over the radio, letting both Bryce and base know she'd heard their transmissions. She loved dogs, and would have liked to have been a dog handler. Her husband was deathly allergic to dogs, and she couldn't have one of her own.

"Your bus ticket will be some puppy kisses." Probably not appropriate radio procedure, but the search was over. Patti had been in search and rescue so long that everybody cut her some slack.

"Sierra's got lots o' kisses for ya. See you shortly. 44 clear"

"47, clear."

Bryce and Sierra made their way out the trail, and Bryce didn't bother to put Sierra on lead. If she did get to the south trailhead, Patti would be there to make sure she didn't get into the road.

As they neared the trailhead, Sierra started walking tiptoe and sniffing the air. *"There's some people here, for sure. I'll have to give her a soft reward for finding them,"* Bryce thought.

But then he heard the crushing of brush, which meant Sierra was clearly working off the trail. He wasn't sure what she was up to, but didn't want her chasing a deer or finding somebody's used toilet paper. There wasn't anybody left to find and he wanted to get back to his truck.

"Sierra, come!" he called, but she was already on the way back. It was odd that she was coming back so directly, and not just wandering back after checking out a random smell. She burst out of the brush a few feet ahead, turned to face Bryce, and sat.

"Hey girl, we've already found everybody we're going to find tonight. You remember Patti? We're going to see Patti!"

In the past, Sierra had reacted to the name. She'd searched for Patti a lot in training, and knew what it meant to "find Patti." But tonight Sierra was having none of it. When Bryce tried to walk around her, Sierra spun, got out ahead of him, and sat again.

"Sierra...let's go...we need to get to the truck," Bryce told her, with some exasperation in his voice.

But when Bryce tried to walk around her, Sierra rose up and put both front paws on his waist. It was almost like she was trying to push Bryce off the trail.

Bryce was tired but he knew to pay attention when Sierra offered a behavior he'd never seen before.

"OK girl, whatcha got? Can you show me?"

This wasn't the sharp "Show me!" of a normal re-find. He used the words so Sierra knew she could set out, but he said them more softly. He wasn't interested in teaching her to find a dead deer or a diaper.

Sierra continued through the brush and took Bryce almost to the road that bordered the forest. He was ready to call her back to keep her from getting out into traffic, when he saw her sit again. A few more steps, and his nose told him why she was sitting. He no longer needed a cadaver dog to know what was there.

He took a few more steps through the brush, carefully, and saw the badly decomposed remains in the brush. The extremities were missing, probably carried off by animals. But the clothing and the overall shape confirmed that this body was human.

"Good girl! You found Digger…you found Diggerrrr!" Bryce said quietly, tossing her ball to her.

Bryce's mind was running in high gear. He'd found plenty of bodies before, but he'd always been *expecting* to find one. To have one appear out of nowhere made it as much a shock to him as anybody else.

He needed to call base, but this would be confusing. The last thing he wanted to do was give a death code over the radio and have horribly wrong information get to the family of the mountain biker. He thought for a minute about what to say.

"Base, Dog 44." Bryce worked to keep his voice calm. He knew the media and scanner hobbyists would be listening. No matter what code he used, if there was excitement in his voice, they would know something was up. He needed to sound as matter-of-fact as he ever had in his life.

"Dog 44, Base. Go ahead."

"Dog 44. We're almost back to the trailhead and, of all people, we've bumped into Nat Sessions. I haven't seen Nat in ages and I'm going to spend a few minutes seeing what he's been up to. If Patti wants to come down, I'm sure Nat would be glad to see her as well."

Nat Sessions had been a long-time and much-beloved member of Bryce's SAR team until his death three years' previous. Using his name was a clue that something odd was up.

"Dog 44, ummmmm…OK. Is Nat here for the search?" The question told Bryce that Ronda was confused, but catching on.

"Nah…he's just here for the day. Completely unrelated to the search, juuuust a coincidence. He said he misses going on searches and misses working with the Sheriff's office."

"The deputy here says they miss Nat as well. In fact, the SAR deputy wants to drop down and see him if he wouldn't mind."

"A fine idea. Have him come in the south entrance and take the first trail to his left. I think we're within hollering distance. 44 clear."

Bryce had managed to keep the secret with the tone of his voice, but Deputy Link gave it away with the sound of his engine. The sound of a Ford Crown Victoria Police Interceptor engine can be heard for miles, especially in quiet suburban neighborhoods. Everybody in the Forest heard the engine wind up as Link went south on Banner Road. He took the corner on Olalla Valley Road in all but a sideways slide, and skidded to a stop at the south trailhead. Those already there looked on with wonder, but didn't question when he got out and strode into the forest with purpose.

Back at base, the question "What's up?" was circulating around the parking lot. Everyone had heard the mountain biker probably would survive his injuries, so a low-flying deputy raised eyebrows there too.

"What was that?" the rider's wife asked Jones. "I thought you said my husband was OK?"

"I'm sorry. That's unrelated to your husband's case," Jones tried to reassure her. "He's being carried out now, and has been talking to his rescuers. Let me have someone run you down to the south entrance so you can talk to him before they load him on the ambulance."

Link located Bryce and Sierra back out on the trail, marking the spot with pink grid ribbon. Bryce had tied bits of ribbon to bushes and branches as they walked out, so that others could find their way in.

"A second body?" Link asked, incredulously. "You found *another* body?"

"Yup, pretty badly decomposed," was Bryce's response. "You'll be able to smell it about halfway there. The clothing looks female but that's up to the coroner."

"Anything around it? A bike? Gun? Bottle of pills?"

"I didn't search. It's a crime scene, so I got out and marked the way back in for you."

Link started in, and followed Bryce's ribbons to the scene. He took a quick glance and backed out himself, for the same reason Bryce had. After giving a statement to Link, Bryce left the scene of the dead body and Patti gave him and Sierra their ride back to base.

"Nice goin', kid," said Ronda, upon seeing Bryce loading Sierra in his truck. "It took me a minute to figure out what you were trying to say. It just didn't compute."

The only thing that made Bryce more uncomfortable than girls was compliments. He tried to turn Ronda's into a post-event debrief.

"Anything I could have done differently?" he asked. "I thought about using my cell phone, but the service is really sketchy here. Half a message could have been more confusing than a coded one."

"You did just fine, young man. Good on Sierra for picking up on the scent. Had you given her a search command?"

"No, she just likes searching and if she picks up odor, she'll react to it."

"Well, I'm happy for you and even better, you really ticked off Granger."

Bryce was completely confused by the remark.

"How so?"

"He was late getting here and really wanted to get in the field. In particular, he wanted to search the south end. I thought he was going to pop a vein when Link told him you were already deployed there."

"Dang it. There's not some scorecard out there. We're not in competition."

"No, but you know how he is. He likes to pick his own search area. It's hard to argue with his success. I guess you aced him out of two notches for his belt. He'd guessed the rider would be in the south west quadrant, and then Sierra got you bonus points for the body."

"Yeah…good for her," was Bryce's only response.

CHAPTER EIGHT
Ugly Carpet

"Look at it from my side, Junior. What are the odds that a dead hooker would get randomly dumped directly, and I mean *directly*, across the street from the home of a registered sex offender?"

It pained Detective Bob Wright to call Misty Combes a "dead hooker." Wright had been a patrol deputy the first time he contacted her, and it was obvious she didn't belong walking the stroll along Highway 303. She'd been a prostitute all right, but was a poster child for how the sex industry victimizes children. He'd tried to get her help, into a program or placed at a shelter, but she was too far gone for anyone to help.

His pity for the young lady aside, Wright had to speak his suspect's language. Junior would never have referred to any girl as an "at-risk youth." He wouldn't have understood the term. "Dead hooker" was what he understood.

"I don't know what to say," Junior replied. "I get it. It looks bad. What more can I say? I didn't kill her."

Junior was a sarcastic nickname bestowed by what was left of the young man's family when he was in his teens. He'd been big at birth, and became huge when he hit puberty. Unlike most "juniors," he didn't share his father's name. In fact, he'd never met the man. Calling someone of his size "Junior" was simply funny on the face of it.

The discussion was also happening in an unusual place. Wright didn't normally confront suspects on the porch of their house. He preferred to do that in an interview room where he controlled the environment. But he decided to toss Junior some rope and see if he hung himself.

"Let me make it easy for you," he said, adopting the good cop persona. "You brought her home and she OD'd in your bathroom. You didn't kill her, but you couldn't get caught with a hooker. So you dragged her across the street and hoped the bears would handle it."

"Nooo. I've followed my program. I've been to all my group sessions, made all my meets with my CCO, and you won't find anything on my computer."

In fact, at that moment a state Community Corrections Officer was going through Junior's computer. He'd found a resume, e-mails to potential employers, and absolutely nothing in the way of pornography.

Junior had been renting a room in the home across from Banner Forest. "Renting" was maybe a generous term, as the couple who'd taken him in knew his history and his financial status. Three years prior, Junior had molested his nine-year-old niece. His current landlady and her husband were devout Christians who volunteered at the minimum security prison to which Junior had been assigned. They spotted him there, worked with him, and came to believe that Jesus could save this troubled young man.

When he got out of prison, they provided the room knowing that they'd only occasionally be paid.

"He's right, there's nothing on the computer," the CCO told Wright. "It's out in the dining room, so not much chance for something to slip by the couple who's renting him the room."

It was a delicate dance they were doing. The CCO could search Junior's residence any time he wanted, but only for parole violations. If the cops were investigating some new crime, a search warrant would be necessary. Wright knew he didn't have enough evidence for a search warrant, but asked the CCO to come along and see if they could gently develop some.

"Anything else in the room?" Wright asked.

"Nope, and Junior's right. So far as I can tell he's met all his conditions. I'd have to check the records to be sure, but I don't recall him ever missing a check-in."

Junior, despite his size and apparent manliness, was starting to cry. He was a big baby, which explained why he couldn't handle a relationship with a woman his age. That he'd turned to a nine-year-old girl was sick, but fit in with the character Wright was seeing.

"I've done everything I'm supposed to and have a job all lined up to start next week. Now this. You won't tell my new boss, will you?"

"He'd better know you're an RSO," the corrections officer called from inside.

"He does, and there's no kids around the shop," Junior hollered back. "It's a good job in the warehouse for an online company. We don't even have customers coming in the front door. I'll be pulling orders and doing the shipping. I'm the only one outside the owner's family who works there."

As Wright and Junior continued their conversation on the porch, a car pulled into the driveway. The couple got out with obvious concern on their faces. Wright's car was unmarked, but only the police drive older Crown Vics with black hubcaps. It was obvious to the couple that detectives were paying a visit to Junior.

The man was in a white shirt and wide 1980's tie, the woman in a long flowered dress that stretched from neckline to ankle. Her hair was in a bun, and her only fashion accessory was a pair of very stylish reading glasses hung around her neck. She still wore the ID card that read "Chaplain" clipped to her dress.

"I'm Anita Harper," she said quietly. "Can I ask what's going on here?"

Before Wright could answer, Junior jumped in. "They think I killed a woman and dumped her body over there. They think I did it."

Junior buried his face in his hands and sunk to a sitting position against the doorframe. He began a series of sobs from deep in his chest.

Anita stepped forward and extended her hand to Wright. Her husband hung back, silently. Wearing a dress or not, it was clear who wore the pants in this family.

"We've kept pretty close tabs on Junior, as I suppose he's told you," Anita said. "He's allowed Jesus to enter his life and seems to be living righteously."

"Yes ma'am. Thank you for all you're doing for him," Wright replied.

"There's a dead woman over there?" Anita asked, pointing with her nose rather than her hands. "We saw all the excitement last night, but the news said it was a mountain biker who crashed."

"Yes ma'am, that's how it started out. While we were out there, one of the search dogs alerted us to the body."

"Oh how horrible. We'll pray for her tonight. You don't really think Junior's involved, do you?"

"We don't know who's involved, ma'am. But like I told Junior… for a young lady to show up dead across from the home of a registered sex offender is a bit of a coincidence. We've got to check it out."

"Well yes, I'm sure you do," Anita replied, and then lowered her voice.

"My husband and I minister up at the prison. We think Junior's doing well on his redemption, but we've learned that the devil has too much hold on some people. How can we help you figure out if he's involved?"

"Well, giving us consent to search your home would be a start. Because he's in community custody, the corrections officer has already searched his room. You'd have to give us permission to search the rest of the house."

"Done. Where do I sign? If Junior's involved he needs to be held accountable, and if he's innocent I want his name cleared as quickly as possible. We've gotten him a job with a fellow church member, which I think will be the final chapter in his redemption."

From the corner of his eye, Wright caught a glimpse of the husband, whose face had gone white as a ghost. The man swallowed hard and quickly regained his composure. Wright filed "the look" for future reference.

"Let me get the form. It would be great if both of you could sign it." In case anything developed of this, Wright wanted both husband and wife on the record as having given permission. He couldn't force the nervous husband to sign, but he had an ace in the hole. While the police can't intimidate someone into giving up their rights, the U.S. Constitution gives husbands no protection from domineering wives.

"Sign here, dearie, and we'll let this nice young man get on with his work," Anita said. She turned to Wright. "Is the body still there? Can we go pray over it?"

"We got the body out early this morning, ma'am," answering Anita but watching her husband. "And it wasn't a pleasant sight. I'm sure God will hear your prayers regardless of where she is."

The husband's hands were trembling as he signed. Wright hoped to run across something else with the husband's signature to see just how poorly he'd done.

Along with the CCO, Wright had brought Davy Jones back to the scene. Wright was among those who recognized Jones as a rising star in the agency. He thought the experience would do him good.

The two of them went through the house with just less than a fine tooth comb. Consent or not, they didn't want to tear the house apart and risk having the Harpers back out of the deal. They had the right to withdraw their consent at any time. Wright and Jones searched the obvious places a killer might have hidden a weapon or left a forgotten item of the victim's clothing.

"The final thing I'd like to do is run a cadaver dog through the house," Wright told Anita. "I doubt we'll find anything but if someone was killed here in your absence, there's almost always blood that the dog can find."

"That's fine," Mrs. Harper replied. "We love dogs, but don't have time for them because of our service to the Lord."

Wright had already arranged for a call to Bryce. This was no team callout. The fewer people who knew about the search, the better. He didn't want the media speculating or reporting that a sex offender lived across the street from where the body was found. It wouldn't be fair to the Harpers, and perhaps not even to Junior. Wright was starting to doubt that Junior had the guts to kill a street-savvy woman like Misty.

Bryce had parked well away from the home. He had learned long ago that if there's a strong odor source in the home, it can waft outside. If you park in the driveway, the dog can be in the scent pool from the time it jumps out of the truck.

They also didn't want to make it obvious to passersby that the home was being searched. The long driveway hid Wright's Crown Vic from the neighbors. Bryce had taken discretion one step further, actually parking back at the Banner Forest trailhead. To the rest of the world, he appeared to be taking Sierra for a walk. They would stroll down the street, casually turn down the driveway to the home, and then go to work for real. It made the search more effective, and kept the whole thing nicely low-key.

"G'morning, Bryce…how ya doin', Sierrrra? How's my girrrlll?" Jones hoped to one day have a patrol K9 of his own, and enjoyed working with the dog team when he got the chance. He knew the secret that Sierra loved butt scratches, and offered her plenty.

"You know what we got?" Wright asked Bryce.

"Yes, sir. We'll make a lap around the outside of the house, and then go inside. I'll take her from room to room and see if she comes up with anything."

The lap around the outside was mostly to let Sierra get used to smells that were present in the local environment. They had the body, so there was no need to check the crawlspace. It would be unusual for someone to take a victim under a house to kill them, and then move their body across the street. They were looking for small evidence, a knife or piece of clothing stained with blood. They'd circle the building casually, and then go to work for real inside.

As they got to the back of the home, Bryce noticed Sierra looking at one particular window. It was open just slightly, and the curtains were blowing out. Sierra's body language didn't change markedly, just two very subtle pops of her head. From the outside, the room appeared to be adjacent to the garage. He'd be sure to check that area carefully.

The house was tidy inside. The furniture was older but in good repair, and seemed to match the conservatively dressed couple waiting outside. Bryce was glad it wasn't the time of year when golden retrievers shed their coats. If it turned out to be a murder scene, dog hair would make extra work for the forensic scientists. If it wasn't a murder scene, he'd hate to leave blonde hair all over such a well-kept home.

They entered the living room, and Bryce repeated the command "find Digger." Sierra immediately began snorting and sniffing around furniture in a very animated way. Bryce was a bit stunned to find her immediately "in scent," and put his hands in his pockets. He didn't want to risk cueing her with any body language.

Sierra turned left out of the living room, down a hall toward the couple's bedroom. She sniffed under the bed, cleared her nose, and immediately left the room. No interest. She moved through the kitchen, and didn't pause for a moment at the cabinet under the sink, where most people have a garbage can. Then it was down the long hall toward the room with the window that had attracted her attention earlier. Bryce was not surprised when Wright whispered that it was Junior's room.

Sierra sniffed the bed, the closet, the desk—all places the CCO had looked earlier. Bryce saw that she kept coming back toward the entry door.

One of the challenges of human remains detection is that scent can collect in a pool. The dog will alert on the pool, where the odor is the stronger, even if the actual source of odor is a few feet away. A handler needs to recognize that the dog is doing its job, even if it seems to be missing the mark.

Bryce had seen Sierra do that many times, and had learned to avoid the temptation to help her. He'd give her a few minutes to work the problem with her nose. He was careful to avoid any body language, not even looking at Wright and Jones to signal something was up.

Sierra left the bedroom, checked the carpet in the hall, and then walked back to the living room. She snorted to clear her sinuses, and then came slowly down the hall with her nose right on the carpet. As she approached the area outside Junior's room, she sat.

"Showwww me," Bryce said softly, just above a whisper. Both Wright and Jones had seen her sit and were paying direct attention to her. Bryce whispered to soften the mood, to help avoid cuing a false alert.

Sierra put her nose down on the carpet directly in front of the door to Junior's room. This was a no-questions-asked-full-on cadaver alert. But because he didn't know for sure something was there, he rewarded softly.

"Good girlllll," he said quietly. He didn't want to alert Junior—now a murder suspect—that something had been found. He whispered his praise to Sierra, in the front room well away from the source of odor. Jones joined in the quiet play, but Wright went down the hall to where Sierra had indicated. He put his own nose down to the carpet, and smelled…nothing?

Bryce and Sierra checked the rest of the house for good measure, just to be thorough. The only source of odor was from the carpet directly outside Junior's room.

The investigation was beginning to focus on Junior as a suspect, so it was time to advise him of his rights. Junior acknowledged them, but said nothing else. At least they'd have his attention now.

"This is more than a coincidence," Wright told the trembling man. "It's one thing for a dead hooker to turn up across the street from a sex offender's house. It's quite another for a cadaver dog to hit right outside the offender's bedroom door."

Wright adopted an almost pleading voice. "Junior, we truly don't know how this girl died. It could have been an overdose, or an accident during rough sex. Maybe she threw up on the carpet as she was dying, and that's what the dog smells. But if you continue to deny, it's only going to look worse."

"I don't know any…" and Junior stopped himself. He was not a sophisticated criminal, but he'd been around the block once. He decided to invoke his right to remain silent.

"I want an attorney," he said, ending the conversation with Wright.

Wright now had a problem. He had a dead girl, an alert from a previously reliable cadaver dog, and not much else. Was this enough to arrest Junior? If he didn't arrest him, would he flee? Could Junior be the Chimera Killer they'd been looking for? The one that James Garrision insisted didn't exist? That seemed ludicrous—Junior didn't have the guts. But if he was the killer and Wright waited to arrest him, would he use the opportunity to kill again?

Wright went outside to speak to the Harpers.

"Folks, I'm sorry to tell you we've had an alert from our cadaver dog," he told the couple. "The home is now officially a crime scene and I can't let you go back in. Do you have someplace you can stay for a few hours, maybe even overnight?

"Well, yes," Anita replied. "But I need to get some clothes, my toiletries…I need things."

"I'm sorry, that's just not possible right now. I'll have a search warrant in a couple of hours and we'll be as quick as possible. It all depends on how fast I can get the warrant and how fast the crime scene team can get back out here."

The Kitsap County Sheriff's Office didn't have enough violent crime to justify its own team of forensic crime scene investigators. It relied on the Washington State Patrol's Crime Scene Response Team to handle the gathering of evidence, and they'd been at the scene in Banner Forest all night. Most of its members would be sleeping right now and it might take a while to get them spooled back up.

Wright put in the call and then turned to write his search warrant. The Harpers had given consent to search, and the two detectives had done a reasonably thorough one. With Sierra's alert, they needed to break out the fine tooth comb they hadn't used before.

In the search warrant affidavit, Wright outlined the careful steps that had led them to inquire of Junior. He didn't want some defense attorney to later claim he'd focused on Junior to the exclusion of all others. Police always talked to those who lived near any crime scene. The fact that one of the neighbors was a registered sex offender wasn't his fault. Wright pointed out that he had consent to search at every step of the way and he laid a solid foundation for wanting to cut up the Harper's carpet.

Wright also had to let the judge know that Sierra was a reliable dog. He wrote, *"In the affiant's experience, K9 Sierra has been exceptionally reliable at alerting to cadaver finds. In particular, she located the victim's body, across the street in Banner Forest, while returning from an unrelated search. She had not been given the command to look for deceased remains but alerted her handler anyway."*

Wright indicated he wanted to search for evidence of a crime, a search that would include removing carpet, padding and any underlayment that might contain evidence. He wanted the judge to sign off on exactly what was going to take place, and clearly approve what would become a significant intrusion into the Harper's home and castle.

Modern technology meant that Wright could craft and print the warrant right in his police car. But when he learned the on-call judge, Barb Stanton, lived in nearby Port Orchard, he took it to her for a face-to-face meeting.

"You're asking for permission to cut up somebody's carpet on the say-so of a dog?" Judge Stanton inquired.

Wright couldn't tell if she was being critical or not. Sometimes those who support you the most ask the hardest questions.

"Yes, your honor. As I note in the affidavit, this particular dog has been very reliable. I've spoken to the sheriff, and if we're wrong, we'll replace the carpet."

"Then you have your warrant," came the reply. "Off the record, is this Junior fellow our…what was the word…Chimera Killer?" Even the judge had been made aware of Garrison's remark and was mocking him.

"I don't know, your honor. I'm just trying to run this one homicide to ground and see where it takes us."

"Good hunting," were Stanton's final words as she showed Wright out of her foyer.

It took Wright just a few minutes to get back to the scene. He noticed Anita Harper was no longer sitting in their car in the driveway. Mr. Harper was getting out of the passenger seat, still looking very nervous. So nervous, in fact, that Wright scanned his hands to make sure he wasn't coming out with a weapon.

"My wife is at the neighbor's to use their bathroom," he asked quietly. "Can I talk to you for a moment?"

"Of course. Do you have some information to share?"

"Not really," was the pensive reply. The man was having trouble looking Wright in the eye. "I need to ask you a favor."

"Well, no promises, of course, but you're welcome to ask."

"You're going to go through the entire home now, right? Not just Junior's room?"

"Yes, the judge gave me a search warrant and we need to go through the whole place. We need to look for anything that might prove the dead girl had been in there."

"OK...um...you're going to find some things...some magazines...that my wife might not approve of..."

"Okaaaay...?" was Wright's careful and confused response.

"They're mine, not Junior's. He doesn't know they're there so don't get him in trouble. Is there any way you could not mention them to my wife?"

Wright was stunned, but at the same time not stunned. He'd seen this many times before. Someone is so nervous about something completely and totally unrelated to a crime that they make themselves a suspect. Mr. Harper's obvious case of nerves had Wright wondering if perhaps *he'd* killed the girl. In fact, the problem was a straight-laced wife and a stack of magazines.

"Where are they and what are we talking about?"

"In the attic. There's a hatch off the loft over the garage. They're nothing vile, just some old *Playboys* and *Penthouses*. I haven't looked at them in years…"

Porn? Today's feminists would say so, but a previous generation had dismissed them as just "girlie magazines." Yet this devout man was so freaked out about them that he'd almost made himself a murder suspect.

"Again, no promises. If they're what you say, and you assure me Junior had no access to them, then maybe we don't have to put them on the inventory list."

"I don't think Junior even knows about the attic access. He's never had a reason to be in the loft and there's tons of stuff stacked in front of the hatch. I'd be very grateful."

The man's trembling had stopped, having gotten his concern off his chest. Wright would do his best to keep the secret, so long as the magazines weren't child porn and there was no indication they were Junior's.

Wright didn't mention the search would involve removing the carpet on which Sierra had alerted. He'd have to answer for that later, but didn't want to have the argument before the work was done. He and Jones set about searching the rest of the house, this time with the fine-toothed comb they hadn't used earlier.

They found a Bible in every room, flipped through their pages and found…scripture. They looked everyplace that a hooker might have tossed a piece of clothing and found…dust. They checked the wastebaskets for condoms and found…garbage. Other than the odor of human body fluid on the hallway carpet, the house was as free of human failings as any home that Bob Wright had ever been in.

Well, except for the magazines in the attic. They were exactly where Mr. Harper had said they would be, and were exactly what he said they'd be. The dates on the covers long predated Junior's residency in the home. They were also the kind of magazines that are available in any convenience store. There was no reason to violate Junior's parole or get Mr. Harper in Dutch with his missus.

Wright decided that in the midst of a situation that was making no one happy, he'd avoid making things worse for somebody.

He heard a car pull into the driveway, and went outside to see who it might be.

The uniform of the day for scientists from the Washington State Patrol Crime Lab doesn't include bed hair. Mostly they wear jeans, with a windbreaker that says "Crime Lab" on the back. They're not star-struck, and don't refer to themselves by the TV name of CSI.

Sarah Clarke had short hair that was normally easy to style, assuming she took the time. In this case, Dr. Clarke was rattled out of bed so quickly that she just threw on the same clothing she'd worn the night before and headed out.

When she got out of her car, both Jones and Wright had to laugh, and knew that they could. Dr. Clarke didn't have an ego, and when they had her look at her reflection in the car window she laughed harder than either of them.

"I slept face down for a whopping three solid hours," Clarke told them. "This bed hair was hard-earned and I'm going to enjoy it."

"Well, apparently the rest of us are going to enjoy it, too. Thanks for coming back, and sorry we had to ask. A cadaver dog hit on the carpet right outside our suspect's room. Care to take a look?"

Clarke grabbed a spray bottle of luminol and a black light from the trunk of her car. "You've got a warrant, or are we here with consent?" she asked Wright.

"Both. We started with consent, and when the dog hit, we got a warrant. Our suspect is a registered sex offender who is renting a room from the family."

Wright looked over and was a bit alarmed to see Jones putting Junior in handcuffs. They didn't have anywhere near enough evidence to arrest him yet.

"He was starting to freak out," Jones explained. "I was afraid he was going to try to run or just melt down. So he's in time out."

"Time out" is a detective's term for detained. It's legal for officers to detain someone while they figure out what might have happened, even if they don't have enough evidence for a full arrest. The person is in limbo—not free to leave, but technically not under arrest.

That slight difference meant nothing to Junior. A woman was dead and he was in handcuffs in the back of a police car. His chin was on his chest and his sobs were growing ever louder.

"OK, but keep an eye on him," he told Jones. "Get the medics out here if he starts to look any worse."

"You got it," was the reply from Jones, who understood his

mentor wasn't fully supportive of what he'd just done.

Wright went on inside, still nervous about Jones' decision. He saw Clarke getting ready with the luminol. She had already closed all the doors and pulled all the blinds she could, to limit the amount of light in the hallway. She then sprayed the carpet with an even layer of the chemical and waited a few seconds before turning on her black light.

Nothing. No blood stain, not even a few drops. Dr. Clarke shone the light along the edges, near the molding where a carpet cleaning machine might have missed something. Up and down the hall she went, as far as the cord on the light would let her. She finally admitted the obvious.

"There's no blood on this carpet."

Wright was stunned, because Sierra had always been reliable in the past. Junior was in the back of a police car about to pop a vein, and there was no blood on the carpet. Wright could see liability building and already imagined himself being quizzed by lawyers about Junior's death.

But there was a second concern—Sierra's alert was the probable cause for the entire search warrant. If she turned out to have been wrong, a defense attorney might be able to get any other evidence they found thrown out. Worse, Sierra would be useless for any search warrants in the future. She would still be able to search, but no police officer would be able to write a warrant based on her alert.

"I really trust that dog. Is your luminol expired? Is there too much light here from the outside, should we wait until tonight?" Clarke was picking up that Wright was rattled, and tried to become the calming influence.

"The light can be a factor. It's barely dark enough for what we're doing, so maybe there's something we can't see," Clarke tried rationalizing. "Let's pull the carpet up and see what's underneath."

Wright now had another problem. Not only was Sierra's reputation at risk, but if they ripped up the carpet and found nothing, he'd have to explain the expense to his boss.

"Can we just pull it up from the edges...without destroying it?"

"I've done that in the past. It never goes back in exactly right, but maybe we can get it up."

Clarke started in a corner, under some molding. She got an edge, and stretched it enough to get off the hook strip below. She was able to start peeling the carpet back.

The pad was next. It also looked clean and Clark didn't bother using the luminol on it. She was interested in the floor underneath.

Her guess was well-founded. When they got the carpet and pad pulled back, there was an obvious stain on the plywood underlayment, right where Sierra had alerted. No special chemicals were needed, it was visible to the human eye. A quick spritz of luminol and the stain glowed like a star in the night sky. It was blood all right, and a lot of it.

.The discovery was both good news and bad for Wright. The blood meant Sierra's alert was valid, so the warrant would hold up. But if Misty Combes died on the carpet, how did her blood get onto the floorboards without leaving any stains on the carpet or padding?

By this time Anita Holmes had returned to the yard, and was waiting outside with her neighbor. Wright decided to talk to them. He adopted the most casual voice he could.

"Had the carpets cleaned recently...?" he asked.

"We haven't had the carpets cleaned…ever," she replied. "We vacuum every Tuesday, but we haven't got the kind of money that would allow us to hire a steam cleaner or anything like that."

"How long have you had the carpet? Have you replaced any sections?"

"The lady who sold us the house put new carpet in the hallway right before she listed the home. She kinda tried to make it a selling point."

Wright didn't normally share investigative secrets with those outside the department, but he decided to take a flyer. He needed an explanation for how there could be blood on the floorboard but not on the carpet.

"We found blood…quite a bit of blood…on the floorboards. That's confusing us, because so far as we can tell, there's no blood on the carpet itself. That's a little weird. Would you know if Junior had tried to clean it?"

"I can't imagine he'd do that. We've left him alone for a few hours at a time, but we'd have noticed if we'd come home to a freshly shampooed carpet. It would have been wet."

The neighbor had been silent through the conversation, but now started to speak up, somewhat hesitating.

"You say there's blood on the floorboards, but not on the carpet? I might know how that could be…."

"Go on," Wright added. The neighbor had lived in her home for forty years, and knew everything about everybody.

"The lady who sold the home to the Harpers was a widow. Her husband died after cutting himself with a chain saw. I heard the yelling and came over. He had run inside and they said he bled to death in the hallway. Is the spot just inside the door from the garage?"

"Yessss," was Wright's frustrated reply. He didn't regularly let himself show emotion, but this had been a promising lead.

"Well, that's it," the neighbor said, sounding like one of those busybody private detectives on TV. "Nobody would have bought the house with blood all over the carpet. They obviously replaced it."

Wright and Clarke exchanged a look of agreement. Replacing the wood underlayment would have been expensive, and if you're trying to dump a house you wouldn't go to the expense or trouble. You'd do the cosmetic fix—the carpet. Just the carpet.

Jones was already heading over to the car to let Junior out. He was not completely off the hook. There was still the fact that a dead girl had been found across the street from his home. But he wouldn't be arrested tonight and Jones doubted he ever would be. He knew Misty Combes, and despite Junior's size, Misty would have scratched his blubbering eyes out if he'd tried to harm her.

It was back to square one. Junior had been a viable suspect, and even Mr. Harper brought himself up on radar. They were oh-for-two on what had become a very long day. The Chimera Killer was starting to piss Jones off.

CHAPTER NINE
Gifts

If Jerome and Verna Carlson had been responsible dog owners, the body of Heather Scott might never have been found.

The Carlsons were that one special couple who seem to reside in every neighborhood. Jerome revved his Harley late at night. Verna drove their minivan down their street like it was her personal raceway. They regularly had drunken arguments which all the neighbors could hear, and over which a few had called the sheriff.

Their house was a dump and hurt property values on the entire road. Worst of all, they let their dog Charlie roam the neighborhood at will. They had no fence and didn't make the slightest effort to keep Charlie on their property. The only reason Charlie hadn't been killed by a passing car is that there weren't many cars passing through the remote part of Kitsap County where they lived.

Once you turned into the neighborhoods off Old Belfair

Highway, most of the properties bordered logging company land. The streets mostly dead-ended into the woods or at gated logging roads. There wasn't any reason for people who didn't live in the neighborhood to be passing through.

Charlie was an interesting dog. Jerome had joked, when he was being civil to his neighbors, that he must have been raised by cats. He had a penchant for bringing things home and presenting them to his masters.

Rabbits were a regular gift. Moles were an occasional offering. Charlie did his part for Darwinism by making sure only the speediest of squirrels survived. Whatever he managed to catch, kill, dig up or find dead was usually deposited on the kitchen floor upon his triumphant return home.

As a result, neither of the Carlsons thought it unusual when one evening Charlie brought home a long bone. They assumed it was a deer or elk femur, maybe even something out of a bear. Those animals were always getting hit out on the main highway, and would frequently survive just long enough to run into the brush behind one of the houses along their side road.

Verna had immediately taken the "gift" back outside because it smelled bad. But she allowed Charlie to continue chewing on it, so long as he did so out in the yard.

A few nights later Charlie came home with a rib, and Verna assumed it was from the same animal from which the femur had originated. She again opened the back door, tossed the item outside, and allowed Charlie some good times chewing on the bone.

"*Rich folks buy those Nylabone thingies,*" she thought. "*We live here in the woods and grow our own.*"

It wasn't until Saturday night, when both the Carlsons had been drinking a bit, that Charlie brought home another gift. This one sobered them up like no cup of coffee ever could.

It wasn't one bone, it was a collection of bones. They were in a bloody sock, which was still contained in a bloody shoe. Verna got to the telephone first.

"911, what are you reporting?" the operator asked in her most businesslike tone.

"Um...my dog just brought home a foot. He's been bringing home bones for a couple of days and we figured they were animal bones. But he just brought home a running shoe and it looks like the person's foot is still inside."

"Do you know where he's getting the bones?" the dispatcher asked. 911 operators are trained to ask questions and this one was no exception as she tried to ferret out whether her caller was drunk or hallucinating.

"He's been bringing home bones for a few days, and we figured they were a deer kill. They're probably still out in the backyard..."

"But do you know where he's getting them?"

"Uh...no...out back in the woods someplace."

"OK, ma'am. We'll have a deputy swing by in a little while. Try not to handle the shoe or other bones any more than you already have."

The wait for the deputy was short, compared to the usual response times for a rural sheriff's office. Every county employee down to the courthouse janitor was dialed into the person now being called the Chimera Killer, though they were careful not to use that name when James Garrison was within earshot. The dispatcher moved this call up to the highest priority, and only a murder-in-progress would have gotten a deputy sooner.

"Yup, it's a foot…in a shoe," the first-arriving deputy told Detective Wright. The deputy needed all of about five seconds to understand this was the real deal and ask WestCom to get ahold of Wright.

"The family also rounded up the other two or three bones the dog brought home," the deputy said. "They've all been chewed pretty bad, but they're the right size to be from a human."

Wright knew that if the bones came from the same place as the shoe, they'd likely be human. What he needed to find was the rest of the remains, and any other clues at the scene.

He got on the phone and explained the situation to Bryce.

"I know you have those GPS collars. Does it take a long time for dogs to get used to wearing them?" was the question.

"Not at all. The hard part is teaching the human how to use their half of the system. I take it you want to put a collar on the family's dog and see where he goes to find bones?"

"Precisely."

"I'm on the way. I can probably hang out for a while. We can put the collar on the dog and turn him loose while we wait. It'll save teaching the family how to use the thing."

As he drove, Bryce wondered what it might be like to search with somebody else's dog. There really wasn't anything in the books for that, so he'd be winging it. There was no way to tell if the dog would pick this day to return to the source of its gifts.

Bryce got to the residence and saw that Charlie was at least big enough to handle the GPS collar with its foot-long wire antenna. He made friends with Charlie before trying on the new collar and it didn't seem to bother the dog. So he fired up the tracking unit and asked everyone to go inside.

"If we're out here, Charlie will want to interact with us," he suggested. "If we all go inside, maybe he'll take off. Even if he goes out of range of my unit, when he comes back we'll be able to download the track from his collar and see where he's been."

Inside, the small talk was about as awkward as it could have been. Jerry and Verna weren't from a world where people routinely deal in decomposing human bodies. Bryce spent a while talking about search and rescue and some other missions he'd been on. Every so often, he'd check the GPS and see that Charlie was still hanging out in the yard going nowhere.

After about another forty-five minutes, the dog icon on the GPS began to move.

"Looks like he's headed out. How long does he normally spend wandering the neighborhood?" Bryce asked the Carlsons.

"We don't know. When he's here, he's here, and when he's gone, he's gone."

Bryce was able to track at least the beginning of Charlie's travels from his hand-held unit. The unit and the collar communicated if they were within a few hundred yards of each other with no hills in between.

"He's down at the corner. I think I saw a fire hydrant there if I recall," Bryce reported.

Charlie continued his trek, and eventually the GPS beeped that it had lost track of the collar. The Carlsons wanted to try and follow, but Bryce nixed the idea.

"Charlie needs to be Charlie right now, doing what Charlie does. If he detects that we're following him he might change his behavior."

The small talk got smaller and smaller, and in another hour Bryce knew more about the Carlsons than he could have possibly cared. Their first date, their second date, their honeymoon and forward in time to veiled references about the alcohol-induced events the neighbors had reported.

Bryce would really have preferred to wait in his car, but didn't want to risk going outside or doing anything that Charlie would hear or smell. He and Wright exchanged looks, but continued trying to make the best of an awkward situation.

"Well, look at that. He's back in range," Bryce announced as the GPS began tracking Charlie again. "He's coming from the back side of the house, out in the woods. That's a good sign. Let's let him get to the yard and see if he's got a gift for you."

When Charlie came into sight, the only thing in his mouth was his tongue. He came to the yard and was obviously looking for one of his earlier finds, but Wright and the coroner had collected all those bones. Bryce went out to download Charlie's full track.

Working with the collar was a nice excuse to get away from the Carlsons, and it took Bryce about five minutes to get the track downloaded. On the GPS screen, it looked like Charlie had been well out into the backwoods, but didn't linger any place in particular.

"Let me fire up my laptop so we can look at this on a bigger screen." Bryce walked to the Suburban, and set his computer up on the center console. He made no effort to go back in the house, and when the track was displayed he called to Detective Wright.

"I don't see any place that he spent a lot of time, except maybe at the fire hydrant. He was probably checking pee-mail there, then moved on to sniff other things. Let me convert this track to a route and I'll take Sierra on a similar path."

Bryce manipulated the GPS so that the record of where Charlie had been would now show up as a path to be followed. He'd lead Sierra through the same route, and see if they came across any bones.

Sierra, having been kenneled in the back of the Suburban for a couple of hours, was more than ready to start searching. Bryce gave her a bit of time to stretch her legs and do some other business, and then asked Wright if he'd like to come along.

"Sure. Let me get some boots on instead of these running shoes, and I'll be ready to go."

Bryce had decided to work Charlie's track in reverse. He didn't need to go visit the fire hydrant down the block, because Charlie's time back in the woods was of much more interest.

"OK, Sierra. Let's go find Digger," was Bryce's standard command. Sierra was off and sniffing the wind, but not in any particular direction.

After about an hour, it was starting to look like Charlie had decided to keep his secret stash a secret. Bryce, Detective Wright, and Sierra followed Charlie's path back to the fire hydrant, with Sierra finding nothing in the way of interesting odors. They came up empty.

"I'll get an evidence search spooled up for tomorrow morning," Wright told Bryce. "Can you come back?"

"Yup, we'll be here. Looking at the map you might need a half-dozen or so dogs to really cover the area in a day. It's pretty brushy back there, and there's no telling how far back Charlie went to find the bones."

"I know you want to be in the field with your dog, but I could really use your expertise at base, helping me design a search plan. Can you do that?"

"Yeah. I'll get maps made up overnight and designate search areas for the dogs. In the morning we can get everybody else deployed, and if there's an area left over, Sierra and I will cover it."

At 7:00 a.m. in Belfair, it was frequently foggy, and today was no exception. The close proximity of Puget Sound meant there was plenty of moisture in the air, and the trees held cool air like a sponge. It was borderline creepy on a good day, and especially so if one was looking for a body.

Bryce had designated eight search areas, and Wright's mission call-out had yielded only six handlers. Three were from Bryce's team, and three from other counties. Five of the six were hanging out chatting, but Alan Granger, "Mason 20," was not one for small talk

Granger did make his way to the command post to ask for his search area. Bryce was still trying to figure out which six areas to search first when Granger came up behind him.

"I'd like to search the area over across Minard Road, between Old Belfair Highway and the watershed," Granger asked in a voice that was slightly stronger than a request.

The watershed belongs to the city of Bremerton, and is the source of the city's drinking water. The road is gated at the property line, and the city does its best to keep everyone out. Though seemingly a good place to hide a body, had someone parked at the gate and set out with a dead body over their shoulder the neighbors would have noticed.

"I've got that down to search, but it's about my lowest area of probability," Bryce tried to explain firmly but politely. "There are higher-probability areas much closer and since we're short of handlers, we'll need to all do those areas first."

"No, I think that far parcel is a higher priority and I'd really prefer to go there first."

Bryce caved. He didn't need to start the day with an argument and he had to begrudgingly give Granger some credit for his prior successes. Granger was also known for not playing well with others, and this did give some separation between him and the other handlers.

"OK, head on over when you're ready and get started. Since you're not following the search plan the rest of us are working under, no need for you to attend the briefing." That probably wasn't the most diplomatic way to speak to Granger, but he was too arrogant to notice he was being brushed off. In fact, Granger didn't feel any need to mingle with people he felt were posers.

"Works for me. I'll let you know what we find."

"Fine."

Bryce spent a few more minutes finalizing the search plan for those who'd be following it, and walked over to brief the other handlers.

"Where's Alan?" was the first question posed.

"He's off working an area he has 'a feeling' about," was a more PC response from Bryce. "He's done that before, and with some success."

It wasn't clear who Bryce was trying to convince, himself or the other handlers. But he got knowing looks from most of the folks and pressed on with the briefing.

"As you might have read in the news, a local family dog has been coming home with human bones. We put a GPS on the dog but he didn't go back to his stash, so we'll have to go proactively find the remains. Our search areas are centered on the family home, in concentric circles out to the quarter mile mark. But I really think the high probability areas are in the woods behind the house.

"I've tried to keep most of the search assignments to about forty acres, but I don't know how difficult the brush is in all of them. We have more areas than handlers, so if yours turns out to be easy let me know and when you're done we'll give you a second assignment."

Bryce handed out maps to all the handlers. One side was topographic and on the other Bryce had printed overhead satellite photographs, which showed homes and vegetation.

Between the two maps, handlers could get a clear mental picture of what they'd be going into.

In about fifteen minutes, the handlers all began to move out, reporting over the radio that they'd started their assignment. The only one Bryce hadn't heard from was Granger.

"Mason 20, I assume you've started your assignment?"

"About half an hour ago. I called but got no response."

Bryce and everyone on the channel knew that was baloney. The radio coverage was good in the area, and there was nothing to interfere with a call. But there would be no argument over the radio.

"Sorry if we missed you. I'll put you down for a start time about thirty minutes ago. Base clear."

Bryce focused on getting his own dog and equipment ready and getting into the field himself. Wright would take over handling base, and there was a radio operator for routine messages. If Wright had a question about dog strategy or capability Bryce could answer it over the radio while he worked his own area.

For about the first hour, there was virtually no radio traffic from the teams in the field. Everyone was doing their jobs, and unless something developed, there was no reason to be yakking on the radio.

At the sixty-minute mark, the base radio operator checked the status of each team. All responded except for Granger. Three calls went unanswered, and the operator followed procedure by waiting five minutes and trying again. If there was no answer then, other teams would be diverted to look for the missing handler and dog.

The five minutes passed, and three more calls went unanswered. The procedure was for base to alert the Operations Leader, which on this day was Bryce.

"Dog 44, Base."

Bryce had heard the failed radio calls, and had expected to be notified.

"I copy that Mason 20 isn't answering status checks," Bryce replied. "Can we have a deputy drive over to wherever he parked his pickup and call from there?" Radios are funny things, and Bryce hoped that being closer might make the difference.

Wright heard the call, and nodded to the radio operator that he'd handle it. If that didn't produce results, Granger would then become the subject of a missing person search himself.

Wright had no trouble finding Granger's truck, and made his call.

"Mason 20, County 128. Status?"

"Mason 20, County 128. Status?"

Wright made the third call, already knowing what the answer would be.

"Mason 20, County 128. Status?"

After the first two calls, Bryce had turned and started heading back to base. He had no fear that Granger was actually down and injured. The guy was a mountain man who oozed through the woods like water down a streambed. He probably just had his radio turned down so he wouldn't have to listen to his competitors. Regardless, as the ops leader, Bryce was responsible for his people. He would take the lead in finding their wayward searcher.

"Dog 44, Dog 34. We're almost done with our area and can come help you search for Alan if you'd like."

"Dog 34, Dog 44…that sounds great. Meet you at base, and we'll head over. 44 clear."

"34 clear."

It took about ten minutes for the two of them to meet at Granger's truck, and work out a quick plan for covering his area. It wasn't large and the two could cover it quickly.

"His dog isn't aggressive, but if Alan is down and injured, it might be protective of him," Bryce warned. "If you spot him, secure your dog and holler from a distance"

They looked at their maps and split Granger's area into two sections. Bryce and Sierra took the northernmost section, and headed out to start searching.

"Oh, don't forget," Bryce added. "Alan doesn't like interlopers in his search area. If it's just that his radio is turned down, he might be pretty steamed when you first find him."

Wright stepped in at that point. "If he gives you any grief over this, let me know. I've noticed his attitude toward other searchers and it needs adjusting. I'm probably going to do that either way this goes."

Bryce and Sierra continued north, and plunged into the brush off the road. They took the paths of least resistance and wound east, rather than gridding. Bryce fully expected to find Granger up and walking around, so they didn't need to look under every bush. Sierra's nose would be more than adequate to find him.

It took about twenty minutes for Sierra to start working further from Bryce, and it was clear she was in scent. Bryce decided to do an informal voice check without calling Sierra back.

"Hey…Alan…you out here?" He hoped that the softer tone would clue Granger that something was amiss, and cause him to hesitate before starting another argument. He heard no response and Sierra seemed to be working further and further away. She definitely had something and was headed toward the boundary of the watershed.

They started to drop down a short ravine and, while Sierra had no trouble getting down, Bryce had to work his way down gingerly to avoid falling. While Sierra took a moment to drink from a stream, Bryce looked up and noticed a flash of orange on the opposite ridge. Granger had been wearing an orange shirt when he left base.

"Hey…Alan…is that you?"

The spot of orange never moved, and there was no response by voice. Bryce called Sierra and said, "Stay with me," his way of trying to get a very active search dog to stay close. It seldom worked but he had to try. As he moved up the opposite hillside, the orange splotch became clearer and it was obviously Granger. He was sitting on a log, perfectly still, with his elbows on his knees and his chin cradled in his hands

The brush was thick, and Bryce was making a lot of noise as he approached. Sensing a problem, he gave Sierra a "Stay!" command and went forward without her.

"*He's almost in a trance,*" Bryce thought to himself. He wondered if Granger's dog had been injured and he was in shock. But as he got closer, he could see the Malinois sitting quietly at Granger's feet, looking back at Bryce.

Granger still didn't move, and he said nothing. Bryce got to within ten feet of him.

"Alan…ALAN! Are you OK?"

At that moment, Granger finally moved, and what moved most was his mouth.

"WHAT ARE YOU DOING HERE?"

"We couldn't get you on the radio for…it's been nearly an hour now. We came to make sure you're OK."

"I don't need you checking up on me. I'm just fine."

Bryce had long ago gotten fed up with Alan's attitude, and, after this disruption to the search, he didn't have any energy left for a diplomatic response.

"Well, you're obviously not 'just fine.' I walked through all this brush to get here and made all kinds of noise and you didn't hear me. You've completely disrupted the search plan for the other areas and I've got two of us searching *your* area looking for *you*."

Sierra had heard the angry words, and although she might not have understood the actual words, she knew something wasn't right. She broke her stay, something she almost never did, and went bounding to Bryce's side.

Bryce's rebuke, a rarity for Alan to hear, actually got through.

"I'm sorry. I must have had my radio turned down. I was just taking a break. You can have everybody go back to their own areas."

"Um, no. You're coming out of the field with me. Detective Wright wants to have a little chat with you. 34 and I will finish your area and then go back to the high-probability areas we wanted to search in the first place."

Bryce started to use his radio to let everyone know that Granger was OK, but when he keyed up his microphone he got loud screeching feedback from Granger's radio.

"If your radio had been turned down that wouldn't have happened. Turn it down now so I can call in."

"Sorry...."

"Base, Dog 44. We've found Mason 20 and he's OK, but he's coming out of the field with me."

"Base copies. Glad to hear he's OK."

Bryce had been so focused on Granger that he'd lost track of Sierra. A short bark got his attention, and he looked over to see her in a sitting position next to a bush. As he looked, Sierra put her nose under the bush, resumed her sit, and gave another soft bark, as if she was afraid to interrupt the discussion.

"Whatcha got, girl? Something there?" Bryce looked under the bush, and immediately noticed the logo on the shoe. It was the mate to the one back at the Carlson's house, with what appeared to be the matching foot inside.

"Good girl! You found Digger you found Digger…yay." Bryce slipped Sierra her ball but didn't toss it. He didn't want Granger's dog to decide it wanted the toy and trigger a dog fight. Search dogs were used to being around one another, but their toy drive can trigger snarls if they perceive another dog is after their paycheck.

"What the hell, Alan? You're in the middle of the crime scene. Did your dog alert?"

"Um, no. Yes. I mean…."

This man who'd been an icon in search and rescue, who had been so arrogant and unpleasant to so many people, was now completely flummoxed.

"You need to go back to base. Now that we've found remains, I've got to stay here until a detective comes to take the scene. Tell you what…you go get Wright and lead him back here. Do you feel up to that?"

"Sure…that makes sense. Let him know I'm coming."

"Base, Dog 44."

"Base, go ahead."

"We've just bumped into Nat Sessions out here and are going to take a little break with him. Mason 20 will be headed back to his car to meet the detective."

"Dog 44…okaaay…you wanna give me some coordinates?"

"Not at this time. Mason 20 will provide them to Detective Wright."

"Understood. Break. Base to all teams. You can return to base."

It took about twenty minutes for Wright to find his way to Bryce's scene. He had another SAR member with him as a guide, but Alan was nowhere to be found. He'd simply told him to wait in his truck, and would deal with him later.

"What's up, Bryce?"

"Do you mean with the remains, or with Granger?"

"Well, both, eventually. What happened out here?"

"It was like he was in a trance. I could see him from the other ridgeline behind you. He was just sitting here on this log, with his dog at his feet. As I was dealing with him, Sierra went over there and found the other foot."

"Had Granger found anything?"

"That's the weird part. When I asked, he couldn't tell me either way. I didn't smell any alcohol on him, but something's not right. He claimed he didn't answer because his radio was turned down, but when I tried to call in I got feedback from his speaker. The radio was obviously turned up and working fine…he was just zoned out."

Bryce was torn between being angry at Granger for behaving so

135

unprofessionally and being concerned for his health. The poor guy's dog had led him to the bones and he apparently couldn't handle it.

"I really hope he's OK. I mean, nobody likes the guy, but nobody wants to see someone go over the edge, either. Maybe he's just found too many bodies."

"That, young man, is for the sheriff to decide. You needn't concern yourself with it except to provide a written report of what you saw. And nice job finding the remains."

"As much as it pains me, all the credit goes to Granger. This is the last place I would have searched, and he demanded to come here. Good on him."

CHAPTER TEN
Back to the Future

Katie hadn't gone forty-eight hours without a shower since she was four years old. She might not have been that typical prissy seventeen-year-old girl, but she did believe in good hygiene. And like every teenager, she had a bit of self-centeredness. She was sure that everybody else could smell her and would be gossiping about it. Her teenage brain had completely forgotten that everyone around her had been shower-less for the exact same period.

Katie was completing her final weekend of search and rescue training. She'd pestered her mother to let her join, and had to convince her that she wasn't just chasing Bryce. Katie's mom really liked Bryce, but wanted to make sure her daughter was getting involved in SAR for the right reasons. Search and rescue meant a huge time commitment and expense, and teenage relationships don't always last. If Katie and Bryce stopped getting along, would Katie lose interest in SAR?

Katie had all the right answers, and her mother finally relented. This final weekend of training was her third in the woods, which involved living out of her pack from Friday night through Sunday afternoon. There were virtually no creature comforts involved. Not only had there been no showers, there weren't even any porta-potties.

"We want you to learn to use nature's bathroom," an instructor pointed out at the start of Katie's first weekend of training. "It sounds icky, but it's really not that bad."

Katie eventually got used to going behind a bush and, by the end of that first weekend, it was second nature. For all that she'd learned, she said later that the major accomplishment was keeping her toilet paper dry, something not all the trainees had managed to do.

As a further test in minimalist living, the trainees hadn't been allowed to carry tents. They'd been shown how to rig shelters with two tarps and a rope, and Katie had gotten very good at the task. This final weekend, she slept very comfortably despite a surprise March snowstorm. She was grateful that her mother had invested in a really good sleeping bag with synthetic insulation. A few of the trainees had gone whole-hog, splurging on high-end sleeping bags with soft, goose down insulation. Those trainees learned a very cold lesson: down insulation is useless if it becomes wet, and in western Washington almost everything gets wet. Katie's synthetic bag kept her warm despite the inevitable moisture that crept in.

For a generation brought up on smart phones, the trainees were also shocked to learn they wouldn't be allowed to use GPS devices during their initial training. They all had to work their way around Green Mountain using map and compass, measuring distance by counting their steps.

The objective that final weekend had been for teams of two to navigate to multiple points around the mountain, noting their arrival time at each and taking a card that would prove they'd been there. The total distance over the forty-eight hours would be nearly fifteen miles.

Katie's biggest challenge hadn't been the navigation, or the snow, or the blisters on her feet. Her biggest challenge had been her teammate, a fourteen-year-old who just didn't want to be there.

The girl's griping started Friday evening, and continued nonstop until they returned to base camp on Sunday afternoon. Her feet hurt, she was cold, her pack didn't fit, she hadn't slept well and the freeze-dried food upset her stomach. Katie had nursed her along, though at one point she stepped aside to discuss the issue with an instructor.

"This is the first time that girl has done anything hard in her life," the instructor said. "It's the worst experience she's been through, because at her age, she hasn't been through much. If you can help get her through this, she'll thank you, and she'll grow. Some of the kids who gripe the most become our best searchers, once they figure out they really can do it."

So, Katie had reluctantly taken on the additional role of mentor. While she was learning to do everything herself, she had to simultaneously teach it to her teammate, and motivate the girl besides. It didn't ruin the weekend, but it did put a damper on what would otherwise have been a great time. Now the training was coming to an end and base was just a few turns of the trail away.

Katie's relief at reaching base, dropping her pack and getting out of her boots, was dimmed by the sight of Bryce's Suburban in the parking lot. Bryce had completed his training nearly three years before, and there was no reason for him to have trekked all the way out to Green Mountain. But there he was, and Katie was simultaneously happy and unhappy to see him.

"I stink!" was her reaction when Bryce tried to give her a hug. She wanted the hug, but stepped back so as not to offend her boyfriend.

"I train cadaver dogs for cryin' out loud," was Bryce's laughing reply. "I've found dead bodies and helped carry them out of the woods. Suffice to say, I'm pretty hard to gag."

Katie wasn't having any of it.

"You'll get your hug back at the house after I've had a shower. Besides, we're not supposed to be displaying affection in front of the other kids."

Bryce had to admit she was right about that part. The hug was intended as one of admiration, not affection, but nobody would know that. He'd wait for the hug and make it worthwhile when it happened.

"So tell me all about it. How did it go?"

"Well, I'm warm and dry and only have a few blisters on my feet. We hit all the points with little fussing. My partner wasn't wild about being out there and griped a lot, but we got through that."

Katie was tired and a bit emotional at having achieved the milestone. She started to prattle on.

"We met this old man and I felt sooo bad for him. He was just sitting in his truck on one of the logging roads. He was staring out the window looking over the valley. I was afraid he was part of our scenario so I went up to him. He might have been planted as a 'witness' that we were supposed to interview."

Katie continued almost without taking a breath. "He wasn't. When I asked him if he was part of search and rescue, he just stared at me. Whatever he was there to meditate about, we ruined it for him.

"Then we had the one navigation issue but I figured out there was a new road that didn't show on the map, so we found the point we'd been looking for. I don't know if the instructors picked that point because they KNEW there was a new road there to mess us up…"

Bryce smiled. "You're tired, aren't you?"

Katie realized she'd been going on and on, but she was very proud of having completed the weekend and that she would get her "ground pounder" SAR certification.

"Yeah, now that I'm back here, the fatigue is starting to kick in. And my blisters hurt more than before. I can't wait for mom to come pick me up."

"Your mom's not coming. I asked her to let me pick you up, and she's cooking dinner back at the house. I wanted to welcome you back from the field. Let's get over for your debrief and then get you home. And I'm going to stand next to you during the debrief, no matter how bad you smell."

By this time, all of the teams had made their way into base, and the operations leader had gathered them off the rear door of the communications van. This particular OL liked to pay compliments with run-on sentences. "Congratulations. You are now all mission-ready, certified, officially designated, proven-in-the-field, card-carrying and well-respected Search and Rescue ground pounders. You are the backbone of this organization and whatever happens in the future, nobody can ever take this weekend's victory away from you."

A chorus of weak clapping and whistles went through the crowd. It wasn't that they weren't proud of the accomplishment, but they were too tired to celebrate at that moment. High-fives would have meant raising their arms…

"It's easy in a debrief to focus on what went wrong, and then everybody leaves feeling bad," the OL continued. "I'd like to start with what went right this weekend.

"The first thing that went right is that you're all back here and beyond a few blisters we had no injuries. That's a huge success in my book. Anybody else got any 'what went right' examples?"

The first person to step up was the fourteen-year-old who'd been Katie's ball-and-chain the entire weekend.

"What went right is that I got assigned the best teammate a scared little girl could ever hope to have. I need to thank Katie Lovering for helping me get through this. I also need to apologize to you, Katie, for whining the entire weekend. You believed in me even when I didn't. I kept expecting to fail, and I kept expecting the next task to be impossible. The impossible never happened, and you're the reason why. I apologize for being such a drama queen and now that I'm through it, I realize how much fun we had."

Katie was tired. For Katie, like most people, tired equaled emotional. The girl's comments got to her immediately.

"You're welcome," Katie managed to blurt through her tears. Nothing else would come out. She wasn't sobbing uncontrollably, but the tears flowed and there was a lump in her throat that kept her from saying more.

"I'm not surprised," Bryce whispered, nudging Katie on the shoulder. "And you smell good, too." Katie laughed a bit through her tears.

Katie heard the rest of the debrief, but didn't process any of it. Her mind was now completely focused on changing out of her boots, getting in the car, and getting home to a shower and a meal.

When the members were dismissed, Bryce and Katie walked back to his Suburban. Bryce let Sierra out of her crate to give her a potty break. It also turned out to be a back-scratch-belly-rub-cry-on-Sierra's-shoulder break.

"I'm really glad to see you, girl. Thank you for bringing Bryce along to take me home."

Katie put her backpack inside next to Sierra's crate and got her flip-flops out of the side pouch. She got into the passenger seat and began to change. She got one boot off and the flip-flop on, leaned back in the seat, and decided to close her eyes for just a second....

———————

"Shhhh, this'll be a great picture for graduation," Bryce said to Pam. "One boot on, one boot off, sound asleep in the truck."

They'd managed to get the creaky door of the Suburban open without waking Katie. Now they just had to get the angle right to get both her face and boot in the shot. Fortunately, when Katie fell asleep, she turned her head toward the door, so the picture would catch the snoring look on her face.

"Let me switch to video mode so folks can hear her snoring," Bryce whispered. "She's loud."

"This truck better be the only place you hear her snoring, Buster," Katie's mom whispered back.

"Yes, ma'am," was Bryce's unthinking reply, until he realized the significance of what Pam had said. They both got to laughing, eventually waking Katie up.

"What're you guys…? Are we home?" Katie was having a little trouble waking up, but eventually figured out what was going on.

"I better not see those pictures on Snapchat," she scolded Bryce.

"I promise I will not put these pictures on Snapchat," Bryce responded.

"Graduation?" Pam whispered. The graduation dinner always included a slide show of the most embarrassing pictures from training.

"Uh-huh. But not on Snapchat…I promised."

As Katie awakened, she managed to get her other boot off and stumble toward the house. About halfway there her left leg cramped up and she almost fell before her mother grabbed her.

"Wow, you stink," Pam said.

"That's what I told Bryce, but he wanted a hug anyway."

"Well, he's a man. That's how they think. He can get his hug after you've had a shower."

"That's also what I told him," Katie replied, looking directly at Bryce.

Bryce bowed his head, conveying the "I am unworthy" look that husbands and boyfriends have for centuries used to appease the women in their lives. Even though he was only seventeen, the look came naturally. Not knowing what else to do, he added the "yes, dear" his romance coach had recommended.

"I wish you'd stop doing that!" Katie started to say.

"Good boy!" was Pam's response. "Katie, if your father had said 'yes, dear' a little more often we might all still be living in the same house. Forget the three little words every woman wants to hear. The two words that really count are 'yes, dear.' Bryce you just keep on doing that."

"Yes, dear…ma'am…Pam…jeez, now I don't know what to say."

"Well, just help me get Katie inside on this bad leg," Pam said.

Bryce tried to salvage the situation with some first aid advice. "Have you got some potato chips for her to eat? She needs to drink a couple glasses of water and eat something salty. That'll help with the cramps."

Pam grabbed a glass from the cupboard and a bag of chips from the pantry, and got Katie up the stairs on only one truly working leg. She came back downstairs to find Bryce standing right where they'd left him.

"Goodness, Bryce. It's not like we don't know you. Grab a spot to sit. When you're here, the house is yours."

"Thanks. I talked to some of the instructors before Katie got back to base. They were very impressed."

"Really?"

"Yes, they figured out about halfway through the weekend that the partner they'd assigned her was a real handful. In the end, the girl got up in front of everybody and thanked Katie."

"Well, that was nice of her. You know…I almost didn't let Katie join SAR. I wasn't sure whether she was doing it for the right reasons."

"I'm not sure I…"

"Was she doing it because she wanted to go help find lost people, or because she wanted to be with you? She likes you a lot but if she's going to take the responsibility of looking for somebody's missing loved one, it needs to be for the right reasons."

"Well, she did pretty well at training, and I wasn't there for any

145

of it. Doesn't that mean she's committed?"

"Yes, and she's attended all the other training and, occasionally when she comes home, she talks about SAR and not you. That's pretty unusual because she talks about you a lot."

"Um...OK."

"Young man, she thinks you're pretty special. I'd say you're probably her first love and I'm glad she picked you."

"Thank you," Bryce said thinly. Now he really didn't know what to say.

"I haven't set a good example for Katie, and maybe I'm not capable. Pardon my language, but I'm what my girlfriends call an 'asshole magnet.' I'm only attracted to men who will treat me badly."

"I knew you were divorced, but Katie didn't share much."

"There's not much to share. I married my ex because he was this rowdy, manly, party-boy, and then I couldn't stand it when he continued to be a rowdy, manly, party-boy. The only thing that changed when we got married was that he developed a memory problem—he kept forgetting he was married."

"Well I hope you don't think that I'm...that I'll..."

"No, I don't. Not at all. What I want you to know is that I think Katie is in love with you and I trust her judgment. First loves seldom work out, but I hope you'll be in our lives for a long time. I'm glad *she's* not an asshole magnet."

Bryce knew he liked Katie a lot, but never having been in love, he wasn't sure what that was. He hadn't thought about the future. He was simply enjoying Katie's companionship more than any friend he'd ever had.

"I hope Katie didn't join search and rescue for me. I wasn't around at all this weekend and she still did great. I hope that means something.

"What's this about you being an asshole magnet?" Katie said from the top of the stairs.

"You never mind that," Pam scolded. "And watch your language. How's the leg? Are you cleaned up?"

Katie came downstairs, freshly showered and only limping a little.

"Are potato chips really a cure for leg cramps?" she asked.

"The salt helps," Bryce replied. "The experts have decided that salt pills really don't work. My doctor just recommends drinking water and eating something salty. Potato chips are about as salty as they come."

"Hey, here's a thought," Pam interjected. "Why don't we forget salty and all eat something meaty? The crock pot's been going all day and the beef stew is really calling my name. We'll put it over rice and it'll be just chock full of carbs and protein."

"That sounds great, I'm starved," Katie said. "I ate every bit of food in my pack plus the snacks they had for us at debrief, and I'm still hungry."

Bryce explained that she'd burned a phenomenal number of calories during her fifteen miles of walking, and even burned a few keeping warm at night in her sleeping bag.

"Your bag won't make you warm, it merely keeps you warm. Your body has to produce the heat in the first place, and that takes additional calories."

Pam's face brightened at the explanation. "You mean if I join search and rescue, I can eat anything I want? Where do I sign up?" She breezed off into the kitchen, thinking Bryce and Katie were following. Bryce started to, but Katie stopped him.

"Now that I don't stink, I owe you a hug." She made it a good one. She held him in her arms just long enough that her mother wouldn't come back and catch them.

"Thank you for being such an inspiration to me," she whispered to Bryce. "You weren't there physically this weekend, but you *were* there. And it wasn't calories that kept me warm in my sleeping bag. It was the thought of you."

"I'm glad I could help," Bryce said, trying a bit of humor to cover his discomfort.

"You helped a lot," Katie said, taking Bryce's hand and leading him into the kitchen. "Dinner time..."

————————————

Three weeks later—

Bryce was busily loading Sierra and his gear into the Suburban when his phone rang for the second time in ten minutes. The first time had been the call out for the search, a missing subject on Green Mountain.

The second call was from Katie. "Hey, can you pick me up? Mom had to run into work for a few hours and I'm stuck without a car."

"Sure, I'll swing by. This one should be a snap for you. It's the north side of Green Mountain, right where you were training."

"Talk about a soft landing for my first search. I even still have my map. I'll have my stuff on the porch and be ready for you."

"See you in a few."

Bryce and Katie were among the first to arrive at base and began getting into their boots and radio harnesses. They checked out radios from the command post and got ready for the mission briefing.

"Hi everybody, my name's Dennis Baker and I'm a brand new SAR deputy. I apologize that my first search is kind of a can of worms…this guy's been gone a long time."

"We're looking for Bill Marcus," Baker continued. "Bill is a sixty-seven-year-old white male with mental health, alcohol and depression issues. He's attempted suicide in the past. Bill left the family home about three weeks ago, but nobody knew where to look. His burnt-out truck was found last evening here on the GM3 by a forest ranger, so we're going to use that as a "point last seen" and search the area around it. We assume we're looking for his remains, as suicidal subjects seldom go far from their vehicles."

Bryce was busy taking notes and didn't see the stunned look starting to come over Katie's face.

"What kind of truck was it?" Katie asked, interrupting the deputy.

"It doesn't matter, it's been recovered. We're not looking for it," the officer replied.

Katie flipped back through her waterproof notebook and interrupted again. "Was it a Red and Black older Ford F150, Washington License AB3812Q?"

"Yeah, how do you know that?"

"I talked to the guy, and it wasn't on the GM3. It was further up near Horse Camp, on the GM4."

"When did you talk to him?" Baker now had laser focus on Katie. Bryce had stopped taking his own notes.

"Three weeks ago when I was up here for the final weekend of WESAR training. Several of us were here and walked past the truck. I talked to the guy thinking he might have been planted as a witness…you know…part of our scenario. He wasn't and he seemed pretty…um…distracted."

"'Spacey' is the word his family used. They wouldn't be offended if you did. But we found the car down here on the GM3 and that's where we're going to search. Miss…you're…?"

"Katie."

"Katie, you and your team leader stand by after the briefing. I'd like to talk more to you."

The Operations Leader for WESAR had decided that Katie would go as support and navigation for Bryce and Sierra, so Bryce was her team leader or "TL." The two of them stayed behind while everyone else deployed to the field.

Bryce was pleased that Katie had spoken up, but it also meant they'd be last in the field. That meant the lowest probability areas and the least likelihood of making a find.

"Call me Dennis," the deputy said. "Great job documenting your conversation with the guy. That was undoubtedly Bill."

"Was I the last person to talk to him?" Katie asked, a bit meekly. Baker picked up on the emotion creeping into her voice.

"You never know, but it really doesn't matter. The family said he was already suicidal, so it's not like you pushed him over the edge."

Katie had expected to deal with people who were already dead when she encountered them. She felt prepared to find a body and help carry it out of the woods. But there was something about being the last person to talk to a suicidal subject that was…odd.

She gave the deputy all the information from her notebook, and everything she could remember about the circumstances. She'd seen no weapons and detected no odor of alcohol. Perhaps there had been a small canister of butane, like the kind she carried for her backpacking stove. She showed hers to Baker, who noted that the truck had burned very hotly and perhaps that added to the mix.

"OK, let's get you two down to the search area. I want to get this guy found and the case wrapped up today. I just hope we find all of him, what with all the bears in the area. I don't want to keep coming back to look for body parts."

"Sir, we haven't met, but could I make a suggestion?" Bryce responded.

"Sure…like I said, I'm a rookie as a SAR deputy."

"Well, I've been to a couple of searches where the subject's car was stolen after they'd left. One was a suicide, almost like this one, and one was a missing hiker. The thief stole the hiker's car from one trailhead and dumped it at another. We spent three days searching entirely the wrong area until the subject found his own way out to a road."

"I get it. You want to go back up and search where Katie talked to Bill. I guess that makes sense."

"It is, technically, where Bill was last *seen*. Down here they only found his truck."

"I agree. You two head up there. Make sure you have good radio contact back to base, that's quite a ways. Do you need someone to let you in a gate?"

"Nope," Bryce said. "These roads all connect. They have to for my theory that the truck was moved to hold up. We'll call you when you get in the area."

Bryce and Katie piled back into the Suburban and Bryce decided to make this a training evolution for Katie.

"OK, my dear. You've got the map and you were just out here. You'll be the navigator and you tell me how to get to the spot where you talked to Bill."

Katie was a step ahead of Bryce and already had her map out. It didn't take long for her to suggest they head out of base camp along the GM3, and go up the hill.

"The spot was on the GM4, just below Horse Camp. I know right where to stop."

The road was rough, and it took a few minutes to get to the area without shaking all their tooth fillings loose. Katie was eventually satisfied they were at the right spot. Bryce then backed the Suburban down the hill about 500 feet.

"What are you doing? The spot was up there," she asked.

"We don't want to dump Sierra out of the truck right in the middle of a possible scent pool. We'll start down here, work away from the spot to let her acclimate, and then move back up the road. Now, think back to your classes. How far should we search from the point last seen?"

"Suicides are usually less than a quarter mile from their vehicles. We should first make a 250-foot circle around the truck for high probability, and then see if the terrain permits a quarter mile circle."

"Good answer. Let's go." They got their packs on, and let Sierra out of the truck. Bryce got her GPS collar in place and worked her away from the PLS. After she'd burned off some energy and left a calling card for the bears and coyotes, Bryce turned Sierra around and had her start working toward the spot where Bill's truck had been parked.

"Base, Dog 44 starting our assignment," Bryce said into his radio.

"Dog 44, Base. We copy you loud and clear, and you're starting your assignment."

Bryce turned to Katie and continued the lesson.

"Notice the wind is coming from our left," Bryce said as they walked up the road. "Sierra's nose is covering everything out to our left, so, as the second human on the team, you need to be looking to our right. There's no way Sierra can smell anything that's downwind of us."

"Got it…I'll watch to the right, although this doesn't look like anyplace someone would try to go."

The brush to the right was exceptionally thick, with blackberries and devil's club. Washington has lots of thorny bushes, but blackberry and devil's club are the thorniest.

"I've given up trying to predict what missing people will do. There are lots of books that talk about percentages, tendencies and other statistics. The problem is that missing people never read the books. While over time there might be patterns that emerge, every individual search is a crapshoot. This guy might be ten feet from where he parked. But if he didn't want to be found, he could be ten miles away in the worst possible terrain."

At that moment Sierra plunged off the road, to their left, and began working through brush that was thankfully less dense that on the right.

"Well, this looks like something worth following. Why don't you hang back about thirty feet, but follow me in. Let's stop talking so we don't distract Sierra."

Katie did as she was told, though a couple of times she caught herself creeping up behind Bryce. It was all so interesting, and she wanted to see Sierra work. She could hear Sierra's bell, and it was clear she was working back and forth, into the wind.

Bryce turned and whispered. "She's working the scent cone. Whatever she's got is up ahead a ways. Can you hear how, each time she goes left or right, it's not quite so far?"

Katie nodded and continued listening to Sierra go back and forth, left to right, but each pass was forward of the next, directly into the wind. The bell went silent for a moment, and then started up again. No back and forth this time, it was coming directly back to them.

"She's got something," Bryce whispered again. She'll probably come back and sit. Let's make some noise so she can find us."

Bryce stepped off the trail and into the brush, and rustled his feet a bit. In no time, Sierra skidded to a halt right in front of him with her butt on the ground.

"Good girlllll. Show me!" They were off at a run now. Katie had seen this numerous times in training, but it was fascinating to watch Sierra do it for real.

Eventually Sierra added a bark to the mix, her sign that she was already at the subject and Bryce was too slow. She wanted her paycheck.

Bryce caught up, took one look at the scene and immediately spun to block Katie's approach. He dropped Sierra's ball to get her reward started, but didn't want Katie going any further.

"You don't need to see this. It's a bad one. Technically it's a crime scene and we shouldn't approach any further anyway."

Katie was a bit hurt at the thought she needed to be protected. "Really, I can't just go up…?"

"You *really* don't want to. I think he shot himself in the head, and he's been here for a couple of weeks. It's not pretty. Let's focus on your training. What do we do now?"

"Well, somebody has to go up to the body and take a set of GPS coordinates. I guess that won't be me. I'll start finding an easy way back to the road and hang some grid ribbon so everyone else can find their way here."

"Good call, but one other thing. We need to play with Sierra and make this a good one. It seems odd to be celebrating a death, but at least the family's not here to be offended."

They played with Sierra, progressively tossing her ball further and further from the body. They worked their way through the brush back to the road, hanging pink ribbon to mark the path back to the body.

"Do you want to make the radio call?" Bryce asked.

"Not really."

For as outgoing as Katie was, she was a little intimidated by radios and microphones. Her very feminine voice went up about six octaves when she talked on the radio, and she usually had to be asked to repeat everything she'd said.

"All the more reason for you to do it. Do you remember what to say?"

"We've just bumped into Nate Sessions and are taking a break?"

"It's Nat, not Nate. He was pretty well loved, so if you screw up his name you'll hear about it. What do you think they'll come back and ask?"

"They'll want our location. You've got the GPS coordinates. You should make the call…"

"Just tell them to have the deputy come to the location we provided before we left. He'll know where that is and then we can download the actual point when we make our report."

"OK…here goes."

Katie took the radio microphone off the clip on her chest harness. She keyed the microphone and paused for a second, and then meekly got out the words "Base, Dog 44."

"Dog 44 this is Base, go ahead."

"Base, Dog 44. We've just bumped into Nate…NAT…Sessions and will be taking a little break."

"OK, Dog 44. Got some coordinates for me?"

"Just let the deputy know we're at the location Bryce gave him before we left. It didn't take long for us to find…to bump into Nat."

"OK, he's nodding his head so I guess he understands. Base clear."

"Good job on the radio. You did fine, so there's no need to be shy. What do you think happens next?"

"Well, the deputy comes out and checks the body, and then calls the coroner. He's far enough off the road that we'll probably have to carry him out for the coroner, right?"

"Yup. We'll need some other teams here for the pack-out, but we can work that in a few minutes. If we start directing every other team to this location all at once, it kinda gives away that we found the body. We don't want some news reporter listening to our frequency and calling the family before the deputy can tell them."

"But we don't want to keep the coroner standing around…"

"That's the funniest thing you've said all day. It takes the coroner a couple of hours to get any place, and given the nature of this road, I'd say it'll be three hours minimum before he gets here."

"So we just hang here, with a dead body, waiting?"

"No, we hang here with a dead body having something to eat. What did you bring for us?"

"Oh, I'm your cook now?" Katie said with a smile. "You're welcome to share one of my freeze-dried meals. I looooved eating them at training."

Bryce laughed and got into the back of the Suburban. "I threw some leftover pizza into my ice chest. That's way better than freeze-dried."

"You like cold pizza? I love cold pizza. We don't have to eat freeze-dried?"

"Once you're out of training, you almost never sleep overnight in the woods and you almost never eat dehydrated food out of your pack. You might search all night, but if you're going to take a rest break they bring you back to base. I always stash something in my truck that's better than freeze-dried. You should get in the habit."

They'd just finished the pizza when Deputy Baker lurched up in his Crown Victoria police car.

"I love the Crowns, but they're not made for these logging roads.

I think I lost my muffler about a mile back. So where's Bill?"

"Almost exactly 250 feet that way," Bryce said, pointing to the line of grid ribbon hanging from branches.

"This has got to be a record for the quickest find. How did you know he'd be here?"

"If Katie hadn't been on the ball, none of us would have. Cars get stolen and trashed in the woods all the time. Finding a burnt-out hulk doesn't mean we've found the PLS."

"Well, young lady, you get the credit for this one. Technically it's a 'found by K9' in the books, but we all know who's responsible for getting this poor fellow back to his family. I'll make sure the sheriff knows, too."

Katie's head knew she'd done well, but her heart was nagging her a bit. Was there something she'd missed when she talked to Bill? Something she could have said that would have brought him out of his funk?

"Stop it," Bryce said. "You did perfectly here and none of this was your fault."

Bryce had to stop himself for a moment, and realize that he'd read Katie's mind. Katie had a stunned look on her face, too.

"How did you know…?"

"I don't know, I just knew. You're the only reason this family is getting their loved one back. We'd have never found him down by his truck, and probably never expanded the search far enough to cover this area. Your work here was a total success, and his decision to kill himself was his own."

"You're right…it's just so sad."

"Well, on that happy note, let's get the coroner started and some teams up here to carry him out," Baker interjected. "We'll have a bit of a wait."

Now Katie was thinking about her mother…her "asshole-magnet" mother. She'd probably never had a man in her life who could read her emotions the way Bryce just had. She went from feeling bad for Bill to feeling bad for her mom.

CHAPTER ELEVEN
Now You See it

""Wally, I think we've caught a break." Sheriff Patterson was on the phone with County Council Chair Wallace Curry, and in public, he always addressed him as "Mr. Chairman." On the phone or in private, the two were on a first name basis.

"A trail runner out near Tiger Lake saw a man who appeared to be forcing a woman into the woods," the sheriff continued. "He had no cell service, but he called as soon as he got back to his truck."

"If this is another dead woman, please explain why you think that's 'a break.'"

The sheriff realized his error. He'd come across as insensitive toward a potential victim.

"I'm sorry. I'm not suggesting that another murder would be a good thing. But if it had to happen, it's good we have a witness. More importantly, the body won't have decomposed for weeks before we find it. Finding a fresh body means there'll likely be decent evidence for the lab to work with."

"OK…that makes sense. Have you got people out searching?"

"It's a little late tonight to start, and the trail runner isn't exactly sure where he saw them. We'll get everybody out first thing in the morning and hopefully find something useful. I just wanted you to know about this in keeping with our 'full disclosure' agreement."

"I appreciate that and I appreciate you pushing us to get ahead of this. How are you doing on the budget side? Is the fifty grand holding up?"

"I really haven't paid attention," Patterson replied. "We're just doing what we need to do. Oh, one more thing. Please don't share this info with anyone until we get out there and search the area. Right now, it's privileged information from an investigation."

"No problem, my lips are sealed." It wasn't the first time a politician had failed to keep a promise. This one was broken as soon as it was spoken.

Council Member James Garrison, who'd opposed the expenditure and refused to believe there was a killer at work, was in the room as Curry took the call. Curry hadn't shared that with the sheriff before, and didn't feel a need to now. Garrison had heard half the conversation and Curry soon filled in the blanks, telling Garrison to keep his mouth shut about the Chimera Killer.

"Oh, now you're busting my chops with that name?" Garrison asked. "It's all over the courthouse and I guess I earned it, but I hadn't expected it from you."

"Sorry, but that's the nickname that reporter hung on the killer and we're all stuck with it now. Let's pretend this conversation was mythological and never happened, OK?"

"No problem. My nose is outta joint, but my lips are sealed," Curry spoke as he finished his scotch and water.

While the sheriff had been talking to his elected counterparts, Bob Wright had been arranging a SAR callout for the next morning. This would be a long night, and he couldn't use the automated system for this particular search.

"We're doing this in stealth mode," Wright told Bryce. "I'm calling a few searchers directly but not notifying the whole world. Can you be at Tiger Lake tomorrow at 0700?"

The next day was a Saturday, and the callout meant Bryce would have to miss training. He could let the rest of his dog team know he'd be gone without telling them why.

"No problem. Who else are you calling?" Bryce asked.

"Just the proven ones. You, Alan Granger and a guy from Clallam County who's impressed us on a couple of searches."

That was more of a problem. It meant Bryce might have to deal with some hurt feelings among his teammates who weren't called. But it was Wright's decision, and there wasn't anything Bryce could do about it.

"One favor…I'm trying to get Katie Lovering some experience as a navigator and K9 support. Can I bring her?"

"OK, but please don't tell her why or where we're looking. Just tell her there's an evidence search tomorrow and leave it at that."

"I can do that, thanks," Bryce replied. He and Wright wrapped up the call, so Wright could notify Granger and the new guy from Clallam. That took about another half-hour, but Wright didn't head to bed. He headed for Tiger Lake and what would probably be an all-nighter.

As if serial killers weren't weird enough, many of them have sick habits that go beyond just the killing. Many keep trophies of their victims, such as a piece of clothing or other personal items. Others revisit the place where they dumped the body, to relive the thrill of the killing. Wright was hoping this serial killer would come back for a visit.

"Does this ghillie suit make my butt look big?" Wright asked as Davy Jones was also changing into field clothing.

"It's not the ghillie suit," Jones responded.

Ghillie suits were pioneered by Scottish gamekeepers as camouflage when hunting. They go far beyond just a wooded pattern on the fabric, such as on military fatigues. Ghillie suits incorporate leaf-like attachments along the entire body, including the head, making the wearer look like a walking bush.

"Y'know, it's rumored that old Honest Abe said the exact same thing to Mary Todd Lincoln the night he was shot. Everyone thinks he was killed by John Wilkes Booth, but it was dark in that theater. Maybe he'd been just a little too honest about the First Lady's butt."

"Well I don't know about your butt, but my whole suit itches," Jones complained. "Do we really have to wear these things?"

"Probably not, but it makes the game more interesting."

Tiger Lake was logging land, owned by the state natural resources agency and leased to a timber company. There were always hikers, joggers, hunters, dog-walkers, wildlife photographers or someone coming through. But that was during the day. Anyone coming through at night was usually up to no good.

Wright and Jones wore headsets with boom mics, so a sudden noise over the radio wouldn't give away their location at the wrong moment. They also had night vision goggles, and infrared laser pointers so they could direct each other's attention to something they might see. All of this in the hope that the mythological Chimera Killer would pick this night to revisit his handiwork. It was a long shot, but it was their only shot. By the next afternoon the search would be on the news.

They couldn't leave a police car at the gate, so they had a patrol deputy from the area drop them off just after sunset. There weren't many houses nearby, and the deputy didn't linger long in his marked car. The two detectives in their ghillie suits got out quickly, walked around the gate, and disappeared down the road.

Jones took up a position a hundred yards or so inside the gate, but on a hill in heavy brush. He was able to see the gate, the parking area beyond it, and about another hundred yards down the road in the other direction. Wright continued walking and Jones radioed just as he was about to lose sight of him

"Pop in right there, and go up to your right. Between us we'll be able to see the gate and about the first 300 yards of road."

Wright got far enough off the road that he couldn't be seen, and then up a little higher for a better view. He set out a small backpacker's chair to sit on and keep him off the cold ground. It would be a long night, and getting cold would make it longer.

Jones was stunned to see a vehicle pull up to the gate only about forty minutes after they'd settled in. His pessimism was so entrenched that he had trouble believing the killer might actually be showing up.

The four-door pickup stopped just outside the gate and the driver got out. He looked up and down the logging road and took a few steps inside the gate. Logging gates are heavy-duty affairs designed to survive being rammed by a vehicle, but they're only intended to keep vehicles out. Those on foot can simply walk around them to enjoy a day in the woods.

"Got one," Jones whispered into his radio. Wright couldn't see the man yet, so Jones kept up a whispered commentary via the radio. "He's about ten feet inside the gate and already headed into the bush."

Wright held his position. While they wanted to catch the killer at the body, this was too close to the road. The jogger had reported the man and woman were further inside the gate when he saw them fighting.

"Wait, he's coming back out and…zipping his fly. Probably just watered a tree."

"Is he carrying anything? A gun? Is he a poacher maybe?"

"Nope, nothing that I can see. He's just walking and looking, almost like he doesn't know where he is. Annnd…upon further review, it looks like he might also be DUI. The rocky ground isn't helping him walk."

The man stood for a full five minutes just looking around with his hands on his hips. Wright could see he was wearing a dress shirt and tie, and shiny leather shoes. Not something to put on for a walk in the woods.

"He's not dressed for a hike," Jones radioed to Wright. "I think we ought to make contact. Even if he's not the killer, he's screwing up our stakeout."

"Concur," was the immediate response. "Take him. I'll come out and we can both talk to him."

"I'm almost down to the road. It's a good thing he already peed, because this outfit I'm wearing would make him go for sure."

Jones came out of the woods and stashed the headgear from his ghillie suit. He hoped to avoid triggering a heart attack or a Sasquatch sighting.

"Sir...sheriff's office. Please keep your hands where I can see them," Jones said as he approached the subject. The subject turned around and Jones' face reacted as if *he'd* seen a Sasquatch.

"Come on down, partner," Jones radioed. "You're not going to believe who this is."

Wright got to the scene as quickly as he could. He could hear the man stammering and talking to Jones long before he could see the pair. He thought he recognized the man's voice, but couldn't remember where he'd heard it before.

He rounded the last corner and the two men came into view. Wright also reacted as if he'd seen Sasquatch.

"Councilman Garrison, what are you doing here at this hour of the night?"

"I was just telling this deputy, I wanted to go for a walk and sort some things out in my head."

"And you just happened to pick THIS night to walk in THIS patch of woods?"

"Yes, is there any law against that?" The councilmember's tone was just short of trying to pull rank on the deputies. He was an elected official, after all.

"No, but there's a law against drunk driving and it smells like you might have violated that one. How much have you had to drink?"

"Just a couple of scotches with Wally Curry. Your sheriff called and said...."

"Said what?" Wright leaned in close. He stared into Garrison's eyes about six inches from his face. "Said...what?"

"OK, I wasn't supposed to know about this, but I was there when the sheriff called. I didn't tell anybody, just like Curry said. But if we do have something horrible happening here, I wanted to see it for myself."

"Councilman, you've put us both in a real pickle. We were waiting to see if your Chimera Killer might come back to visit his handiwork. They do that, you probably didn't know. Not only have you screwed up a stakeout, but Brownsville PD just fired an officer for failing to arrest a city councilmember who was DUI. That was in the news, do you remember?"

"Yes."

"So what am I supposed to do with you? I've made a lot of DUI arrests and you reek of alcohol. We're away from the car, out in the woods with a breeze blowing, and I can still smell you. I'd bet you're half-again over the legal limit, maybe more. I don't want to arrest you, but I won't kiss off my career for you."

"Can you call me a cab, or have my wife come get me?"

"No, and no. I've already told you I won't put my entire family in that position. Jones, get on the radio and ask dispatch to send us a state trooper."

"Yes, sir," Jones replied. State Troopers liked arresting DUIs and, despite their remote location, he had no doubts a trooper would be there quickly. Then he and Wright could go back to the stakeout, assuming the whole thing hadn't already been blown.

While they were waiting, Wright checked his cell phone to see if he had service. If the jogger would have had service, they might have caught the killer in the act. Jones had only one bar, but it was enough to call the sheriff. In the official chain of command there were three or four people between him and the sheriff. On this case, Wright reported directly to the big guy.

"Sir, I'm with Councilman Garrison here at the Tiger Lake Gate. He wandered right into the middle of our stakeout. He said he was in the room when you were talking to Curry. To make it worse, he's obviously DUI and we've got a trooper coming to take him into custody."

The thing that separated Elroy Patterson from mediocre executives was his ability to keep calm in the face of things that would have lesser men throwing tantrums in all directions. There were lots of police executives around who had dealt with murder and mayhem in the street, but couldn't handle political intrigue without blowing their stack. Patterson was as comfortable in a board room as a back alley.

"Thanks, Bob. You've handled this perfectly and please continue as you have." Patterson said in the most even of tones. "Make the arrest, or have the trooper do it. If there is any political heat, I'll take it. But given that Curry violated my confidence and Garrison drove into an active criminal investigation, I don't think anyone will be throwing stones at us. Please ask the trooper to send us a copy of his paperwork when it's done."

"Yes, sir. Thank you. Dispatch said the trooper would be here in about another ten minutes."

It was fifteen.

"Sorry it took so long," the trooper said. "There was a truck at the other gate, but it was almost at the bottom of the hill. It took me a few minutes to figure out I had the wrong gate and come up here."

"It's no problem, but we're in the middle of a stakeout here. How quickly do you think you can clear the scene with this guy? There's still a chance our suspect might show up."

"Let me buzz through the sobriety tests, and get a tow started for his truck. I know the towing company owner, and he'll put a rush on if I ask.

Garrison spoke up quietly. He knew cooperation was in his best interest. "I'll take your tests, but if I fail them will I be put in jail?"

"Probably not," the trooper replied. "Your county's jail doesn't have enough room for us to book someone for simple DUI. So long as you don't try to kill me or escape, I will run you through the DUI process, but you will sleep in your own bed tonight."

Garrison knew enough about the jail to know that if he wasn't booked, his name wouldn't show up on the morning roster. Reporters on the police beat always made that the first stop of the day. Keeping his name off the jail roster would enhance his chance of keeping the entire incident under wraps.

"Thank you," Garrison said meekly. "You don't have to worry about me. I'll do your tests or whatever you need."

Garrison failed all three of the standard sobriety tests, and by a wide margin. The trooper asked the councilman to turn around and put his hands behind his back. He pushed Garrison's shirt sleeve up when placing the handcuff, and noticed a bandage.

"Are you injured?" he asked.

"The cat scratched me pretty good the other night," Garrison responded. "If I say it really hurts, will you skip handcuffing me?"

"No. I just have to ask," The trooper responded, not giving the bandage any additional thought.

It took about twenty minutes in all to get Garrison, his car, and the trooper out of the scene. Jones had watched carefully and no one had driven by the remote location. The road curved enough that someone approaching wouldn't have noticed the trooper's lights until it was too late to turn off. Wright and Jones took up their old positions, but the secret agent mood of the evening had been broken. They stayed for a couple more hours, and then called dispatch for a patrol deputy to take them back to their cars.

The trip back to their cars took them past the other gate, the one that had confused the trooper. Wright began to wonder why someone would have been there at this hour. He'd allowed himself to get radar lock on Garrison and failed to go check out the other truck. That possible mistake would ruin the couple hours of sleep Wright had been hoping to get.

0700 Saturday – Tiger Lake Road at the logging gate.

"We're looking for a fresh body…here less than twenty-four hours," Wright began. His briefing for the dog handlers would be short, because there wasn't much to say. "The jogger couldn't tell where they went into the brush, only that the male was clearly forcing the female along against her will."

"We don't have any reports of missing females, though our previous victims have all been under-the-radar types. It might be a few days before any of their fellow hookers or drug buddies notice they're missing."

"So what you're saying," Bryce interjected, "is that there might not even be a body here."

"That's right. The couple could have left when the jogger went to make his call. The cell service here is bad, and he had to go a ways to get a signal. That said, this Chimera thing is too big not to bring you out."

"I'm sorry, I wasn't being critical."

"No worries…fair question."

The search plan Wright had devised would cover the three most likely areas. The handler from Clallam County would handle the area north of the logging road. Alan Granger would handle the south side, and Bryce would take a third area further south of Granger's. Bryce's area would extend almost to the other logging gate that had confused the trooper. Wright's inner voice was still gnawing at him, and he wanted to give that at least some cursory coverage.

Bryce and Sierra, with Katie as support, had the furthest to go. They would get to the area south of Granger's by taking a spur road off the main line. The road was narrow and the scotch broom scratched along the sides of the Suburban, but they eventually got to the northwest corner of their assigned area.

"Let's put the coordinates in your GPS and you can keep us in the area," Bryce told Katie. Having a navigator would free Bryce to pay more attention to Sierra and not have to worry about where they were.

The three of them set off, finding a suitable place to get through the roadside brush. They'd spend the next couple of hours looking around, and either find a body, or not. Bryce had no idea there was a third possibility.

0700 – By phone

"You don't really think he's a suspect, do you?" Curry asked the sheriff.

"That's not the point. I asked you to keep quiet about the search and you broke a confidence. And it wasn't just a political confidence; it was about an active criminal investigation. You can consider my promise to keep you informed in the future officially revoked. You and the rest of the council will get monthly reports, not a syllable more."

"You might need more money in the future…"

"Don't start that…blackmailing. Understand this. You broke a confidence and Curry ended up ruining a stakeout. On DUI arrests, we always ask the person where they were last drinking. Curry told the trooper he was drinking with you, in your office. So you're both hip deep in this. I'll do everything I can to avoid drawing attention to that, but if it gets out, you'll both have a lot of explaining to do."

"It sounds like you're trying to blackmail *me*."

"I'm trying to give you good political advice and preserve my criminal case. I might not think Garrison is a suspect, but to a defense attorney, he's terrific reasonable doubt."

"I don't get it. If you don't think Garrison is your serial killer, what's the problem?"

"When we arrest the killer, the first thing his attorney will do is point the finger at everybody else who even touched the case. They don't need to prove their client is innocent, they just need to create reasonable doubt in the jurors' minds. Now that Garrison has interjected himself into this situation, he's the textbook definition of 'reasonable doubt.' I'm angry, but wait until the prosecutor finds out about this. He'll be more than furious, and we can't control him. He's elected by the people and doesn't report to either of us."

"OK, what do we do?"

"Councilman Garrison should take what's called a deferred prosecution. By now, I'll bet his attorney has explained the whole thing. He goes into court, pleads guilty and asks for the deferral. That puts all the paperwork on hold for a year, and if he keeps his nose clean, it goes away."

"That sounds like political favoritism."

"That's the deal any first-time DUI gets. Any other path and Garrison is blowing up his own political career and probably yours. With the public disclosure laws in this state, I won't be able to keep the reports private. Any reporter who asks will get everything. The goal here is to avoid giving anyone a reason to ask.

"Now for the political part," Patterson continued. "I was truthful the other night. My guys have been very careful about overtime, and we've not had to spend the entire $50,000. That won't change because of this. But if I decide I need more money, you *and* Garrison will give me your unconditional support, right?"

"Well, now you are trying to blackmail me. But arm twisting in politics is nothing new. Yes, you'll have my support. Garrison's you'll have to get from him. He also doesn't work for us."

"Thank you. Teams are searching for a body now. If they find one, you'll hear about it when you get our press release, and not before. You've lost the privilege."

0830 – East of Tiger Lake Road.

Clearly someone had been in the area. Even Katie could tell that Sierra was in scent and looking hard for something she just couldn't pin down.

"This is why we try to keep the ESAR ground pounders out of an area if we're going to search it," Bryce explained to Katie. "Sierra knows somebody has been here, but she can't find a source. That complicates what we tell the detective."

The two of them continued to watch Sierra make circles into the wind, instead of the usual cone. She eventually tightened the circle down to a small patch of underbrush…stopped…sniffed… and sat.

"Good girlllll," Bryce intoned quietly. "Show me."

Sierra put her nose to the ground as Bryce walked up. The underbrush had been beaten down by something bigger than Sierra. There was a clear impression that something had lain there, but there was nothing for Bryce to see. He moved the brush just in case there was something underneath, but it was for naught. Sierra hadn't given many false alerts in her time, but there was nothing there to substantiate what she was trying to tell Bryce.

"Base, Dog 44. Is Mason 20 anywhere near the south end of his area? We've got a spot of interest and would like another dog to check it out."

"Mason 20, are you copying 44?" the base operator relayed.

"Yes and yes. I think we're pretty close. I'll bet if he just yells, I'll be able to hear him."

Bryce and Katie yelled "Alan" together, and soon Granger was tromping through the salal to their location. They were north of the area where Sierra had alerted, which would allow Alan his own opportunity to find or not find whatever might or might not have been there.

"The area is basically due south of where we're standing, by a couple hundred feet. Sierra had interest but couldn't really pick out a source," Bryce explained, deliberately not telling the whole story. He omitted that Sierra had alerted, so as not to cue Granger that an alert was appropriate. He wanted to see what Granger's dog did on its own.

"OK, we'll go down and check that out. Wait here and I'll let you know what we find."

Bryce used the intervening time to explain protocol to Katie.

"If your dog smells something, but can't pin it down, you put your ego aside and call another dog. Sometimes they find something you missed. More often the other dog alerts also, and nobody figures out why either of them did. It's amazing how often two different dogs will alert in the exact same spot, but there's nothing visible to explain why."

"Crittering?" Katie asked, meaning Sierra might have alerted on a spot where another animal had slept, or urinated.

"I don't think so. I've worked hard to make sure Sierra doesn't alert on the smell of other animals. I've proofed her off animal bones, and animal poop. My folks thought I'd gone completely crazy when I bought a bottle of bear urine at the hunting store. There's a lot more bear poop in the woods than dead bodies, so if our dogs were alerting on it, we'd notice."

After about twenty minutes, Granger returned with an impatient look on his face.

"Nothing there. Not a whiff of interest," Granger said, almost rolling his eyes in disgust.

"Did you see the spot where the salal was all tramped down…just big enough for a body?"

"Your dog probably did that before you got there," Granger said, the irritation showing in his voice. "I'm tellin' ya, there's nothing there. I'm going back to my area now."

Bryce opted against arguing with Granger, because the only thing to argue about was the tone of his voice. All that mattered was whether Granger's dog found something and, since he didn't, the matter was settled.

"Thanks. We've got a little bit of our area left to do and we'll be headed back to base."

Bryce told Sierra "go find Digger," and moved off a few feet, out of Granger's sight. Then he circled back to where Sierra had alerted and where Granger's dog hadn't.

"Why are we back here?" Katie asked.

"Keep your voice down," Bryce replied, getting into his first aid kit. He removed all four of the rubber gloves he kept there for patient treatment. He put two on, and then grabbed a wooden tongue depressor.

"I need to figure out what's here that Sierra's alerting on. We'll take some of it home and let the rest of the dogs on the team take a run at it." Bryce used the tongue depressor to scoop up some of the dirt, and put it in the third rubber glove. He tied the wrist tightly, and then put that inside the fourth glove, tying that wrist tightly also. The result was that the dirt was double-bagged inside two rubber gloves.

"But what if the deputies find out you've tampered with a scene?"

"What scene? You heard Granger, there's nothing here. If there's nothing here, it's not a 'scene,' right?"

"I guess so," Katie opined. "It just seems odd."

"I'm a cadaver dog handler. We're all sick puppies. I just need to find out if other dogs do or don't alert on this dirt."

"Why?" Katie pushed.

"*Because I don't trust Granger,*" Bryce hissed, immediately regretting his tone with Katie. "I'm sorry, I didn't mean to snap. I just don't trust the guy, that's all."

"You think his ego is so big that he'd shut down his dog to avoid you getting credit for a find? We all know he's an ass but nobody's that big an ass."

"No," Bryce answered. "It's more than that. I don't even like thinking what I'm thinking, and I'm certainly not going to say it out loud. Let's just finish the rest of the area and get back to the truck."

Back at the Suburban, Bryce quietly locked the sample of dirt in his glovebox and never told Jones or Wright what he'd collected. At home, he found an old locking cash box his parents had in the attic. The dirt went in the box, and the box went at the very back of the Finn family freezer. The key stayed with him.

He never offered his teammates a chance to run their dogs on the dirt.

CHAPTER TWELVE
Firing Pin

"You're both in on this. You want to put drugs in my body and keep me locked away. Well, I'm done...I'm outta here!"

Janice Arnold had been as nice a lady as you'd ever meet, until she went completely, totally, crazy. She was married after college, was still with the same husband twenty-seven years later, and had one child. The family had a storybook life until Janice's brain chemistry changed.

No one knows why people develop mental illness. For some, it's genetic. Some get brain tumors. In some cases, it's voluntary use of recreational drugs. But for others, it's the saddest reason of all: no reason.

Janice had been fighting her demons for about five years, and her husband Leo had stayed with her. His fight was to remember the woman he loved and married, and know that somewhere inside she was still there.

He'd urged her to get treatment, but that had been labelled a conspiracy. Leo was the ringleader, with her doctors and their daughter as cohorts. Janice spiraled downward, yet Leo remained at her side and faithful. He took her from doctor to preacher to spiritualist without success. He'd have taken her to an Indian medicine man if he'd known one.

Still, the tantrums continued. Leo was always the focus. He'd been the victim of assaults on several occasions, but never called the police. Janice repeatedly threatened suicide, and Leo always talked her out of it.

"Honey, remember, you need to take your medicine. You don't think straight when you're not on your meds," he would patiently remind her.

The inevitably shouted response would always be to blame Leo. "You just make me take those pills so you can keep me docile, like the good little wife you want me to be."

The arguments got worse, and tonight Janice was more delusional than she'd ever been.

"I should have divorced you years ago, you cheating bastard. I know you've slept with every woman in the neighborhood. Every time I'm not looking, you're with somebody else's wife."

The accusation hurt Leo like none of her previous rantings ever had. He'd been completely faithful, and had gone so far as to find his own source of counselling to help him deal with such a troubled wife. He could feel his own anger building and wasn't sure he could respond lovingly. He tried one last time.

"Honey, I love you. I've never cheated on you and wouldn't. We've got to get you back on your meds."

"I'm going for a walk...and I'm not sure I'm ever coming back."

And with that, Janice put on her coat and stormed out of the house. Leo decided it was better to let her cool off, and didn't try to follow. She stopped by the barn, came out wearing boots instead of her tennis shoes, and headed into the thick brush that adjoined the property.

Like many houses in north Kitsap, the Arnold home was set in the woods and secluded from the neighbors. It bordered on a greenbelt that spanned nearly a mile to the next paved road. It wasn't a great place for a walk, as there were no trails. But it was a great place to get lost.

"We're looking for a white female, sixty-three years old, her name is Janice Arnold. She was last seen wearing a gray barn coat over a yellow blouse and jeans," was the briefing from the deputy.

"She's had some mental health issues, but her family says she's never been violent." That wasn't true, but the deputy didn't know it. Leo's embarrassment about her condition had caused him to lie. The deputy merely repeated what he thought was true.

Bryce, Katie and Sierra wouldn't start at the house. They'd instead begin at the other end of the greenbelt, along the paved road. That way they'd have containment on Janice, as opposed to chasing her through the woods. If she ran from them, she'd run into the deputies at the house.

The three of them were delivered to their starting point by a sheriff's deputy in an SUV. The deputy dropped them off and left, and Bryce reported by radio that they were starting their assignment, leaving from the paved road.

Bryce worked Sierra up and down the ditch before finding a spot to turn into the greenbelt.

"The brush is always the worst right along the roadway," he told Katie. "It's because of all the sunlight. Once we get in a hundred feet or so, the trees shade out some of the underbrush and it'll be easier going."

Bryce turned and made a pass parallel to the road about one hundred feet in, right where the brush thinned out. He'd found people in this transition area before. Missing people make their way through the thinner brush, but give up when it gets thick. They don't realize they're often only yards from a trail or road.

And Bryce was pleased to see Katie with her own spritz bottle, spraying a fine mist into the air and watching which way it drifted. She was careful to watch downwind to cover the areas Sierra's nose would miss. As navigator, Katie's primary job was to check her compass frequently and keep Bryce going in the right direction.

"Those bushes pushed us a little bit right. Bend it a little bit left now that we're clear, and get back on your track."

They worked the transition area all the way through the greenbelt, to a utility substation with a chain link fence. Janice obviously hadn't climbed it, so it was time to make a pass in the other direction.

Neither that pass nor the next two yielded any results. But on their fourth pass Sierra suddenly turned left and headed off. Bryce didn't follow.

"Shouldn't we be going with her?" Katie asked.

"She'll be back in a minute. Check the wind."

"I already did, she's headed downwind."

"Well, does that tell you anything?"

"Oh…Sierra can't smell what's downwind of her. So why is she going that way?"

"Human scent blows through the woods much like smoke. Sierra is following the scent as it rolls downwind. It'll eventually peter out, the way smoke thins out. Sierra will pretty quickly figure that out and…ah, here she comes now."

Sierra had returned, and was working the cone of scent back to its source. She paid no attention to Bryce and Katie as she worked past them, directly into the wind. Now Bryce turned and began to follow.

They'd only taken a few steps in their new direction when suddenly a figure stood up about thirty feet in front of them.

"Get that damn dog away from me. I don't want to get bit."

"Sierra's a search dog, she won't bite you. She loves everybody," Bryce replied in as cheerful a voice as he could. "You're probably Janice, right?"

"So that cheating bastard of a husband sent the dogs after me, did he? Well I'm not going back. He's just trying to keep me locked up in the house and make me take those drugs."

"Janice…gosh…I spoke to your husband before we came out here. He seems really worried about you."

"No, he doesn't care for me at all. He just wants me locked up like the 'good little wife,' and he's even turned my daughter against me. I'm NOT going back."

"OK, well…that's for you to work out with your husband. We're just out here because you were reported missing and we wanted to help."

As Bryce was talking, he closed the distance to Janice so he could be heard while speaking in a soft voice. If he yelled to be heard, Janice might interpret him as arguing.

"Katie, will you get on the radio and let Leo know we've found his bride?" Bryce was careful not to mention police, correctly fearing that would aggravate the situation even more.

"Sure, I'll call Leo and let him know Janice is OK. I don't have very good radio reception right here…I'm going to move over there a ways."

Despite being a rookie, Katie had picked up that by being out of earshot, she'd be able to give base a better explanation of what was developing. She moved well away from Bryce and Janice and got on her radio.

"Base, Dog 44," she whispered into her radio. "We've located our subject and Bryce is talking to her now. She's not happy to have been found and we might need a deputy to come talk her into going home."

"Dog 44, Base copies. Send your coordinates and we'll get a deputy out there. The husband says she's quite verbal but has never been violent."

Leo's little white lie was about to be exposed.

Bryce moved as close to Janice as he felt he could, and plopped himself down on a log a few feet away. He hoped the closer contact and non-threatening body language would build a rapport.

"So what was your plan? How long were you going to stay out here?" Bryce asked.

"That's none of your business and you should just leave. You can tell that no-good husband of mine I'm not coming back…AND I DON'T LIKE DOGS!" To Bryce's complete surprise, Janice pulled a small revolver from her coat pocket and pointed it in Sierra's direction.

Bryce made a split second decision and moved toward Janice instead of away from her. He grabbed at the gun and managed to get a grip on the cylinder. He put his shoulder into Janice and they both went down, with each of them having two hands on the gun pulling it back and forth, each trying to wrestle it from the other.

"Are you out of your mind?" was the only thing Bryce could say. She obviously was, that was the whole reason he'd been called. But he was still incredulous that someone he'd tried to save would point a gun at his dog.

Sierra, seeing her master in a fight, did what any dog would do and became protective. She grabbed Janice at the waist and began to yank with her teeth, growling in a tone that Bryce had never heard.

"Sierra…no…leave it." Search dogs are *never* supposed to show aggression toward humans.

Janice screamed in pain and took one hand off the gun to slap at Sierra. It didn't work, but it did give Bryce a chance to get better control of the weapon. He pushed forward against the weaker muscles of her forearm, and used both arms to push the gun down to the ground, right next to Janice's head.

Janice continued beating at Sierra, who never released the grip on her waist.

Those who go through stressful situations report thinking odd things at the height of the crisis, and Bryce was experiencing exactly that. His mind was racing in two directions, both bad. In the short term, he had to get the gun from Janice before she killed him AND Sierra. In the long term, was Sierra finished as a search dog? What would the sheriff's office say when the "rescued" subject came back with a shredded hip?

"Sierra NO! Leave it! Let her go!" Bryce managed to shout. Janice continued to slap at Sierra, occasionally connecting but only increasing Sierra's level of aggression.

"Sierra...I said NO! Leave it!" Bryce said, knowing that if Sierra did obey him, Janice would again have two hands to fight for the gun.

Sierra obeyed, and backed away a few steps with her hackles still up. She was crouched down, as if ready to spring back onto Janice if she thought it necessary. She continued making a low growl that Bryce had also never heard.

Katie had heard the commotion and came as quickly as she could through the brush.

"No, get away. Take Sierra and run. I can hold her until the deputies get here."

"Forget it. I'm not leaving. They told us in training that mentals can get super strong. You might not be able to hold her yourself."

Janice was twisting herself around, though she hadn't yet managed to get a second hand on the gun. Bryce was holding it on the ground, his full weight straight down on it. She had managed to raise herself up a bit, and bring another weapon into the fight... her teeth.

"Katie, dammit. I'm your team leader and telling you to take Sierra and run."

"Well, I'm your team, and I'm not running out on you. What do you need me to do?"

"It would be nice if she'd quit biting me," Bryce managed to eke out. Blood was beginning to run down the arm closest to Janice's mouth.

Katie leaned in and put both hands on Janice's left shoulder, pinning her flat on her back. That put Bryce's right forearm out of biting range, and he continued to stiff-arm the gun into the ground. He stayed over it in the same way he'd been taught to do CPR. Elbows locked, body weight directly over, and pushing down. If the gun went off now, the bullet would probably pass along the ground behind Janice's head. Probably. Unless it hit a rock and ricocheted up, at which point any of them could be at risk.

Bryce and Katie took a few breaths and assessed their predicament. Janice was now kicking, but she didn't have much leverage and the two of them were able to keep her pinned down. Sierra had stepped back a few feet, but remained on high alert, her teeth bared and the low growl continuing.

Bryce decided to take a chance, and get on the radio. He put all of his weight over his stiff right arm and used his left hand to key the radio mike. "Dog 44 emergency! She's got a gun and we're wrestling her for it. Have those deputies step it up!"

"Dog 44, base copies. We'll let 'em know."

The base operator said nothing else. He knew that Bryce and Katie might well be fighting for their lives, and yakking at them on the radio wouldn't help. He stuck his head out of the comm van and yelled at the one deputy who was still in base.

"Get on your radio and tell your buddies step it up. She's pulled a gun and the team is fighting her for it."

The two deputies got the radio call just as they got close enough to hear the commotion on their own.

"I...will...kill...you...ALL!" Janice screamed. She had gone completely delusional, and homicidal to boot.

"She's getting stronger," Bryce said to Katie. "It's the adrenaline kicking in. If you want to run, it's OK. I don't know how much longer we can hold her."

"I'm not leaving. Can you get the gun out of her hand?"

"I don't think so. She's got a death grip on it, so to speak. Let's just try and hang on until we get more help."

With all of Janice's screaming, they hadn't heard the two deputies arriving through the underbrush. In trying to run, they'd each fallen multiple times. But they eventually got to the scene and started grabbing at Janice, yanking her away from Bryce.

"Don't do that!" Bryce said, despite being grateful for their presence. "I've barely got control of this gun. If you go yanking on her and pull her out of my grip, we're all in trouble. Let's all just take a breath and freeze things for a minute."

The deputies weren't used to taking orders from searchers, but Bryce's words made sense. They backed off and each leaned on one of Janice's legs to stop her kicking. The senior deputy spoke next.

"OK...good call. What do you want to do?"

"I need to get her to release her grip on this gun. I think my hand's caught in the mechanism and it's hurting like hell. If you use your TASER, will it shock both of us?"

"You might feel a little tingle, but she'll get the big jolt. Wanna try that?"

"YESSS, please. Do it."

"OK…she'll thrash and scream and hopefully wear herself out a little bit. Wait until she's ridden the full five seconds and when she's had enough of the pain you can try and pry it loose."

The deputy hollered "TASER TASER TASER" per procedure, though his partner knew exactly what would happen.

Bryce heard the crackling sound and felt Janice's body stiffen. She screamed even louder than before. She flailed a bit, but Bryce was able to hold onto the gun until she went limp. She'd clearly had enough of the pain, and the gun came free with surprisingly little effort. The two deputies rolled Janice face down and handcuffed her.

Bryce stepped back, now with his own death grip on the gun. He'd fought for it for so long, he couldn't bring himself to let go. The pain he'd felt was getting worse as his own adrenaline began wearing off.

"OK, I'll take that," the deputy said. But when he started to hand it over, Bryce winced in pain of his own.

"I'm hooked or something," he said. The deputy could only stare. Bryce opened his hand and the gun didn't fall. It hung there, as if attached by Velcro.

"My God, I've only seen that in training. Have you been taught how to take a gun from someone?"

"No, but can we get it loose…please? It's really starting to hurt."

The deputy carefully cradled the gun, taking its weight in his own hand. He pulled the hammer back slightly and Bryce's hand immediately came free. The trick was to then lower the hammer gently enough that the gun wouldn't fire.

"It really is just like they taught us in training," the deputy explained. "When you grabbed the gun, she'd already pulled the trigger. That little web of skin between your thumb and forefinger got between the firing pin and the bullet—at just the right moment. She was sure as hell trying to shoot your dog."

Bryce could see a small hole in his hand made by the firing pin. It went all the way through the web of skin. The pain was decreasing, but now his head was starting to spin.

"Here...sit down for a minute," the deputy said. "It's normal to be upset after something like this. Do you need some water or something?"

Bryce started to shake, and his voice cracked. "I just want Sierra. I can't imagine somebody shooting her." Sierra had been off to the side, her normal self once the struggle had ended. Dogs may react, but they don't hold grudges.

"Oh, girl, I'm so sorry I got you into this."

Bryce began to cry. He wrapped his arms around Sierra, who wriggled and wagged, and then began licking the tears off his face. Bryce just held her and shook.

Katie walked up and put her arms around both of them. Bryce stopped in mid-sob, and remembered his role as team leader and mentor to Katie. He immediately tried to stifle his emotions.

"Oh no you don't, mister," Katie said in a tone that was both scolding and supportive. "Don't you go all macho on me. You got one hell of a fright and you *should* be upset. Let's get it out of your system or it'll be worse later."

Katie's words got through to Bryce. Her message: it was not only OK to cry, it was probably a good idea. His head fell onto her shoulder, and he sobbed at the thought of losing Sierra.

Katie let him go for a bit, to really get the emotions out. Only then did she speak. Quietly, so the deputies couldn't hear.

"One of the things I love about you is that you're strong, without being macho. I've seen those kinds of men around my mom, and they've always turned out to be asses. You not only saved Sierra today, but maybe me too. And your first thought was to get me away while you fought for your life. You did all the right things today and there's no way you could have known the woman had a gun. It's OK to be upset. It makes you a better leader and a better boyfriend."

Bryce was coming around. The sobs were lessening, having been truly vented on Katie's shoulder. He was also starting to realize that she was right. The deputies would have to figure out where Janice got the gun, but that hadn't been his fault.

He continued to hug Sierra, but the tension was leaving his body. He'd never felt anything like that, and knew only that Katie had brought it about. He'd read her mind earlier, and now she was reading his. That meant something, only he wasn't sure what.

One problem remained. Janice was still refusing to leave her spot. The brush was just thick enough that she couldn't be forced to walk through it, even with deputies holding both arms. She was passively resisting in a spot where she couldn't just be dragged to the back of a police car.

"Base, Dog 44." It was Katie using the radio.

"Base, go ahead."

"Dog 44…the deputies are asking if we have enough people for a pack-out. The subject has mild injuries and is not compliant. They don't think they can make her walk through the brush."

"Base…yeah…I think we can scare up enough people to pack her

out. We'll gather them up and send them out with the Stokes."

"Dog 44, thank you. We'll be standing by."

It took about twenty minutes for the team to show up with the Stokes. They had more than enough people for the pack-out. The only question was whether they had enough people to get an angry, flailing mental case into the Stokes.

"Janice, we're going to take you out now," the senior deputy offered. "Since you won't walk, we're going to put you in this litter and carry you. Will you let us put you in the litter?"

"I just said I wasn't going back," Janice yelled. "I meant under my own power. If you TAKE me back and he kills me, that's on you. Put me in your damn litter and carry me anyplace you want to."

Janice's twisted logic escaped the deputy, but he didn't care. He just wanted her in the litter. Janice let them put her in and didn't even complain when they pulled the straps extra tight. Nobody wanted her getting loose halfway to base.

The twenty-minute trip out with the litter turned out to be nearly an hour with a patient on board. They passed the litter over downed trees, and then hand to hand through narrow spots between blackberries. Eventually, Janice was back at base and loaded in a fire department aid car. They'd take her to a hospital for a mental evaluation and then probably to jail for her antics with the gun.

The senior deputy turned to Janice's husband in a very unhappy tone.

"OK, Leo. Where did she get the gun? She almost killed a couple of kids out there."

"I had one hidden in the barn, I didn't even know she knew

about it. I moved it out of the house the last time she…she…"

"She what? *You told me she wasn't violent. Did I mention she almost killed a couple of teenagers? We don't send teenagers to look for people who might have guns.*"

"I'm sorry…she went to the barn and came out with her boots on. I didn't think she knew about the gun, so I never connected it up."

"But she has been violent in the past, right?"

"Well, she's hit me a couple times and threatened suicide. But I never thought she'd be a threat to anyone else."

"Jeez, Leo…I could take you to jail right now for recklessly endangering our searchers. The only reason you're not going to jail is because I don't arrest people while I'm mad. You can bet I'll be having a conversation with the county prosecutor in the morning. I might be at your doorstep tomorrow afternoon."

"I'm sorry…if you have to arrest me I'll understand. But our daughter has emotional issues of her own. I need to go talk to her right now and help her understand why her mother is in handcuffs."

Bryce, in the meantime, had put Sierra in the truck. He was sitting in the driver's seat, staring into space. He'd need to have a discussion with somebody about Sierra's getting involved in the fight. Would she now be aggressive toward other humans, having learned the behavior while possibly saving Bryce's life?

More than that, could he ever put her in the field again knowing she could be shot? It had been sooo close, and with no warning. His eyes started to tear up again.

"Hey…I said something wrong out there." It was Katie. Bryce

was so caught in his own thoughts he hadn't noticed her walk up.

"You did not," Bryce replied. "I was freaking out and you said exactly the right things. I'm still shaking and could probably stand to hear them again. What do you think you said wrong?"

"Remember I was telling you about mom and all those macho men in her life? I said, 'One of the things I love about you is that you're strong without being macho.' Remember?"

"It was a bit of a blur, but I remember something about that."

"Well...the fact that you're strong without being macho isn't something I love *about* you. I said that wrong. It's one of the reasons *I love you.*"

So many times with Katie, Bryce had been unsure of what to say. He'd never had a girlfriend, didn't have a sister, and generally had no idea how to communicate with women. Today, despite the near-death experience and skyrocketing emotions, he'd never had a clearer picture of what needed to be said.

"I love you, too."

CHAPTER THIRTEEN
Now You Don't

"I couldn't get ahold of Wright and since you're working, it makes sense to give this to you," Robinson told Jones over the phone. She'd taken the 911 call and would normally have radioed it to a deputy working in the area it had come from. But her "dispatcher sense" told her the call could be related to the series of cases that Wright and Jones had been working.

It was also a call she thought shouldn't go out over the radio. There was no way to tell who was listening, from the media to the bad guys themselves.

"Thanks and thanks," Jones said. "Good call on getting this to Bob or me, and better call keeping it off the radio. I'll contact the family."

"Should I let the sergeant know what's up?"

"No, I'll take care of it," which meant he wouldn't be telling anyone but Bob Wright, at least for the time being. "Let's keep this just between us for now."

Both Jones and Wright had been frustrated at their failure to find a body at Tiger Lake three weeks before. The trail runner had appeared sane, sober and clear of head. Despite what he'd seen, there was no body. Jones, in his role as an apprentice detective, was beginning to learn why investigators keep information from even other police officers.

Jones dialed the number, and it was answered midway through the very first ring.

"I'm Davy Jones with the sheriff's office," he explained. "Our dispatcher said your daughter is missing…?"

"She is," the woman interrupted. "She's disappeared before but never for this long. It's been way more than forty-eight hours since we last saw her, so we're hoping you can put out a missing person report on her."

Jones was immediately frustrated with the old wives' tale about people needing to be gone forty-eight hours before police would take a missing report. It wasn't true, and the rumor only created unnecessary delays.

"Ma'am, we can put out a missing person report anytime we think someone's in danger," Jones replied, trying not to show his irritation. "There was no need to wait any time at all. What's your daughter's name?"

"Maria Angelica Santiago," the mother replied, proudly using her daughter's full name. "She's seventeen."

"When did you last see her?"

"About three weeks ago. Like I said, she sometimes disappears for a while, but most times she runs out of money and comes home.

We're worried that we haven't heard from her. Are you able to do…what do they call that…an AMBER Alert on her?"

Jones barely heard the question, his mind stuck on the timing. It had been exactly three weeks since the trail runner had reported the incident at Tiger Lake.

"I'm sorry, you mentioned…Amber?"

"I think that's what it's called. We see the alerts on TV."

Every single parent of every single missing child wants an AMBER Alert. The criteria for AMBER Alerts are based in good logic and good police procedure, and are completely impossible to explain to panicked parents.

"Oh, an AMBER Alert. No, I'm sorry. We only do those when an abduction is actually witnessed, and we have enough info to tell the public what to look for."

"So you won't take a missing report? My daughter is a seventeen-year-old Hispanic girl and you don't care about her? We're here legally, you know."

"Ma'am, wait a minute. We're absolutely going to do a missing person report, just not the AMBER Alert. All the local police and shelters will get notified that she's a runaway."

"We don't think she's a runaway this time. It's worse. For her to be gone this long…something bad has happened."

Most routine runaway reports were taken over the phone, but Jones was developing a feeling about this one—and it wasn't good. He decided it would be worth a personal visit.

"Where are you now, ma'am? I think it's best if I come over and meet with you in person."

Jones got the location. It was the furthest you could be from his patrol district and still be in Kitsap County. "It'll take me about thirty minutes to get there. Could you gather up the most recent pictures you have of Maria for me?"

"We've got lots of pictures and we'll have them all for you when you get here. Please hurry. We're really worried."

Unlike Jones' last call, this one was definitely NOT answered on the first ring. Wright had to climb down from a ladder and barely managed to snag the call just before it went to voice mail.

"This had better be good. Don't you know I'm hanging lights in my basement?"

"Sorry to interrupt such important work, but yeah, this should be worth it. I'm headed out to the north end to take a missing that seems to line up with Tiger Lake."

"OK…how so?"

"Timing's right, mostly. They haven't heard from her in about three weeks and when she runs away, it's normally not this long."

"Clothing?"

"Mom doesn't remember what she was wearing when they last saw her. The height/weight part is close. We're comparing a general description from mom with a fuzzy description from the trail runner…mostly it's just a feeling."

"OK. Your intuition's been good in the past. Call if there's anything you need, but I'd like you to handle this. It's why the sheriff and I have you on the case."

Jones was a little surprised that Wright wouldn't want to handle this personally. He was flattered at the show of confidence.

Instead of half an hour, it took Jones nearly forty-five minutes to get to the residence. He had the address, and the house was easy to spot. It was very clearly the nicest home in an otherwise terrible neighborhood. The family was low-income, but what they did have they apparently kept nice. The inside of the house was threadbare, but just as neat.

"My wife tells me you won't send an AMBER Alert for my daughter," the husband asked almost immediately. "Why?"

"I'm sorry, sir. This doesn't fit the criteria for an AMBER Alert. We reserve that for when someone has actually seen a child dragged into a car. We have to have a description of the car to tell people what to look for."

"You know we're here legally. My wife told you that, right?"

Jones was glad he decided to come over in person. If he'd relied on the wife to relay his answers, the husband would almost assuredly remain angry.

"Yes, sir. It's not about your status or anything like that. If we sent an AMBER Alert every time a seventeen-year-old ran away from home, people would stop paying attention. It would become meaningless. Please give us a chance to show what we CAN do for you."

"Here's a picture of Maria," her mother interrupted. "Can you at least do a wanted poster, or whatever you call it?"

"Of course. She'll go on our website, our Facebook page, and the State Patrol's missing person system. We send a press release to the news people, too. The only thing we can't do is call it an AMBER Alert."

"Would a reward help?" We have a little money...."

"Not yet," Jones counselled. He knew this family didn't likely have the means to offer a real reward. Fortunately, the truth about rewards was an adequate explanation.

"The biggest thing about a reward is not how much you offer. It's making the announcement, which gets you additional publicity. In order to talk about the reward, the media would have to talk about your daughter again. Let us do the press release first, without mentioning a reward. Then, if we think it'll help, we can offer a reward later to generate a second round of news coverage."

The family took the explanation gracefully, and began answering Jones' myriad other questions about their missing daughter.

Yes, she was a frequent runaway.

Yes, she'd dabbled in drugs, but had never been arrested.

Yes, she'd lived on the street. She frequently hitchhiked down Highway 3 to Belfair to hang out with friends.

That set off alarm bells for Jones. Highway 3 passed just south of the Tiger Lake neighborhood. If an abductor had picked her up there and needed a close place to make his kill, Tiger Lake would be perfect.

"One more thing," Jones asked. "Do you have anything that would have Maria's blood or hair on it? We'd like to get her DNA in our database. It doesn't mean I think something's happened, but you watch those CSI TV shows, right?"

"We've washed everything since she left. If she came home, we wanted her room to be nice for her."

"OK, then maybe I can take your DNA? We can tell when there's a family relationship."

"Do you have to draw blood?" the mother asked. "I hate needles."

"Not at all. We just swab the inside of your cheek with a big Q-tip thing. It doesn't hurt at all. I have the kit in my car…"

Jones turned and started walking, without giving the parents a chance to object. Neither did, but Jones was surprised that the mother followed him to the car.

"You didn't need to come out here, ma'am. I could have grabbed the kit and come back in," he said.

"No, I wanted to talk to you away from my husband. I wanted to tell you something else about my Maria that my husband doesn't know."

Whatever this was, Jones knew it would likely be gold. It's routine for detectives to separate witnesses to make sure their stories are told independently. When witnesses voluntarily choose to separate themselves, they tend to drop bombshells.

"I think my daughter has been selling herself," the mother said, not able to call her daughter a prostitute.

Bombshell, indeed.

"That doesn't change anything for us. We'll still try to find her. What makes you think she's a…been selling herself?"

"A mother just knows these things. I could see it in her eyes. They were different. Well, that and the box of condoms I found in her purse."

In fact, the revelation about prostitution *did* change things. It meant Maria Angelica Santiago fit the Chimera Killer's victim profile to a T. Jones didn't say that, however.

"I appreciate you telling me, ma'am. I know that must have been very hard."

"Please don't tell my husband."

"Well, I'm certainly not in any hurry to tell him, but I think you should start getting ready to break the news. If she is…selling herself…it's likely going to come out sooner or later."

"I know…but it'll kill him. She was his baby until she tried those drugs. Everybody in the neighborhood gets drunk or high, and we tried to keep her away from all that. We can't afford to move to a nicer neighborhood…"

"It doesn't matter what neighborhood," Jones counseled. "I see it everywhere. With some drugs, you take one hit and you're hooked. My younger brother got into heroin, and we've had no luck getting him help."

"Wouldn't you like to find the person who gave your brother that first hit? I would. If I could find the person who got Maria into drugs, I'd kill him with my bare hands."

"That's maybe not a great thing to say to a police officer, but I get it. Um…if there's nothing else, I should get back to the office and get Maria entered in the computer."

Jones left, and on the way back called Wright again.

"This felt right when dispatch gave it to me, and it feels even righter now. Turns out mom thinks she's a hooker, and she hitchhikes Highway 3 out to Belfair a lot."

Belfair straddled Highway 3, just to the west of Kitsap County. It was a mostly rural town, in neighboring Mason County. It had a few businesses clustered around a couple of stoplights along the highway.

The internet has brought civilization, good or bad, to rural America. In the past, when a man in Belfair wanted a prostitute, he had to travel to Bremerton or Tacoma and drive slowly up and down just the right street. Now, he merely needed a reasonably fast broadband connection and could arrange to meet the girl of his choice at any hour of the day or night.

"That does fit. I know a gal over at Mason County who's been working the online angles with the sex trade. I can give her a call and see if she knows the girl."

———————

"The gal" at Mason County was Detective Ada Wills, and to say that Wright knew her was an understatement. Ten years before, the two had been deeply in love until Wright realized he needed to quit drinking. Ada continued to party hearty, and Wright knew where his life was headed if he didn't stop.

"I love you, but I can't do the booze thing, and for the time being I can't even be around it," he'd told her.

Professionally, they still got along. Ada was as addicted to putting away sex traffickers as she was to her Irish whiskey. Wright knew he could call and get not only everything in Ada's computer, but her personal take as well.

"Buy you a drink?" Wright said when she answered her phone.

"A drink, or a *drink* drink? How are you, old friend? I miss your voice."

"Yours too," Wright responded, remembering the friendly tone that had won his heart a decade before. "I'm pretty solid now. I could probably buy you a *drink* drink and just have a soda myself. We'll have to do that sometime."

"Sounds good, buuut…it also sounds like that's not why you called."

"It's not, and I kinda need to jump right to business. You know anything about a possible street urchin named Maria Santiago? She's seventeen and maybe hung out in Belfair."

"Funny you should ask. I got a call last night from one of her fellow urchins, as you call them, who was worried about her. We didn't have a last name, but seventeen and Maria makes it a pretty sure bet. Who called you?"

"Her folks. Mom thinks she's hooking, and can't bear to tell Dad. We'll be doing a bulletin on her later this morning."

"How about I scoop up her friend and we all meet at the Airport Diner? They all hate the cops unless you're buying them lunch. You got a picture to show my little friend?"

"I've got a whole portfolio. The family provided more pictures than I can use, mostly to prove what a sweet little thing she used to be."

"Most of the girls I work with were good kids…once. Let's say 11:30 unless you hear otherwise. I think I know where to look for my informant."

———————

"Call me Brux. I don't have to give you my name and birthdate, do I?"

The Airport Diner sits just off the tarmac at Bremerton International Airport, and is well known throughout Kitsap and Mason Counties for putting out a more-than-decent plate of food. The booth they'd selected was as secluded as the restaurant offered. The 11:30 start would give them a little time before the place filled up.

"Nope…Ada has all your info if I need it. I just need to show you a picture and see if we're talking about the same Maria. I really appreciate your help."

The waitress arrived with water and menus. "How are y'all doin' today? The special is our fish and chips. Three pieces with coleslaw and pie is $8.99."

"Oh my God," Wright replied. "Your 'pieces' of fish are huge. Three of them would put me in a food coma." He feigned thinking about it for a few seconds. "Actually, a coma sounds good today. I'll have that."

Ada opted for the club sandwich and Brux went with a burger and fries. Wright figured she'd also eat this third piece of fish and maybe his pie.

"How did you pick a nickname like Brux?" he asked.

"Brussels is this wonderfully mysterious place I hope to live someday. I used to hang with a guy who'd lived there. He's in jail now, but he told me all about it."

"Right...well, I hope you make it there someday. It's gotta beat Belfair."

"For sure...that place is a dump."

Belfair was actually a nice community when you got off Highway 3 and into the hills around. Nobody had a lot of money, but they were honest folk who made the best of what they had. It was just the highway itself that seemed to attract scum.

"So, can I show you some pictures and see if we're talking about the same Maria?" Wright asked.

"Sure. It's probably her, and that guy probably killed her."

"What guy?" Ada jumped into the conversation. "You didn't say anything about a guy."

"No, I told you. The guy in the big pickup. He picked her up near the light at Safeway."

Ada and Wright shared a look that each understood. Dopers forget and remember things at their own convenience. Brux probably believed she'd told Ada about the guy and his truck, but she hadn't.

"Honey, I'm sorry," Ada said, trying to retreat from any conflict. "If you said anything, I missed that part. You saw her getting in a truck with a guy?"

"Of course. Why else would I have called you?"

Ada decided to not make an issue of Brux's omission. "OK, what kind of truck was it? Did you happen to see the driver?"

"Like I said it was big and white. I'm not a car person so I don't know much else."

"How about the driver? Could you see him at all?"

"Older guy, looked like. Maybe with a beard but there was a reflection on the window. I couldn't see in much."

Ada knew she'd now have to ask the dumbest question of the century.

"Brux, did you happen to see a license plate?"

"No…I might have been a little loaded that day. I probably couldn't have read it even if I'd been close enough to see it."

"We understand…that's no problem and we appreciate your honesty. Did you see which way they went?"

"Back toward Bremerton."

Back toward Bremerton was also back toward Tiger Lake. While none of this made Maria a definite murder victim, neither did it rule her out.

Wright offered up the most recent picture of Maria.

"That's her," Brux said without hesitation. "She was really pretty."

"You're talking about her like she's in the past tense," Wright said, looking her directly in the eye. "You already 'forgot' about the car. Now you're talking about Maria like she's already gone. Do you know something else you're not sharing?"

"No! I mean…I don't know who'd want to hurt her," she replied, not looking away or avoiding his gaze. "It's just that all those girls have gone missing and I see her get in that guy's truck and then nothing…"

The fact that she looked directly back at Wright when answering the question carried a lot of weight. Liars tend to avoid the direct stare.

"No pimp, no drug dealer…nobody in her life like that?"

"We're 'casual labor' if you get my drift," Brux replied, still looking Wright in the eyes. "We hit the street if we need cash but nothing formal. I'm definitely not handing over my hard earned money to some pimp."

"Brux, I'm sorry for having to push you, but when you speak in the past tense it sounds like you know more than you're sharing. We all want the same thing, and that's to get Maria back, right?"

"Uh-huh."

"Then I need to ask straight up—do you know where Maria is or anything about what might have happened to her?"

"No, and I don't like being accused. I came to you, remember?"

At that moment lunch arrived and the conversation stopped. After the experience with Garrison at Tiger Lake, Wright wasn't even trusting waitresses. They figured out who got the fish and who got the burger, and Wright used the break in the conversation to adopt a softer tone.

"We really do appreciate you coming to us, honestly. But I have a job to do and part of that is asking hard questions. I accept what you say," Wright said, closing the matter. "I shouldn't have ordered the special...it's too much. Want a piece of fish?"

"Sure."

———————————

Jones, in the meantime, was working with the sheriff's public information officer Deputy Lem Smith to get out a bulletin about Maria. Bulletins were routine, but in light of the killings, they were starting to get an increased level of attention from both reporters and the public.

"Let's think about when we send this," Smith said. Even though he held the rank of deputy, Smith reported directly to the sheriff and was his advisor on all things media. He wasn't just a mouthpiece, he helped develop strategy.

"I don't want to send this at four o'clock and then be taking calls all evening," Smith told Jones. "I'd rather get it out this morning if we can get it written and approved."

"Can we also do something on Twitter and Facebook?" Jones asked. "Who reads press releases anymore?"

"Yes, we do all of that. But actually, I like having the old-school media involved," Smith replied. "If they write a decent article, then everybody on social media links to it. If we just have people 'passing the word' on Facebook, things get screwed up."

"Whatever, I just want to get it out there. Dammit, I left all her pictures in my car. Let me run and grab those while you're writing."

Jones had to walk through the lobby to get to his car and ran into Bryce at the counter.

"Hey, Bryce, what brings you in?"

"I gotta renew my ID card, and they want an updated picture. What's going on?"

"Well, we've got a lead on that missing persons case you went on up at Tiger Lake. A seventeen-year-old girl who matches the description was last seen getting into a truck down in Belfair the same day we got the call from the trail runner."

The case had weighed on Bryce since the day of the search. Sierra had given a very strong alert at Tiger Lake, and he hadn't been able to let it go.

"All we have to do now is figure out where she is," Jones continued.

Bryce hesitated for a second, and drew a breath.

"Well, I might not know where she is, but I think I know where she was," Bryce replied. He knew the risk he was taking on about a dozen different levels. He decided to tell Jones about his frozen dirt regardless.

"You remember the spot where Sierra hit?" Bryce asked.

"Sure, but you had another dog check and it didn't confirm her alert."

"I took some of the dirt. It's in my freezer."

"YOU WHAT?" Jones asked. "You tampered with a crime scene?"

"It wasn't a scene," Bryce reminded Jones. "Nobody thought there was anything there. I just wanted to see what other dogs would do if they had a chance to sniff the dirt."

"Well, did they hit?"

"I don't know. I haven't gotten around to it. Our last training got cancelled for a real search, so the stuff is still sitting in my freezer."

"Let's go on back to the office. We gotta talk to Wright and figure out what we're going to do. I wish you'd asked us before doing that."

"I know. I should have. Even good dogs like Sierra sometimes alert when we can't figure out why. Sierra was solid on this, but I didn't want to look defensive."

As they walked to the office, Jones' mind was going 100 miles per hour. If Bryce had tampered with a crime scene, it could be the end of his SAR career. On the other hand, if this turned out to be THE big break in the case, it could catapult him to stardom.

And if the body HAD been there, when was it moved? It took the trail runner less than an hour to get back to cell coverage, and deputies were on-scene quickly. If someone had been thrashing about in the woods, they'd have noticed.

The only time someone could have moved the body was while he and Wright were fussing with Councilman Garrison. Nobody had gone in or out via the main road. Even while they were trying to sneak Garrison's car out of the scene, one or the other of them had been at the trailhead.

That was it...something the trooper had said when he showed

up. He'd gone to the wrong trailhead, where a pickup was parked.

Jones dialed Wright's number from the office. He answered, obviously in his car.

"You alone, buddy? Got some info for ya...maybe."

"Yeah, what's up?"

"Bryce Finn is here. He's on the speaker phone with me. He's convinced his dog's hit at Tiger Lake was a good one, and he snagged some of the dirt."

"OK, that's dangerously close to tampering with a crime scene, but we didn't think it was anything at the time. Go on."

Bryce jumped in, fearing his entire SAR career was at risk. "I just wanted to see if other dogs would hit, to confirm Sierra's alert. But when I thought about it...if the other dogs do hit then it's retroactively a crime scene."

That wasn't entirely true. There could be other explanations for why multiple dogs would hit on dirt in the woods. Sometimes multiple dogs will hit on a spot and nobody ever knows why.

"OK, I'm tracking," Jones replied. "Where is this dirt now?"

"Home, in my freezer."

"Who else has access to that?"

Wright was already thinking about the chain of evidence. The Sheriff's Office had enough trouble with defense attorneys attacking their very formal system for storing evidence. The killer's attorney would have a field day if what turned out to be key evidence had been stored in somebody's home freezer.

"I don't suppose your freezer locks?"

"No, but our basement does. It's just my family and nobody else has been in the house."

That was a partial victory. It meant that the entire family would likely be subpoenaed to testify they hadn't tampered with the evidence. Wright put that out of his mind—it would be the prosecutor's problem when the time came.

Jones jumped in. "Do you want to have some other dogs sniff the dirt and see what they do?"

"No need," Wright responded. "If the dogs did hit, all we'd do is send the dirt to the lab. The more we mess with it, the more likely it is to get contaminated. Let's just run it over to the lab and see if they can pull blood out of that dirt."

"Can they do that?" Bryce asked.

"You'd better hope so, young man. I'm glad you spoke up today, but I wish you'd said something sooner. You have a very good reputation in this agency. If you'd pushed it, I'd probably have sent the dirt to the lab regardless of whether the other dogs hit. I don't know if three weeks in the freezer has degraded it to the point of being useless."

"I know. I just didn't want an argument with Granger." Bryce lowered his head, and his voice. "I made a really bad call."

"OK, here's what we're going to do. Davy, call the lab and see if they can get blood out of frozen dirt. At the very least we need to know if it's human or not, and then hope they can type the DNA. If they can, haul ass over to Bryce's and drive it to the lab yourself. Take a cooler so it stays frozen until it's in their hands, got it?"

"Yup...easily done."

Wright continued. "Bryce, I'm really peeved at you right now and I don't want to make decisions when I'm bugged. If we get another body case tonight, I probably won't use you and your dog. I'll be talking to the sheriff when I'm a little more calm and we'll see how he wants to respond in the longer term."

"I understand."

Jones killed the speaker phone and turned to Bryce.

"I don't know what to say. I see both sides, but this is a huge case. I know you weren't trying to tamper with evidence but that's how it's worked out. For what it's worth, I hope this ends up being nothing more than a great lesson learned."

"It's already a lesson learned," Bryce blurted out. He was trying not to lose his composure, but the thought of screwing up a major case was starting to weigh on him. Even if the sheriff didn't kick him out of SAR, how could he face his team if this went bad?

"Can you tell the sheriff I know I made a mistake and I'll never do anything like this again? I'm really sorry and if there's anything I can do to fix this…"

"The sheriff's a good guy, and has forgiven more than one mistake of mine. This is a big one, but he's normally pretty good about things when you 'fess up. I admire that you did that, by the way. I'll make sure the sheriff knows."

"Thanks."

"OK. I'll meet you over at your house…do your folks know what's in your freezer?"

CHAPTER FOURTEEN
Blood from a Turnip

Crime labs prioritize their work in mysterious ways. It's not a case of first-come-first-served, nor do even the most serious cases get worked first.

The first priority for labs is a very practical one, driven by the courts. Scientists have to first work the cases where a suspect's speedy-trial rights are at risk. Suspects are often arrested and charged based on other evidence, and the lab work is done to merely confirm their involvement. But if the lab work isn't done before trial, defense attorneys can accuse the state of hiding evidence.

Getting the lab to push Bryce's dirt to the head of the line would mean calling in a multitude of favors, and perhaps adding a carrot to the stick.

"This is a huge case, and this is our best break," Jones told the lab manager, Jim Oliver. "We'll both have very public egg on our face if the media thinks we sat on this. How soon can you work it?"

"We talkin' that…what's it called…the 'Chimera Killer?'" Despite a multitude of college degrees, the manager always spoke plainly.

"Yup," Jones replied. He went on to explain why the dirt was important, how it came to be wrapped in a couple of rubber gloves, and that it had been frozen for almost three weeks.

"How long was it out there before it was frozen?" the manager asked.

"Less than twenty-four hours. We got the report late in the afternoon and the handler scooped it up the next morning."

"If that's the case, we probably can get DNA out of it. The issue is how badly the blood degraded before it was frozen."

"That's great news." Jones was trying to be patient, but his question was timing. "How long…?"

"We'll get started on this right away. Results will be a few days out."

"The most important thing is that we need to know if there's human DNA there at all. One dog thinks there is, another dog thinks there isn't. The case will turn on who's right."

"I'll call ya when we have that much. This will be a cool professional challenge for us. It's really hard to get DNA out of dirt."

"I'm pulling for ya. Thanks."

———————————

"So why aren't we out there processing the scene?" Sheriff Patterson asked those who'd gathered in his office.

"We were waiting for something from the lab," Wright answered, knowing immediately it was the wrong answer.

"If there's enough reason to send something to the lab, then there's enough reason to go back and work the scene. Let's at least get our own people out there ASAP. I could see waiting to call CSRT until either we or the lab find something."

"Yes, sir," Wright responded. "Jonesy and I will get out there this afternoon. I might need to call Bryce to help us find the spot. Since we considered it a negative, I don't have the coordinates in my notes."

"Yeah…Bryce," the sheriff said softly. "You want to tell me how this all played out, and why we're just finding out about this now?"

"The kid made a mistake…a teenage error in judgement. If he'd pressed me, I'd have taken the dirt and sent it to the lab that night. He just wanted to make it a training opportunity, and was maybe a little defensive about the other dog not alerting. The other handler is kind of a jerk, and they've butted heads in the past."

"One could argue he tampered with a crime scene." The sheriff never, ever raised his voice. But there was as much emphasis in his words as Wright had ever heard. "If this dirt turns out to be evidence, a defense attorney will tear us apart."

Wright had calmed since his discussion with Bryce, and continued trying to soften the blow for his young friend.

"It wasn't a crime scene when he took the dirt. When he got more information, he didn't hesitate to tell Jones what he'd done. He 'fessed up immediately."

"OK…well…part of me hopes this dirt isn't connected to the case and part of me hopes it is. We need the break. When you talk to Bryce, make me the bad guy. Tell him I was on the roof and ready to toss him out of SAR. You talked me out of it, and only because he 'fessed up. Got it?"

"Yes, sir," Wright answered, knowing immediately that he'd be insubordinate and tell Bryce exactly what happened. The sheriff was a kind, thoughtful man, and wouldn't end anybody's career over one mistake. Bryce needed to know what kind of leader the sheriff was.

Besides, Wright knew that no one was being harder on Bryce than Bryce himself. He had little worry that anything of the kind would ever be repeated. He didn't go to his cubicle to make the call. He went to his car, where he had privacy.

Katie had no idea what was wrong. She knew men could have quiet times, but Bryce had been exceptionally close-mouthed. She wondered if she'd done something wrong. Her feelings for Bryce had continued to grow and she thought his had too.

But the last two days there had been no spark, no kind words. He'd even cancelled a date, and didn't seem truly present on this one. She was about to ask if everything was OK when Bryce's phone rang.

Bryce took one look at the caller ID and picked up immediately.

"Hey Bryce, it's Bob Wright. Got a minute?"

"Yes, sir. Am I still in SAR?"

Katie's jaw dropped and she stared at Bryce. He turned away and tried to avoid looking at her.

"Yes...you're still in SAR," Wright said. "And I have a message from the sheriff. He and I are both very proud of how you handled this. You could have tossed the dirt away and never said anything to anybody. Coming forward was the right thing to do."

"The sheriff's not mad?"

"He wanted me to lie, and tell you he was absolutely furious. He wanted me to make it out like I had saved your career by defending you. But in fact, he and I see it the same way. You had no malicious intent, you admitted your mistake and have clearly learned from it."

"Thank you," Bryce managed to get out. Now his problem was to avoid breaking down on the phone. He'd kept the matter to himself, saying nothing to Katie or his parents. The bottled-up emotions were at risk of breaking through. Wright had talked to plenty of people on the verge of losing it and recognized the condition in Bryce. He changed the subject.

Katie would see him shaking. She tried to walk up and touch him on the arm, but he remained focused on the phone call.

"Did you happen to note the location where you grabbed the dirt?" Wright continued. "We want to go back out and work the scene, and since we considered it a negative, I didn't get the coordinates."

"Yeah, I've got 'em. Did the lab say there was blood on the dirt?"

"Haven't heard yet. We've decided not to wait for that. If anybody lost a piece of their behind today, it was me. The sheriff thinks I should have been out there as soon as we talked to you."

"I don't have my notes with me, they're back at the house. I can head there now and text you the coordinates."

"That works...thanks. Take care."

"Right…bye."

"You wanna tell me what that was all about?" Katie asked.

"The dirt I took from up at Tiger Lake. They weren't happy I did that…"

"I told…never mind…why is it coming up now?"

"They've got a girl who went missing from that area at about the right time. I decided to let them know I had it. I still think Sierra was right."

"Are you in trouble?"

"Apparently not anymore. I was really worried."

"YOU were worried? I was afraid I'd done something…you hardly spoke to me."

"Oh, God…no. It was never you, it couldn't be," Bryce said, looking at the ceiling. "Jeez, I've really screwed things up. I maybe messed up their case and I've hurt you. I should have just argued with Granger."

"Is that what this is about? That competition he seems to think is between you? You need to not worry about him so much."

"I know, but he's a really successful dog handler and I'd like to learn from him. He just always acts like he's in some kind of ivory tower."

"Well, that's *his* problem, and you need to not make it yours."

"Yes, dear," Bryce said. This time the phrase was automatic… reflexive.

Katie tilted her head forward as if she were looking over a pair of glasses. "Really? Yes, dear? Am I going to have to get used to you saying that?"

"I dunno. Your Mom seems to like it."

"Well, Mom's my…*Mom*. She's old. Isn't there some other way you could convey complete acceptance of my womanly advice?"

"I bow my head, don't I?"

"You just keep working on that. We need to get over to your place and get those coordinates for Wright," Katie responded, trying to move the conversation along. "Are your parents home?"

"OK, got 'em," Wright told Bryce on the phone, repeating the coordinates back to him. "I think I can run the GPS well enough to find the spot. I might need you to come out if I can't get it to work."

Bryce's parents were in fact not at home, having gone to the coast for a long weekend. Bryce and Katie were the only ones in the house, besides Sierra. Bryce was focused on the call.

"Just make sure your coordinate system is UTM and your map datum is WGS 84. If you're on the old NAD 27 system you'll be about 200 yards off. You'll want to make sure you've got at least four satellites and make sure 'follow roads' is turned off. Oh and you absolutely don't want to forget…."

Wright interrupted. Bryce might as well been telling him how to program his VCR. "Tell ya what, I'll call if I need any help. You feeling OK now?" Wright asked, hoping Bryce had calmed down after their last call.

"Yeah. I'm feeling a little better. The chewing out I didn't get from you I got from Katie," Bryce said. That prompted a faux slap on the arm from Katie, who was standing next to him.

"We all need that in our lives, buddy. Hang onto her, she's a keeper."

Bryce turned to Katie and held up the phone. "He says you're a keeper."

"He's right. I am, and don't you forget it."

"Yes, dear," Bryce said for the second time that day. And for the first time, Katie didn't glare back at him for saying it.

Bryce turned his attention back to the phone. "Call if you need anything. OK?"

"Yup, you're in my speed dial. But if you're with Katie, I'll try to leave you alone. Put a move on her."

"Um, yeah…we appreciate that. Bye."

Katie had another quizzical look for Bryce. "What do you mean 'WE appreciate that?'" she asked. "What did he say to you?"

"He just said he'd try not to bother us this evening."

"Oh really? I suspect some guy-talk there. Big plans, mister?"

"Um, I…really…I'm hungry. You wanna go get dinner?"

"We don't have to go anywhere. Other than bloody dirt, do you have any actual food in your freezer?"

"We don't know there's blood on the dirt, but yeah, we have food. I had Mom pick up some of those little frozen corn dogs for while they were gone."

"I am not cooking you frozen corn dogs. Eww." Katie went to the freezer, and found a pound of hamburger. "Where's your pantry?

Got any pasta or tomato sauce?"

The pantry was big enough for them both to walk in, and look. Katie was the first to spot the package of Hamburger Helper and reached across Bryce for it. The move put her face close to his.

Bryce kissed her on the cheek. "Thank you."

"For what?"

"For being here for me…for putting up with my geekiness…for being you." He slipped an arm around her.

"I can't think of anybody I'd rather have 'put a move' on me."

"You could hear the phone?"

"Yeah, you had it turned up too loud. I heard everything. If a kiss on the cheek is your best move, you need work."

Katie turned to face him full on, wrapping her arms around him while still holding the Hamburger Helper in one hand. They kissed and hugged for almost a full minute.

"Much better move," she whispered, disengaging from Bryce's arms. "I'm starved, and I think a good meal would do you good, too. Pots and pans?"

"Lower cupboard, next to the sink."

———————————

"I'm pretty sure it was right over here," Wright told Jones, staring at the mysterious GPS.

"Nah, I thought it was further west," Jones replied. "What does the gizmo say?"

"'Lost satellite reception.' That's a big help. I think the trees are too thick here."

"Bryce's worked. All the SAR guys GPSs worked. What's up with that one?"

"I dunno, but we're tromping around getting nothing done. We could walk right through the scene and not know it. All these trees look the same."

That was a problem in Western Washington. The trees and brush were so thick, optimists would say "lush," that once you got out in the woods everything did look the same.

"Did you set whatever that was Bryce said...the data?"

"Yes, the datum. WGS 84, just like he said. That has nothing to do with receiving the satellites."

The two decided to stop, and make their way back to the logging road they'd walked in from. They didn't want to wander around too much more and get themselves lost. Getting out of the trees didn't help. The GPS still wouldn't lock onto the overhead satellites.

"Can we call Bryce?" Jones asked.

"Ummmm, he's having...dinner...with his girlfriend."

"I think we better call him. Assuming your cell phone works better than that GPS thing."

Wright put aside his hope for Bryce's evening, and called. The call was scratchy, but it went through.

"Get to first base yet, my friend?"

"Um...we're just finishing dinner," came Bryce's puzzled reply. "What's up?"

"Our GPS won't work in these woods. It keeps losing its connection to the satellites, even out on the road."

"Yeah, some days the satellites are all low on the horizon. Even if you've got a clear sky overhead, the trees are still in the way. What kind is it?"

"Garmin," Wright replied. "It's a little yellow thing…a Trex?"

"My God, an e-Trex? How old is it?"

"Fifteen years, at least. I don't know how long the sheriff's office has had it."

"OK, I wish you'd told me that before you went out there. Those were the gold standard of GPSs in their day, but it's old technology. The newer e-Trexes work way better in the trees. Hang on a sec."

Bryce turned to Katie but she already knew the question—and her answer.

"Yes, we can go help them. Let's just get the dishes in the dishwasher and go. I don't want your mom coming home and thinking I'm a slob."

"You're awesome…hey, Bob. How about if we just come out there and I can show you the spot?"

"That's kinda what we were hoping, but I know you're on a date."

"We had dinner and just need to pick up a bit. I'll bring Sierra too, maybe she can look around a little more."

Wright and Jones decided to hang out at Wright's Crown Vic while they waited for Bryce to show up with his GPS.

"OK…well, Garrison's Chimera Killer has killed at least seven times, and this could be number eight, if we can just find her,"

Jones said. "I've got another six that my street contacts say they haven't seen in a number of weeks. Some are probably elsewhere, but I'm betting at least a couple end up being victims."

"Suspects?"

"Tough when we're just finding bodies and don't know when the women were killed," Jones said. "I checked Junior's whereabouts for the other night, when the trail runner saw the woman being dragged in. He was at his new job."

"I thought he was a great lead for about fifteen seconds, until I saw what a giant wimp he was," Wright replied. "He wouldn't have the courage to kill anybody. But it's comforting to officially rule him out. What else?"

"Our best shot was right here, when Garrison screwed up our stakeout. Did you ever hear an outcome on his DUI?"

"He got the same deal as anybody else. A first time DUI gets a deferral, well, except his deferral happened at eight o'clock in the morning in the empty courtroom of a friendly judge."

"No special treatment there. Noooo."

The two were just getting back to talking over the case when they saw the headlights from Bryce's truck coming up the road. They watched the two get out. Katie was carrying a sack.

"Have you guys eaten?" she asked. "It's just Hamburger Helper, but we had plenty left over. It's probably not even cold yet."

Katie had packed two portions in separate plastic containers, and wrapped them in foil. The two detectives realized they hadn't eaten, and took them graciously from Katie.

Wright turned to Bryce. "See, I told you she was a keeper."

"I have some freeze-dried brownies in my pack if you'd like dessert," Bryce responded. "If I'd known providing food would score points I'd have done it sooner. So…while you're eating, what are we looking for here?

"I don't know," Wright said between bites. "I suppose the same things we'd look for if there was a body, except that there ain't no body."

The two detectives finished Katie's offering of pasta and meat in stroganoff sauce, and declined Bryce's military-grade brownies. Bryce gave his GPS a little time to get locked onto the satellites, and they set out to find the exact spot where Sierra had alerted.

Wright and Jones had been close, actually. Their earlier guess had been about one good blackberry thicket away from the right location. Bryce sent Sierra in first, just to see what she'd do.

Sierra circled around, snorted a couple times, and came back out of the clearing. Without a command from Bryce, she walked to the opposite side and started back in.

"She went to the downwind side," Bryce whispered to Wright. "She does that by herself, I didn't teach her. I wouldn't know how."

Sierra began working a small cone, went to a spot and sat. Her trained indication. Bryce walked over to her and said, "Show me."

Sierra dipped her nose down and touched it to the ground, just as she had done that night nearly four weeks ago. This time there was something funny about the dirt.

Bryce gave Sierra a quiet "good girl," but didn't give her the ball she'd normally get. Bryce had no way of knowing if something was really there. He took Sierra a short distance from the spot, petted and praised her, and nodded to Wright to go take a look.

"There was something there…maybe just a rock…I couldn't tell. It was right where she put her nose."

Wright carefully went over, and dropped to his hands and knees as he approached. He carefully pushed the brush first to one side, then the other, trying to get a look at the bare dirt. When he got to "the spot," he noticed the same thing Bryce had.

Mantrackers, people who make a living out of following people in the woods, have a saying that "there's nothing straight in nature." Rocks are jagged, branches are crooked, animal paws are rounded. If a mantracker sees a straight line in the dirt, whatever left the mark was man-made.

Wright could see a small straight edge sticking up out of the dirt. It was right where Sierra had placed her nose. It wasn't an indentation, though, it was a ridge. Wright put on a rubber glove and gently brushed over the ridge. In doing so, he removed a layer of dirt and the item shined like gold.

Wright brushed again, and cleared a little more dirt off the item. It was definitely not something that occurred naturally in the woods.

"Got something here," Wright said. "You can reward Sierra."

"Woo-hoo…yea…Sierra gets da belly rubs and butt scratches… yes she does!" Bryce and Katie praised the daylights out of Sierra, and eventually tossed the little dog her ball.

"I'll be damned," Wright mused. "It's a cufflink. Bryce, that dog of yours found a flipping cufflink in the middle of the woods. Do you have a tennis ball made out of steak you can give her?"

Wright put the cufflink in a small paper bag they used for

evidence.

"OK, we're clear with the cufflink. Let's have Sierra come back and see if she finds anything else," Wright said, more energized about the case than he'd been in weeks.

Bryce put Sierra back in the area, and she quickly resumed snorting and circling. But she didn't sit...gave no trained indication... meaning she'd found nothing else.

"I never call it a negative based on one dog," Bryce told the detectives. "We should bring another dog in here to see if there's anything else."

"No," Wright responded immediately. "I appreciate that you've put your ego aside and are willing to have another dog find something yours missed, but no. We're not telling any more people than we absolutely have to about this. If anybody asks, you weren't even here, and you definitely didn't find any cufflink."

At the exact same instant, Bryce and Katie both responded with the same word. "Understood!"

"Wow, you two are meant for each other, aren't you?" Wright said. "Answering for each other is something that husbands and wives do after years of marriage."

Usually it was Bryce who couldn't think of something to say. At that moment, neither he nor Katie had any kind of snappy comeback to Wright's observation. They were in love, but they were teenagers. To use the M-word was something they hadn't even considered. Bryce did what he always did when confused and changed the subject.

"Look, I already messed up here. You can bet I won't do it again. If you say we were never here, then we were never here."

Jones had stepped away from the conversation, and the others noticed he was talking on his cell phone. Given the poor coverage in the area, he seemed to be having trouble hearing. They heard him say, "You gotta be kidding," and then he hung up. He walked back to the group with a stunned look on his face.

"That was the sheriff," he announced. "The lab called."

From the look on Jones' face, Wright, Bryce and Katie assumed the news was bad.

"No blood?" Wright asked, his voice falling. Finding the cufflink was still great work, but if Sierra's initial alert had been false then the entire effort could be for naught. Cufflinks were rarely worn in the woods. Fresh blood was all that made the scene relevant to anything current. A cufflink could have been there for decades.

"There's blood," was the response, Jones voice trailing off.

"Then what's the problem?" Wright demanded. "Was it degraded? Too old to test? Any idea who the person is?"

"It's not person, it's persons…plural. They haven't had time to extract the DNA yet, but they found two different blood types in the dirt."

"Wait, what?" Katie jumped in. She'd normally stayed in Bryce's shadow at searches, but the news was too intriguing. "Two people died here?"

"We don't know that anyone died here," was Wright's response, still stunned himself. "The lab says we have blood from two different people and we just found a cuff link…that's all we know."

"But the blood was fresh enough that they're able to test it," Bryce interjected. "That means somebody bled here shortly before I took the dirt…about the time that girl was being dragged into the woods. It all fits."

"It would if we had one person's blood. Two…I dunno. We need to wait and see what we get from the DNA typing. Maybe that will tell us just who these people were."

CHAPTER FIFTEEN
Lip Service

The sheriff had been forced to take a single political science course in college and hadn't liked it much. He wanted to be a cop, and didn't see how Poly Sci 101 related to his degree. At the time, he had no inkling that he'd one day be an elected official, one of those awful politicians, himself.

With nearly three decades of retrospection, Elroy Patterson came to believe the course had one bit of value for him: studying the styles of various successful politicians.

President Abraham Lincoln had been the Great Emancipator.

President Ronald Reagan had been the Great Communicator.

And President Lyndon Baines Johnson had been the Great Ear Grabber. Mocked for literally picking up his beagle by the ears, Johnson figuratively did the same thing in political negotiations. He picked his opponents up by their ears, and told them what he'd do if they didn't compromise.

That was not Elroy Patterson's style.

Not normally, anyway.

Today, however, he would do his best impersonation of the late LBJ. He was going to turn up the heat, literally and figuratively, on someone who'd been a political pain in the rear, and who now owed him a big favor.

The sheriff walked over and closed the window. The courthouse was an old building, and while his third-floor office was ornate, it was always hot. Closing the window would make it positively stifling.

He'd asked Dana, his secretary, to bring him a pitcher of water and two glasses. Glass glasses, not Styrofoam ones. The light from the window reflected in the curves of the glasses and made little rainbows. He focused on the bright colors and used the time to get in the zone for one of the most political conversations of his career.

For all the criminals he'd interrogated, all the witnesses he'd interviewed, the sheriff had never had a conversation like the one he was about to have. If all went well, it would be a non-event. But if it went badly, his political career could come to a crashing halt.

His thoughts were interrupted by the intercom. "Sheriff Patterson, Councilman Garrison is here."

"Show him in, please." Show him in, not send him in. The sheriff's secretary would open the door herself, squire the difficult county councilman in with a flourish, and ask if he needed anything before she left. She knew how to make someone feel important, and the boss had asked her to do that today. She felt like Miss Moneypenny from the old James Bond movies.

"Sheriff, good to see you," the councilman said as he came through the door. "I was a little surprised you asked to see me, but I couldn't turn down your invitation."

"Sir, do you need anything? Coffee or water?" the secretary asked.

"No, I'm fine, thanks. Just had lunch," was the councilman's reply.

The secretary left, and the two men sat at the sheriff's conference table. The sheriff chose his seat carefully so as not to be across the square table from Garrison. He sat ninety degrees to Garrison's right, in the same way investigators sit "just around the corner" from suspects.

The position has several advantages. The table isn't seen as a barrier to their relationship. The investigator can lean in and speak softly if he or she is doing the "good cop" routine. The ninety-degree seating position also puts the investigator within a suspect's personal space, offering the opportunity to make someone uncomfortable when necessary.

"Thanks very much for coming," the sheriff said in as helpful a voice as he could muster. "I figured there would be less tongue-wagging around the courthouse if you dropped by my office than if I went to yours...."

"Stop, sheriff," Garrison interrupted. "The thanks go from me to you. I really appreciate how you kept my recent...issue...on the down-low. I know I shouldn't have been out there at all and your guys could really have made me look bad. I actually wouldn't have blamed them if they had."

The sheriff pretended to appreciate the comment. "One of my roles as sheriff is to mentor my personnel. I try to make them understand that piling on doesn't help change someone's behavior, and it doesn't make friends. They handled the case as expected, but leaking it to the newspaper isn't how we punish those we believe broke the law."

"Well, I *did* break the law," the councilman replied. "And I have only myself to blame for that. But you asked me to come here… what's on your mind?"

"We were talking about making friends. I need one."

"Hmmm, OK….?"

"This serial killer thing is eating my lunch. We continue to run down leads and it's costing me a fortune in overtime. I'm pretty much through the $50,000 the council approved and there's no indication where it might end."

"Thank you for not calling him the Chimera Killer like the newspapers and everybody in this courthouse. I really put my foot in my mouth on that one. But if you want more money, you have to know I got elected by people who want to cut budgets.

"I know, and I understand," the sheriff replied. "I'm elected too. The people who contributed to my campaign also have certain expectations."

"Indeed," Garrison responded. "Of all the agencies in county government, yours is the one I'm least worried about. You've always run a tight ship. But my backers from the business world expect me to keep the pressure on. I'd get a lot of hard questions if I rolled over and gave you what…another $50,000."

"You do recall that we found another body about the same time you were making that first investment, right? I've got more missing women and some additional bodies since we made that deal. The situation has changed."

"Mine hasn't," Garrison shot back. "I am dealing with an unholy alliance of supporters. I have the ultra-right wingers who think cutting dollars will hamper the government conspiracy against them. They're allied with the business community, which isn't political at all except that they hate paying taxes."

"I think I can give you some cover," the sheriff offered softly.

"With my constituency? That'd be a neat trick, but please explain."

"Have you looked at the numbers from the county's Risk Management Division? Lawsuits against the Sheriff's Office are down dramatically in the last two years. I told you I was working to mentor my folks, and we've ended up saving the county a ton of money."

"How'd you do that?"

"Coupla strategies. Driver training was the big one. Most people are worried about cops and their guns, but car wrecks are what cost us the most money."

"How much did you save us?"

"We were averaging about $150,000 per year in payouts for as long as anyone could remember?"

"150 grand from cops wrecking their cars and nobody was getting fired?"

"You have to be reasonable with the law of averages," the sheriff pointed out. "Deputies put a lot of miles on their cars and I'm not going to fire someone for honest human error. As long as they weren't hot-dogging, they get some discipline but escape with their career. The other big saving that the training got us was a reduction in our legal bills. With attorney's fees these days, it can cost you fifty grand to win a case. People sue hoping you'll settle quickly for something less than your defense costs."

"I've heard. The road department just settled a case for $250,000, and the lawyers called that a victory. They said it could have been millions."

"Exactly. So, as I said, we hit the driver training hard. You can't get sued over a wreck you don't have. If an officer does mess up and gets in a wreck, we take care of it quickly and I apologize personally to whoever we hit. You'd be surprised how much impact a sincere apology can have on litigation. Finally, if somebody files a truly bogus lawsuit we tell them to pound sand. We found some real pit-bull attorneys to handle our cases."

"So you've saved us…?"

The sheriff sidled up to Garrison's corner of the desk…as a friend might…and showed him the papers. "As I said, we'd been averaging around $150,000 per year forever, and everybody assumed it was just the cost of doing business. In the last two years, with this new program, we've had half the number of lawsuits against us, which means half the legal bill. For actual damages in the past two years, we've paid $27,000 and $32,000 respectively."

"That's nice, but I still don't get how this affects me, or your big case."

"I haven't told anybody this yet," the sheriff responded, waiting for the light to go on in Garrison's head. "This is something I need to roll out in public session at a county council meeting. If I do that, then I can turn around and ask for a bit of the savings to beef up my case."

"Nope. Too thin. I mean, it might work with the other council members, but it's too thin for me to suddenly support you. My folks will be saying your program should have been business as usual and you shouldn't be rewarded for just doing your job…"

The councilman's voice trailed off at the end of his sentence. Sheriff Patterson was again in his personal space, and now not in a good way. He'd shifted his body position and just stared.

"I'm disappointed," the sheriff finally said, very softly. "I not only kept your issue on the 'down-low' as you put it, but I convinced my staff to do the same. Do you have any idea how hard it is to get sheriff's deputies to keep a secret like that? You know the three lines of communication: telephone, telegraph, and tell a cop."

The sheriff's attempt to make Garrison laugh didn't work, so he decided to channel LBJ and grab his opponent by the ears. He didn't raise his voice, but it took a sharper edge.

"I've brought you in here and showed you that I've been a very good steward of the county's money. A legitimately good steward regardless of any other drama that might be going on. Now I need a little of that money back for a case that's not of my doing and that I don't control."

The sheriff was on a roll, and didn't give Garrison a chance to interject.

"It's not like my office built a new jail and went over budget. This isn't some 'project' we've mismanaged. We can't help it that somebody's out there killing women. If my deputies see you failing to support this, I can't guarantee one of them won't dime you out to the paper. I'd never encourage that, but mentorship only goes so far."

Garrison was starting to sweat and the antiquated courthouse heating system was only part of the reason.

"I get it. I don't have a problem with you, and I don't have a problem with giving you the money you need. I just can't make a complete U-turn on the people who got me elected."

The sheriff reached for the pitcher of water, and one of the glasses. "It's stifling in here today. You sure you don't want some water?"

"Sure, pour me one. That's about all I'm drinking these days anyway," Garrison replied, reaching for the glass.

"Let's remember the full scope of your issue." The sheriff was lifting this beagle completely off the ground now. "You didn't just get a DUI. That paperwork's been filed, and some enterprising reporter might already have it. What the reporter won't know is that you mis-used confidential information and wandered into the middle of a stakeout."

"I've seen the report. The trooper didn't include that part."

"That was nice of him, but plenty of my people know what happened."

In fact, very few employees of the sheriff's office knew about that part. Wright and Jones had kept a tight rein on the information, at the sheriff's request.

"Alright," Garrison conceded. "You've got the power in this situation. I guess I can stand a one-time beating from my people."

The sheriff immediately went back to being the good cop.

"I don't think there has to be a beating at all. I have a distinct recollection that, right after I was elected, you encouraged me to 'think out of the box' on how to save money for the county."

"I don't remember saying that," Garrison interrupted. "But it sounds like something I'd say."

"That's the whole point. Nobody's going to remember whether you said it or not." The sheriff was growing frustrated. "I'm not going to claim that I've personally saved the county a couple hundred thousand dollars, I'm going to give you the lion's share of credit. You prompted me to really think hard, which is what leaders are supposed to do. It wasn't my program that saved the money, it was your leadership."

"OK…this is sounding better." Garrison's tone was lightening a bit. "But as arguments go, I still think it's a little thin."

"Not to somebody who doesn't know the back story. They'll just see it as an elected official sharing some good news and trying to share some credit. Politicians scratch each others' backs all the time."

"You give me the credit, and then follow up by asking for another fifty grand? You think that sleight of hand will work?"

"Oh people will definitely think I'm sucking up to you for more money. But that's all they'll think. And it'll be on me, not you."

Garrison finished the first glass of water and poured himself some more. He was wishing it was gin, but a condition of getting his DUI case deferred was no alcohol.

"I guess I'm gonna have to trust you on this…but…OK. My support will have to be grudging, but in light of the other money you saved, I can have a weak moment."

"Alright, let me call the council secretary and get on the agenda." The sheriff might have put the beagle back on the ground, but he was wasting no time setting the deal in concrete. "I'll have her put the litigation report first, and then piggyback the request for more money. The meeting's not for another three weeks, so we've got some time to work out the actual numbers."

"Yes, I will want to see the hard numbers. They have to be in a range I can support, however grudgingly," Garrison said, starting to rise from his seat.

"I know I'm pushing you, but I want you to know I'm going to give you all the cover I can. It's remotely possible I won't even need your vote. If it turns out the others speak in favor before it's your turn, then you can go ahead and scold me. Just don't speak first and poison the well."

"That I can do," Garrison said, heading toward the door. If someone could be damned with faint praise, someone could be supported with faint criticism. Anything was better than having his issue become public. The sheriff had already proven his ability to keep the lid on things, so he'd count on that for another few weeks.

"I'll be in touch," the sheriff said, shaking Garrison's hand. "I won't hang you out on this, I promise."

"I'm counting on you" were Garrison's last words as he strode to the outer office and then down the hall. Patterson had no way of knowing that when the councilman got on the elevator, he pushed the button for the second floor. His office was on the fourth.

———————————

Undersheriff Bill Burns had been waiting in his own office, right next door, during the meeting. He couldn't hear the conversation, but he hadn't heard any voices raised, either. That was a good sign. He'd kept his door open and, as soon as he saw Garrison leave, he hooked around the corner into his boss's office.

"Get what you were after?" he asked.

"Got exactly what I was after," was the sheriff's reply. Patterson was already picking up his telephone, and dialing a number. The call was answered on the first ring.

242

"I have the item we discussed. Are you ready to work it?"

Burns couldn't hear the other person, but knew exactly who his boss was talking to.

"OK," the sheriff said into the phone. "We'll set it in one of those cardboard carrier things that coffee shops give you to hold four cups. We'll put that in a paper bag. We'll make sure nothing touches the lip of the glass."

Burns could tell from the look on his boss's face that the lab was indeed ready to look for saliva on the lip of the cup from which Councilman Garrison had sipped.

"Bill, let's get to the car. I want you with me through all of this, both as a witness, and to make damn sure the thing doesn't fall off the seat or something."

The two left Patterson's office by the back door, which didn't go through the courthouse lobby. They left via the jail elevator at the back of the building. They got directly into a car that Burns had previously staged in the courtyard out back. Although they were captured on the jail surveillance video, no one actually saw them leave or had reason to wonder why the boss had a paper bag in his hands.

The sheriff looked over at Burns with a half-smile on his face. "And the good Mr. Garrison thought I wanted money."

———————————

"Hey Jenny, how are ya?" the councilman asked.

"Councilman Garrison, as I live and breathe. What brings you down to the finance department?"

Jenny Buchanan was the cornerstone of the county's Budget and

Payroll section. Even though the sheriff was elected separately from the council members, the council controlled his budget and Jenny paid his bills.

"I just need a little...shall we say...unfiltered information," Garrison said.

Jenny's job was pretty straightforward, and a little boring at times. Nothing made her feel as important as a little conspiracy with an elected official.

"Sure...department heads not giving you the straight scoop again? It's public information, and you don't have to be a councilman to get it. Anybody can. I never understand why they try to fool you guys."

"Well, it's happened enough that I like to do my own research," Garrison replied. "The sheriff is telling me he's saved us a ton of money with a driver training program that's reduced crashes. Are you seeing a difference?"

"Oh, wow...yes. I'm seeing a *huge* difference. I wasn't sure why, but it makes sense. The number of crashes that deputies are having has dropped by a ton. I was starting to think he had them all working foot beats."

"So at one point, wrecking cars was a problem?"

"Deputies are human, and they drive a lot, so things are going to happen. But yeah, there was one body shop I had in my speed dial. And the legal bills...my God."

"How much do you think we were spending?"

"Oh, it'd be 135 thousand one year, 170 grand the next. It varied, but was always in six figures. Y'know, this adds up. A couple years ago I started writing checks to this retired Seattle cop who runs an emergency driving school. He was coming over three or four times a year to put on classes for the deputies. Guess he's earning his money."

"Indeed. How have the recent expenditures been?"

"Without looking it up, under fifty thousand in payouts, and the legal bills are down too. That's odd, because he hired attorneys who charge us through the nose—their hourly fees are astronomical. But they seem to get the job done in far fewer hours than our old firm."

"Well, you get what you pay for, I guess. This is great. I'm really happy for the sheriff, and even happier for the taxpayers. Thanks."

Garrison started to leave. "Oh, one more thing. You remember that extra fifty grand we gave the sheriff's office? How's he doing on that?"

"He's just fine. You know the sheriff runs the tightest ship in the courthouse. He throws pennies around like they were manhole covers."

"Well how many manhole covers has he tossed around on this case?"

"Not many. There's been a little bit of overtime for one detective, and a bigger chunk for one deputy…Jones, I think. But he's got plenty of the fifty grand left. We just finished a payroll report, so I know things are up to date."

"He begged for that money, but now he's not spending it?"

"Not so far," Jenny replied.

"Well, there you go, Jenny. That's why I come to you. At the next meeting when the sheriff tells us he's spending money wisely, I'll know he's telling the truth."

"That you will. I assume we never had this conversation?"

"I appreciate your discretion. The sheriff would be offended if he thought I was checking up on him and, if you hadn't noticed, he carries a gun."

———————

"Let's go through this again," Wright said to Jones. "We have a body dump with no body. How does that happen?"

The two men were back at their secluded booth at the Airport Diner. Just coffee and pie today, no coma-inducing lunch.

"We'll learn how it happens when we find whoever dumped, and then un-dumped, the body," was Jones' reply.

"Well if somebody dumped and then un-dumped a body, they must have re-dumped it somewhere. I doubt the killer took it home and put it in his freezer."

Wright's phone rang. It was the supervisor's number from WestCom.

"This was about to go over the radio and I shortstopped it," the supervisor said. "A hunter was chasing a wounded deer and stumbled across a body. It's pretty decomposed, but the hunter said the clothing appeared female. He thought the clothing matched what we put out in that press release on…what was her name? Santiago?"

"Maria Santiago. Where is this?"

"Off DeWatto Road, just inside the D11 gate. Hunter says it wasn't that far into the bushes."

The hunter had been walking back to his car after an unproductive day, and spotted a legal deer about one hundred yards from the gate. He wounded it with the first shot, and then pursued the blood trail—running across the human body first.

"Tell no one. *No one.* Talk to the operator who took the call. I don't even want them discussing this in the break room. Complete silence, radio and everything else."

The supervisor wasn't aware that Maria Santiago had apparently been dumped and then moved. It wasn't unusual for 911 operators to dispatch calls by phone because the media listens to their radios. But everyone who worked at the center was "in the club." To limit even those conversations was taking investigative security to a new level.

"Don't you need a uniform car to meet the complainant?" the supervisor asked.

"Nope, we're headed there now. We're not far, so just tell the hunter to wait for us at the gate."

"OK...I've already got a call created in the dispatch computer and those can't be deleted."

"Fine," Wright said. "Just change it to a 'suspicious circumstances' code and assign it to me, then show it cleared. It's not to come up on anybody else's screen."

"Thanks...will do...is there a reason...?" the supervisor hinted.

"Yes, there is," was Wright's response before hanging up the phone. He turned to Jones.

"You're driving, bud. I gotta make some calls while we're en route. Head out toward Holly, and hit DeWatto Road. I think I remember where the D11 gate is, but it'll be the only gate with a hunter standing in front of it waiting for us."

"Santiago?"

"I think we just found out where she's been re-dumped."

"OK. Hang on…this'll be a quick ride."

Wright didn't need to hang on. Although Jones was among the department's fastest drivers, he was also among the smoothest. Wright was able to dial his cell phone and never miss a digit.

The sheriff's caller ID reflected a call from his lead detective. Despite the urgency of his own task, he took time to answer.

"Hey, Bob. What's up?"

"Hi, sir…it's Wright. WestCom got a call from a hunter who's found a body. Sounds like it might be the Santiago girl…the one we think was moved. Jones and I are on the way out there now."

"They didn't put it over the radio, did they?"

"No, sir, I shortstopped that. The call-taker is being told not to even discuss the call with her co-workers. The only ones who know about this are the operator who took the call, the supervisor, Jones, me and now…you."

"Let's keep it that way."

"Well, I gotta call the Crime Lab. We'll need them to work the scene…and eventually we'll need to have the coroner come out."

"All in due time, but let's get this worked first. And you don't need to call the lab, I'm there now."

"What are you doing there?" Wright asked, momentarily forgetting his place. It was none of his business where his boss was, or what his boss was doing.

"Just a routine meeting," the sheriff responded in as even a tone as he could muster, given the magnitude of his lie. Call me back when you get an exact location and I'll have the manager get

CSRT headed your way."

"Yes, sir. I'll definitely keep you posted. We're less than two-zero minutes out, and you'll have a call ten minutes after that.

"Thanks." The sheriff hung up his phone.

Jones, though driving, was staring at Wright. "What's the sheriff doing at the Crime Lab?" he asked.

"On any other day it would be none of our business what the sheriff did or who he met with. But I got the impression it was more than a routine meeting."

"Come to Jesus meeting to get them to work evidence faster?"

"No, he didn't seem pissed. He just didn't want me to know why he was there. There! Left up the hill…that's DeWatto Road. The D11 is just ahead, on the right."

There was indeed a hunter at the gate. Although he hadn't camouflaged his face, it was a shade of green that matched his camo jacket. Wright and Jones knew this was a man who'd just found a body.

CHAPTER SIXTEEN
Re-Dump

Bryce didn't get a lot of calls on his cell phone. It was usually either the SAR callout system, his parents or, of late, Katie. He was a little surprised to see the caller ID come up as Bob Wright's phone.

"Hi Bob, what's up? I hope I'm not in trouble again."

"Not at all, and quit worrying about that. It's history. You up for a little search this afternoon?"

"Sure...on the sly again?"

"Yeah, just you, Granger and...do you know a 'Lefty' from Yakima County?"

"Know him? He gave me my last recert test," Bryce replied. "I'm still not sure why they call him 'Lefty.'"

"Well you can ask him. It's a long drive but he comes highly recommended, and I wanted somebody from a long ways away.

The guy from Clallam is out of town."

"OK…how soon and where?"

"No hurry. It'll take Lefty about five hours to get here. We don't need to wait for him to start, but no need to rush, either. It's the D11 gate on DeWatto Road, just outside Holly."

"We've trained there…know it well. Whatcha got?"

"You can't tell anyone, not even Katie, OK?"

"OK."

"A hunter found a body a couple hours ago. We first hoped it was the Santiago girl, but it's too decomposed to be her. We want to search the rest of the area. If the killer had to dump this body in a hurry, we're hoping he went back to a spot he already knew when he needed to move her body from Tiger Lake."

"Makes sense. I guess if I can't tell Katie that also means I can't bring her."

"Correct. We want as few people as possible knowing about this."

"I'm just repacking my gear from this weekend's training. It'll take me an hour or so to get out the door and another hour to get there. Does that work?"

"Yup. Granger's stuck at work in some big meeting. He can't get off till later anyway. We'll start with you, and he and Lefty can join up when they get here."

Bryce took a moment to feed Sierra. It was a little early for her normal evening meal, but he didn't want to stop in the middle of the search to do it. Feeding her now would give her time to digest the meal before the physical activity of searching.

He also took his time loading the Suburban, and even had a

quick bite himself. There was no need for urgency. The time lost didn't matter…everyone they were looking for was already dead.

Wright and Jones were at the D11 gate, along with a truck carrying State Patrol license plates. Bryce assumed that vehicle belong to the Patrol's Crime Scene Response Team, who were civilian scientists, not troopers. Wright confirmed his guess.

"We wanted to get them out there before dark, but they're only working right around the body," he said. "Does their scent mess up Sierra?"

"Nope, it's no problem. I'll give her the 'Digger' command and she'll know she's looking for dead things. Live bodies won't matter."

"There's also a dead deer out there. The hunter was too upset to go after his kill."

"Also not a problem," was the reassuring response from Bryce.

"All good…OK, we're thinking of having you and Sierra hit the opposite side of the logging road from where this body was found. If this is a multiple dump site, the guy might have gone right one time, left the next."

"Um, maybe not. Like I said on the phone, we've trained out here. The left side was logged about three years ago and it's a mess. The next generation of trees are about head height, but the old branches are still on the ground and the underbrush has grown up through them. You can't see where you're setting your foot down. It's a total ankle-breaker, and would be especially hard for someone lugging a body. But the right side is easy going for quite a ways out the road."

"OK. We'll want to get the left side sooner or later, but let's have you go down the right side for now. There's flagging tape on the road adjacent to where the body was found, and we've beaten a trail in. Why don't you go a couple hundred feet beyond and consider that the near boundary of your search assignment? That'll keep you out of the way of the lab folks. Go as far off the road to the right as you think someone could reasonably carry a body."

"That works. Whatever we do, it'll be on my GPS."

Bryce got his pack on, after first removing some of the heavier items. He wouldn't be deep enough in the woods to need two days' worth of food, nor his water filter. After thinking about it, he left base with only water, first aid kit, and Sierra's toy ball in his pack.

As they passed the trail to the hunter's find, Sierra naturally turned right and headed in. Bryce didn't want her in the way of the CSRT and called her back. He turned on his best positive voice to say, "We're going this way."

The two of them got about one hundred yards past the trail, and Bryce checked the wind. If the wind was blowing from the hunter's find, Sierra's nose would lead them back that way. Instead, it was blowing from the opposite direction which worked in their favor. They'd start there, and be working into the wind. If a body was out there, each pass would make it more likely Sierra would pick up the odor.

Before stepping off the road, Bryce's final task was to reset both his own GPS and the one on Sierra's collar. That way, they'd record the day's search effort, without other searches or routine hikes left over in the unit's memory. GPS tracks from searches are legal documents, and Bryce didn't want anything extraneous that a defense attorney could use to make mischief.

The two of them stepped off into the easy brush and Sierra soon took the lead, ranging about one hundred feet in front and to the left of Bryce. The two of them went a couple hundred yards into the brush, further than anybody could carry a body They turned left, went about 150 feet before turning left a second time and heading back toward the road. They'd grid the area in what was essentially a saw tooth pattern—back and forth until they hit impenetrable brush or the detectives asked them to stop.

At least that was the plan, but a search dog's nose is the ultimate authority. As they left the road for their fourth pass, Bryce noticed Sierra looking to her left. She gave a few "head pops," and then turned left for good. After a while she started ranging back and forth following the traditional scent cone that emanates from a source of odor.

"Whatcha got, girllll?" Bryce asked Sierra. She moved into an area of particularly heavy brush and sat, looking at something next to her. As Bryce moved closer to look, even his second-rate human nose picked up the odor.

Next to Sierra was a body, moderately decomposed but still basically intact. This decomp *was* consistent with the timing of Maria Santiago's disappearance. The body was unclothed, with the arms crossed at the chest. Bryce was a bit surprised that animals hadn't disturbed the remains, but it was hunting season and maybe the noise and smell of hunters had kept them out of the area.

What struck Bryce was the position of the body. It was obviously posed. He knew some killers did that, but the other bodies he'd found had been so badly disturbed by animals that it wasn't noticeable.

Bryce tossed Sierra her ball, away from the remains so she didn't obliterate evidence playing with it.

His next quandary was how to tell Wright and Jones he'd found something. This had been kept such a secret that other SAR member hadn't been called. A deputy had driven the SAR van so they'd have good radio communications, but no other members of SAR were around. Bryce doubted the two detectives knew his team's normal death code, but he didn't want to announce over the radio that he'd found a body.

"County 132, Dog 44" Bryce called. He was one of only a few SAR members given permission to operate on sheriff's office radio channels.

"132…" came Jones' answer.

"Dog 44…I've found something interesting…not sure if it's related to the case or not. I think it would make sense for you or Wright to come take a look at it."

"132, what is it?"

"I think it would be best if you saw it for yourself."

Jones finally figured out that Bryce was being cryptic for a reason, which meant it was likely something important.

"Understood. How do I find you?"

"We've been gridding the area, and each time we came back to the road, I tied a piece of pink surveyors' ribbon on a bush. Come out to the fourth piece of ribbon and turn right into the bush. Come straight in about 250 feet and we'll be within yelling distance."

"132 copied."

"Dog 44, clear."

It took Jones a surprisingly long time to arrive, and when he did, he was accompanied by a woman from the CSRT.

"Whoa, I guessed right," Jones said, acknowledging the odor that swept over them all. "I assumed that when you didn't want to talk about it over the radio, you'd found a body."

"Yup…it's over here," Bryce said, turning to the scientist. "Ma'am, I assume you're with CSRT?"

"Yes…wow…don't really need a dog to find this one," she replied.

"Actually, we did. This is further into the brush than I'd have expected. Sierra picked up the odor a couple hundred feet away and got me into the neighborhood." Bryce turned to Sierra and scratched her on the head. "Good find, little girrllll! You're a good good good good girlllll."

Jones took one look at the body and then turned to Bryce. "I assume you also didn't mess with this, right?"

"Ugh, no. But I know why you're asking. Yes, she's posed. What do you think the timing is on this? She's decomposed, but she's all here. There's not a lot of animal activity."

"Dunno," Jones responded. "Maybe it's got something to do with the body being killed one place and dumped in another."

"You mean after pulling her out of the other spot…"

"Right. He'd already disposed of one body here, the one the hunter found, and knew the terrain. He gets wind that we're planning to search Tiger Lake and wants to move that body in a hurry. He snatches her up and hurries out here."

"But who knew we were searching Tiger Lake?" Bryce asked, fully exceeding his charter as a SAR dog handler.

"Fair question and all I can say is we're looking at some options."

"OK. Want me to go back to base, download my tracks and write this up?"

"I don't see any point in running you back and forth on the road and I'd like to search as much of the area as possible before dark. Can you save your GPS track to this point and then start a new one from here?"

"Sure, that's easy. I can download them all at once whenever I get back."

"OK, let's do that. Maybe you should make a few notes in case there are other bodies…so your mind doesn't blur them together."

Bryce took the suggestion and made a few notes, but there really wasn't much to write. He described the path they'd taken in, where Sierra picked up the scent, and the exact GPS coordinates of the find. Then, he called Sierra to him. She'd been given an extended chance to play with her ball, but it was time to go back to work.

"I need your ball, girl. There's more Digger out here. We gotta go find Digger."

Sierra obediently dropped the ball at Bryce's feet, and immediately turned away. She went directly to the body she'd just found, looked over at Bryce, and sat. Both Jones and the scientist were laughing.

"Nice try, girl, but you already found that one. We know about that one! Yes, we do! You're a good dog, but there's more out here…let's go find more Digger."

Sierra took off, continuing the grid pattern they'd begun at the start. The two worked another hour and forty-five minutes with no additional finds. Bryce got on the radio to Jones.

"132, 44. We've worked this side of the road all the way to a big swamp. We can use the road to get around the swamp and go back in, or return to base."

"44, 132, you can RTB." Granger and Lefty were just pulling into the parking lot. Jones thought it would be a good idea to get them all together before sending out the new arrivals.

"44, returning to base. Thanks."

Bryce and Sierra walked into base to see Lefty and Jones chatting amiably. Lefty had his dog Dingo on leash, and it was calmly licking itself. Granger was sitting in the driver's seat of his truck. Alone.

"Get some food and water on board—both you and the dog," Jones called to Bryce. "Meet over by my rig in about fifteen for a briefing on the second round."

"Will do." Bryce turned to Lefty. "Hi, sir. Good to see you."

"Good to see you, Bryce. Sounds like nice work out there. Go get hydrated."

"Thanks."

Bryce took time to wolf down a power bar, and got some water and a bit of food into Sierra. He didn't want her stomach full, just enough calories to keep her working well.

Jones called the three dog handlers together for the briefing.

"Thanks for coming today. You probably know bits and pieces of this, so let me give you the big picture. A hunter following a wounded deer came across the body of a woman—we thought it might be the Santiago girl we've been looking for, but it's far too decomposed to fit her disappearance. Bryce, on the other hand, just found a second body that's much more recently dumped.

The medical examiner will have to confirm whether either of them is the girl we're looking for."

Jones didn't give the three any time for questions or comments, and went on with his briefing. "We want to scour the rest of the area and make sure there aren't any others. Remember, the Green River Killer dumped five in one place.

"We assume the killer didn't have a key to this gate, and had to carry the bodies from right here. That means any bodies won't be too far *down* the road nor too far *off* the road. CSRT has finished with the first scene and is now working the second…both scenes are to the right of the road.

"I'd like to get the left side of the road covered, as well as the area beyond the swamp where Bryce stopped. I know that's a long way, but this guy has fooled us before. Alan, I know you like to pick your area—any preferences?"

"Nah, I'm good," Granger replied. "Whatever you need."

Bryce was a little surprised. Granger had always made a big deal out of picking his own areas.

"OK, let's have you head for the other side of the swamp on the right," Jones said.

"Sure," was the one-word response.

Jones continued. "Bryce, you've already busted your butt for a couple of hours. Let's put you just inside the gate on the left side. I know it's gnarly, but at least you won't have to walk far to get there."

"Works for me, sir," Bryce answered, still wondering about Granger's response.

"Lefty, for you that leaves the more distant area on the left—no pun intended. Let's call Bryce's area the first 500 yards down left side of the road, and you can pick up from there. Don't go any further off the road than somebody would likely carry a body."

"Fair enough. I'll get my stuff."

All three dog handlers went back to their vehicles, and went through essentially the same procedure. They got out their packs, radios and GPS devices. Vests went on the dogs, and their GPS collars were checked. All three teams got to the gate about the same time.

Bryce looked at Granger. "Good luck, Alan." No response.

He then turned to Lefty. "Good hunting, sir."

"You too. And please stop calling me 'sir.' My name is Lefty."

Bryce turned into the brush and told Sierra to find Digger. She immediately started pushing her way through what was indeed gnarly brush, not ranging as far from Bryce as she might normally. In a few particularly difficult places she circled behind Bryce, and let him break trail.

They moved slowly, each step taken cautiously. They'd go around especially difficult areas, but always on the downwind side. It took them about two hours to work the 500 yards to where Lefty's area started. Just as they got there, Bryce heard Lefty call Base on the radio.

"Base, Yakima 27. Dingo has some interest, but can't work it out. Can I have another dog here to see if they can find anything?"

"Yakima 27, Base. Where ya at? We can have one of the other dogs swing by."

"Far end of my area. I'm on the opposite side of the road from the swamp that Dog 44 mentioned."

261

"Base, understood. That puts Mason 20 closest to you. Mason 20, are you copying?"

No response.

"Mason 20, Base. Do you copy?"

Crickets.

"27, Base. Maybe he can't hear us from base. You're a lot closer, why don't you try?"

"Copied, break. Mason 20, Yakima 27. Do you copy?"

Still nothing.

"Mason 20, Yakima 27. Do you copy?"

"Break…Base, Yakima 27. He's not hearing me either. Not sure what you want to do."

Jones slipped, and allowed himself to sigh audibly over the radio. "Hmmmm, well, let's run Dog 44 out there and at least get your dog's interest checked out. If we haven't heard from two-zero in a while we can go searching for him."

Bryce bit his tongue, and skipped the temptation to point out they'd done that before. "Dog 44 copies. We were just finishing our area anyway so we'll head right out."

"Base copies, thanks 44. 27, why don't you meet 44 out on the road, and direct him and his dog in from there."

"27, will do. Thanks."

Bryce walked the additional 500 yards out the road when he saw Lefty sitting on a stump with Dingo at his feet. The two dogs gave each other play bows, but weren't allowed to play when they had their search vests on. Both handlers shortened leashes while they talked.

"So what do you need me to check?" Bryce asked.

"Straight in from here, about 150 feet. The dog went into scent but could never resolve it."

"OK, we'll go check. What's the wind doing out there?"

"It's blowing in from the road, so there could be scent from here blowing in. But Dingo's on his cadaver command, so he shouldn't be telling me about passersby."

"Thanks, we'll go see what's up."

As is common in those situations, Sierra reacted exactly as Dingo had. She sniffed and snorted, clearing her sinuses for a better smell. Yet in the end, she found no source of odor and didn't sit to indicate. Both Dingo and Sierra were "honest dogs," and didn't alert just to please their masters. Bryce went back out to the road and spoke to Lefty.

"Got nada. Sierra was in scent alright. There's something out there, right where you said it would be. But she never sat or put her nose anyplace specific. Let's mark it on our GPSs and if the deputies want, ESAR can come out and manually dig through the brush."

Lefty was grateful for the confirmation, even if it didn't lead to a find. "At least my dog's not hallucinating. Have you heard Granger on the radio?"

"Nope. Let's give him another try." Bryce reached for his radio microphone.

"Mason 20, Mason 20…Dog 44. Radio check."

No answer. Bryce didn't want to gossip, but he felt Lefty deserved to know some history.

"You know we've had to go looking for him before. He spaced out on a search over by Bear Creek. We found him daydreaming, just sitting on a log."

Lefty was incredulous. "And they let him continue to search?"

"The guy has a very strong track record. I don't know what the sheriff's office did about it, but he was back searching in a month or so."

At that point Jones called back over the radio.

"Dog 44, Base. How did your search go? Find anything Dingo didn't?"

"Base, 44. Sierra had interest too, but was likewise unable to resolve. We've marked the spot and can talk about it when we get back to base. Have you heard from Mason 20?"

"No…that's the other thing. You guys want to go see if you can find him?"

Not really, was Bryce's first thought. For the second time that day, he held his tongue.

"Sure. He was working the right side of the road, beyond the swamp, right?"

"That's correct. You're heading out?"

"Roger. We'll let you know what we find. Dog 44 clear."

"Base clear."

Bryce and Lefty decided to split up Granger's area. Bryce would take the area immediately past the swamp, and Lefty would go further out before turning into the brush. Bryce and Sierra were about fifty feet off the road when they heard voices. Lefty, walking further out the road, had simply bumped into Granger walking back toward base.

Bryce turned and popped out onto the road in the middle of a heated conversation.

"...searching my area is 'where I've been,'" Granger told Lefty, with a slightly raised voice.

Lefty wasn't taking any crap. "We've been calling you on the radio for over half-an-hour. You haven't been answering and base just had us start looking for you. I've been told this isn't the first time."

"That's none of your business. I assume young Mr. 44 here has been running his mouth."

Lefty was starting to get his dander up. "Talk to me. Bryce isn't part of this. If you're going to be part of the team, you need to do a better job of playing in the sandbox. I'm all the way from the other half of the state and have heard about your antics."

"Well my 'antics' work. We go out and we find people. The rest of you are just doing dog tricks and I'm not going to answer to you or any other dog handler about how I operate."

Lefty got on the radio. "Base, 27. We've located Mason 20 and we'll all be returning to base."

"Base copies. We'll be waiting. Base clear."

Bryce joined the two angry men as they walked down the road. After a few hundred feet of tense silence, he spoke up. "Are you OK, Alan?"

"What is that supposed to mean...am I OK? I'm fine."

"It means what it means, no hidden agenda," Bryce said, keeping his voice as even as he could. "This is twice I've been around when you've gone MIA on the radio. If there's a problem or something's bothering you, you have friends who would like to help."

"Well shucks, that's nice 'o you kid. Ah really appreciates it. Ah do. I'm fine. I've seen worse stuff on searches than you will ever see, so you have no business worrying about me. What I can't believe is what you're doing out here."

"Sierra and I have had some success too, Alan."

"Yeah, you're young and fit, and you've got a decent dog. But there's no excuse for somebody your age seeing the things you're seeing. That's just completely nuts, and I can't believe your county allows it. Out here…just now…you have no business seeing a dead body with its hands folded across its chest. That's just creepy, and nobody your age is ready for that."

"It's not fun, I'll grant you that. But we have a good support system in my county and gore just doesn't seem to bother me."

Bryce sensed that the conversation needed to be over, lest it turn ugly. He'd done the right thing by offering an olive branch. The fact that it came back singed and smoldering was, as Katie had reminded him, Granger's problem. He allowed himself to join in the awkward silence that Granger and Lefty had begun.

When the three teams got to base, each of the handlers put their dogs in their trucks, made sure they had water, and offered them treats. Granger completed the task first, and went to the command post to download tracks from his GPS. Bryce was just getting to the CP as Granger was leaving.

"I'm all downloaded," Granger grumbled. "Knock yourself out, kid."

Bryce went inside and connected his GPS to the computer. He made sure the program was ready to accept data from his model of GPS, and downloaded three tracks. The first showed his search and discovery of the second body, on the right side of the road. The second showed him continuing that area out to the swamp. Bryce's third track reflected his efforts on the left side of the road, moving further out to check Lefty's area of interest and finally the initial effort to find Granger. Bryce had saved his track at that point, not wanting to clutter the map by including the long walk back to base.

Bryce looked to make sure his track displayed in a different color from Granger's, so anyone looking at the map could tell which track was whose. The lesser side of him also wanted to see if Granger had actually searched or if he'd spaced out again and simply sat down.

Granger's trail, displayed on the computer map in red, showed that he had indeed searched his assigned area. Bryce noted that Granger walked directly down the road from base, passing the two earlier scenes, with no side trips.

He turned away from the computer to talk to Jones. "You gonna do a debrief?" he asked.

"Not much to say," came the reply. "Granger said he had to leave, Lefty didn't find anything, and we really don't want to talk too much about this case anyway. What do you see here that's missing?"

Bryce was taken aback by the question and looked around.

"Our cars and the comm van are here…there's fewer cars because you didn't call the rest of the team. What am I missing?"

"News media. What you don't see here is a gaggle of those danged professional looky-loos peeking at us from behind crime scene tape. I think we've kept this one completely under the radar."

"Wow, pretty cool and doesn't happen all that often."

"Tell me about it," Jones continued. "The dispatch supervisor kicked this off right, and I gotta hand it to her. I think there's only about ten people, even including the crime lab, who know there's a scene here at all. Even fewer know you found a second body. If the hunter can just keep his mouth shut, we might get away with the killer not knowing we've found this particular dump site."

"My lips are sealed," Bryce reassured Jones. "Katie hasn't heard from me and will probably accuse me of being out with another woman, though."

"You were! Sierra. Ow, that's a little weird. Forget I said that."

"Yeah...weird...already forgotten. How much do Lefty and Granger know?"

"What, about all this? That's also a kind of a weird question. You heard the briefing, and I haven't discussed anything in detail with them. Why do you ask?

"Oh...no reason," Bryce replied, remembering he was talking to someone who spotted lies for a living. "It's just that sometimes I feel like I don't always have the big picture when I'm searching. I'm trying to figure out who gets what info and how the...I can't remember the term...compartmenting works."

"Compartmentalization. I think the Army coined the term. Yeah, we do that. If somebody doesn't have a need to know, we don't tell 'em. But if that's affecting your searches, then we need to adjust. We don't want you missing something important because we played it too close to the vest."

"If you don't mind, I'll point it out the next time it comes up, so you'll know what I'm talking about."

"Absolutely. If I haven't said it, we really appreciate all you do for us. We're grateful for any feedback you have and thanks for all you do."

"You're welcome," Bryce said, only partly sure he'd gotten away with his lie.

CHAPTER SEVENTEEN
Half the Story

""Hey bud, you awake?" Wright asked, knowing the answer.

"Ugh…not so much. What time is it?" was Davy Jones' weak reply.

"'Bout two…in the afternoon. You work last night?"

"Yeah…off the road at oh-seven-hundred, had to sit around till nine for court. I just got to bed an hour ago. What's up?"

"The boss wants to see us."

"The sheriff? Did we screw up?"

"Yup and nope. Yes, I mean the sheriff. I doubt we screwed up or we'd be hearing from Internal Affairs. His secretary just said he wants us both in his office by three. I think it's good news, but I don't know what."

Jones took a minute to clear his head. Wright had received such calls himself, and knew why there was silence. After a bit, he spoke, to make sure Jones hadn't fallen back to sleep. "Still there, bud?"

"Yeahhh. In the sheriff's office in about an hourrr. In uniform?"

"No, I think this is about Chimera, so plainclothes is fine. But it's the sheriff, so no grubbies, OK?"

"OK. Geez, an hour. I gotta go. It's a good thing the county lets us take our patrol cars home. If I take time to shave, I'll have to run code to get there..."

"Definitely shave...look sharp...be there," Wright said as Jones' hung up.

Jones hopped in and out of the shower in only slightly more time than it took to get wet. He shaved quickly, and was grateful his close-cropped hair meant no time lost to combing and styling. Most officers had taken to wearing the "tactical" styles of casual clothing. Jones selected a long-sleeved polo, cargo pants and boots of synthetic fabric that didn't need shining. He had just enough time to get to the courthouse without using his lights and siren.

The two men pulled into the parking lot about the same time. Wright and Jones walked into the courthouse together and took the elevator up to the sheriff's office. Although the sheriff's secretary wasn't commissioned as a deputy, she handled the sheriff's correspondence and knew every detail of every case. Today, she was white as a ghost.

Wright and Jones shared a look of recognition, but said nothing. "Go right in, gentleman," as she shut the door behind them.

At the office conference table were the sheriff, Undersheriff Bill Burns, and a man Wright and Jones didn't know. The stranger stood up and offered his hand.

"I'm Jim Oliver. Good to meet you."

The sheriff interjected. "Jim runs the State Crime Lab. I asked him to be here to share some news and answer any questions you might have."

Jones was instantly 100 percent awake, but it was Wright who fired off the first question.

"I assume this is about Chimera?"

"It is," Oliver responded. "But the news only comes as a result of some very courageous work by your sheriff. I appreciate his invite but I think he should be the one to share it with you."

"Well you're killing us with the suspense," Wright said. "Nice to meet you, Mr. Oliver, but I really don't care…somebody just tell us."

The sheriff spoke next with no trace of excitement in his voice.

"We have a match to the DNA found at Tiger Lake. Some of the blood was Maria Santiago's as we'd suspected. The lab has also identified the blood of a male who is probably her killer."

"Awesome! Let's go hook him up. Any idea where he's at?"

"One floor up," the sheriff responded.

"What?" both Wright and Jones responded simultaneously.

"It's James Garrison."

Jones, now more than fully awake, jumped into the conversation.

"There's no way. We grabbed him when he showed up at our stakeout. He never got near the spot where the body had been dumped."

"Right," was the sheriff's answer. "If he didn't make it out there when you contacted him, then when was the only other opportunity for him to have been at that spot?"

The light went on for Jones. "Jesus…a few hours earlier when the body was dumped. It makes sense. Much before that and the blood would have been too degraded to test."

Wright, the more experienced detective, shifted to another concern. "What made you think to get Garrison's DNA, boss?"

That was Burns' signal to enter the conversation. "Because our boss is a genius. He had something today's cops aren't allowed to have: a hunch. He invited Garrison up to chat about something political and held onto his water glass."

Oliver took that as his cue to jump back into the conversation. "We got his saliva off the lip of the glass and his DNA matched what we extracted from the bloody dirt, along with Miss Santiago's" he said. "Your young dog handler did all the right things to preserve that evidence. We'll have a fight in court about chain of custody, but the matches are solid."

"Jeez, sheriff, what if you'd been wrong and he found out? The political heat would have been unbearable."

"That's why I couldn't ask you to do it," the sheriff replied. "I wasn't trying to cut you out of the action, and it's not that I didn't trust you. You're both on this case because of the trust I have in you. But I couldn't ask you to risk your careers on a hunch. Now, what are your thoughts on how we go about 'hooking up' the esteemed Councilman Garrison?"

"Well, I for-darned-sure don't think we want to rush upstairs and just cuff him."

"I tend to agree," said the sheriff. "But I'd like to hear your

274

thoughts on why."

"Unless you have another surprise in your pocket, for now, the DNA match is all we've got. It's conclusive for all of us, but his eventual defense attorney will claim it's not enough. We've got to at least check his alibi for earlier in the afternoon, when the jogger saw Maria being dragged into the woods. He had to have returned and gotten the body before we got out there."

"Then why would he show up at all while we *were* there?" Jones asked.

"I dunno. Maybe with the stress of it all he got drunk and made a mistake," Wright answered. "These guys always make a mistake. If they don't make a mistake, we generally don't catch them."

"True enough," Jones replied. "But it'll take some time to *discreetly* check his whereabouts for the time period you're talking about. We can get cell records, receipts for gas and credit cards, and surveillance video from the lobby downstairs. But that'll take time."

The sheriff took on a note of concern. "We've had one security breach on this case, and we can't risk another one. If he finds out we're looking at him he might decide to go out in a blaze of glory. Maybe he snatches one last girl or shoots up the courthouse or who knows what."

"Can we have our narcs do a surveillance?" Wright asked. "They're really very good."

"Nope, I simply can't trust anybody inside this building. We know who the leak was last time, but we don't know all of the allegiances that might exist among those who work here." The sheriff was adamant.

Wright offered a solution. "How about the FBI? They do

surveillance all the time."

The sheriff considered the suggestion. "The SAC over in Seattle called me a couple months ago to offer his assistance. Maybe I could take him up on that." He turned to his phone and dialed the intercom for his secretary.

"Dana, can you get me Jim Keiron over in Seattle. Yeah, he's the Special Agent in Charge at the FBI. I need to talk to him right away...yeah, thanks." He hung up the phone.

"Dana's tracking him down," he said, pointing to the gadget on the table. "If she gets him live, she'll put him on the speaker phone."

He turned to Wright. "So, Bob, we put him under surveillance while you check out where he was when the jogger saw Maria being led into the woods. Assuming we won't be able to prove he was elsewhere, then what?"

"Then we see if we can get him to lie to us. We can ask him some questions to which we already know the answers. Catch him in a couple of small lies and then drop the bomb."

The sheriff was starting to go from politician to investigator. "I like that. Get him to offer an alibi for the time in question. If we can get his cell phone pings quickly enough, we'll know where he really was."

Jones interjected. "The area where the jogger saw him...saw someone...doesn't have cell coverage."

"That still works," Wright said. "We might not have cell coverage that puts him there, but his house, his office, most local restaurants...they all have cell coverage. If it's a 'no ping' response from the cell companies and he claims to be someplace that has coverage, we'll know he's lying."

The sheriff took command, and meddled a bit in Wright's investigation. "Then get the cell phone companies started first. They can be a pain in the rear. Once they're rolling, we can start with the credit card companies and see where he was spending money. Warrant?"

"We'd better. I know a judge who can keep her mouth shut."

"I will go with you, and have a conversation elected-to-elected. It's a conversation you can't have."

"Happy to have you along. If she knows you're personally interested, all the more likely she'll buy our probable cause."

"I don't give a crap if *she* buys it. You write that warrant for the Supreme Court, not for some local judge. You know damn well it'll end up there."

"Roger that, sir."

Dana knocked on the door, but didn't wait to be asked in. "Sheriff, Mr. Keiron is on line two. You can pull him up on speaker."

"Thanks." The sheriff pushed the button for line two. "Jim, how are you? Sorry to call in such a rush. I hope this is an OK time."

"Sheriff, it's always good to hear from you, even when it's not good news. Your assistant…Dana…said you needed some help with something."

"We do indeed. First, let me tell you you're on speaker. In the room with me are Undersheriff Bill Burns, whom I think you've met, Jim Oliver from the Crime Lab, Detective Bob Wright and Deputy Davy Jones."

"Hey, good to meet you all. So what can we do for you?"

"We need some surveillance done, and it's pretty politically sensitive. We need a team, tonight, on one of our county councilmembers."

"I thought this was about your serial killer. If you've got a politician with his hand in the cookie jar…"

The sheriff interrupted. "Jim, this *is* about our serial case."

"Oh, my God. Seriously?"

"DNA at the crime scene, my friend. We're not ready to make an arrest, but we don't want him scouting any more victims while we get our ducks lined up. Can you send us some folks to sit on his house, and follow *very* discreetly if he goes anywhere?"

"You bet. Gimme an hour to round up the right people. With traffic, it might take a couple hours to get them on your side of the pond. Will that work?"

"Three hours, yeah. That'll work. He'll probably be upstairs in his office for the next two. You'll be getting to his house about the same time he does. We'll need a team to watch the councilman's driveway, and maybe somebody in camouflage for the back of his house. His property borders on a public greenbelt."

"Roger…let me ring off and we'll get 'em going. This is unreal. I'll call ya."

"Thanks." The sheriff turned to the others in the room. "OK, assuming we get him locked down for the night what's our next step?"

"The warrant," was Jones' immediate reply. "The cell companies are willing to give us info with a request on letterhead, but that's for missing people like Alzheimer's patients. We know we're looking at Garrison for a crime, so we'd better have a warrant."

"Not my area of expertise," Oliver said. He had a crime lab to run, and they were woefully behind on their massive caseload. "If you don't mind, I'll leave this in your good hands."

"Actually I'd like you to stay," the sheriff said. "I want the warrant to fully disclose the how we got both DNA samples, the chain of custody on the dirt, and your level of confidence that the dirt is a viable source of DNA. I don't want anybody claiming we held back exculpatory information from the judge."

"No problem. Let me make a call and let my secretary know I won't be back today."

"We appreciate that," the sheriff said. He turned to Wright and Jones. "This needs to be the best search warrant you ever wrote. Keep in mind that when this is over, it'll all be public. We'll ask the judge to seal the warrant until charges are filed, but eventually, everybody and their brother will be reading this one."

"Understood," Wright said. "Let me make sure I'm tracking with you. We're getting the warrant and then, in order, we'll serve the cell companies, the credit card companies, and then check surveillance video from downstairs. If the credit card companies show him buying stuff, we'll verify it was really him using the card. Only then will we hit his office and home. Am I getting this right?"

"Yes, that's perfect. Here's a quick thought. Budget and Payroll has online access to his county credit card account. There won't be any personal charges there, but if he did anything on his county card, it would show up immediately. It's the county's card, no warrant needed. Call it a good faith effort to rule him out."

"The county hasn't trusted me with a card, sir," was Wright's reply. "How do we get the statement?"

"It would require seeing Jenny Buchannan down in B&P. I'm breaking my own rule, but I think we can trust her."

"She doesn't have to know we think he's Chimera," Jones interjected. "She cleared up a payroll error for me awhile back and was really helpful. I think I can get access to the records without creating a security risk. Besides, in a couple hours the FBI will have their surveillance up and running. It won't matter"

"This works. Davy, you head downstairs while Bob works on the search warrant. Jim, do you need an empty desk while we're waiting? Maybe you can get some work done, at least."

"That would be great. Let's have Bob write the first draft of the warrant and then I can fill in about the dirt and why we think the sample is scientifically valid."

The sheriff was in his element, acting like a combination of cop and coach. "Ready...break," was his sign that everyone should get moving.

Jones went downstairs to Budget and Payroll, and was relieved to see Jenny at her desk.

"Hey, Jenny, got any more forgotten overtime you want to send my way? That back pay made for a nice Christmas."

"Hi, Davy. No, I think we got your timecards all straightened out. What brings you down?"

"It's confidential. Got someplace besides this cubicle to discuss it?"

"Sure, the conference room's empty." Jenny led the way, and Jones shut the door behind them.

"I need to look at Jim Garrison's county credit card account."

"Well, it's a county card so there are no confidentiality issues. I heard he got a DUI or something awhile back...just rumor. Is this about that?"

"Sort of, but I really can't say. I need to check his credit card statement for charges around the time we're pretending he wasn't arrested." He gave her the date.

"I can pull that up," Jenny said. She went back to her desk, pulled her laptop out of its dock, and returned to the conference room. But the effort had given her time to think and her mind was going someplace she didn't like.

"Is there some kind of political war going on?"

"Why do you say that?"

Jenny was starting to feel like her position was putting her in the middle of...she didn't know exactly what. She'd honor confidentialities, but had to look out for number one. She had a child at home, and no husband. If she was in the middle of a mess, she needed to know it.

"I wasn't supposed to say anything, but a few weeks ago Councilman Garrison was down here checking on the sheriff's budget. He wanted to know how much you were spending on car wrecks, and overtime for you and Bob Wright on this Chimera thing. Now it's the reverse. You're checking up on him."

Jones was adept and looking calm when he wasn't. "What did you tell him?"

"All good. I praised the daylights out of the sheriff. You guys have had a lot fewer wrecks, and the sheriff is keeping a tight rein on the special account for your case. In fact, are you putting in for all the overtime you're working, my friend?"

"Probably not. Did he say why he was asking?"

"The sheriff had claimed to be saving the county a ton of money by reducing civil judgments for car accidents. He wanted to verify that. On the way out, he asked about the special account."

"I can't say why we're asking for his credit card statements, but we'll take the heat for making the inquiry," Jones replied. "If anybody asks, I beat it out of you with a rubber hose."

"Good enough for me. Here's the statement."

Jones scrolled through the screen without telling Jenny what days he was interested in. It was quickly obvious that Garrison had put nothing on this county card the day of the disappearance, nor on adjacent days.

"Thanks, Jenny. I appreciate you sharing that info with me and we'll definitely take the heat for any political fallout. But I have to give you a bigger warning than he did. He might get you in trouble at your job for talking out of turn, but this is a criminal case. If you talk about this, you could end up getting charged."

Jenny went white.

"I'm sorry you're in this position, but you are. So I absolutely need you to keep this between us. I'll make clear in my report that I demanded the info from you...not that you came forward or anything."

"I appreciate that." Because of her role with finance and peoples' paychecks, Jenny was naturally discreet. But a political war was different and usually fodder for entertaining gossip. She'd have trouble not telling anyone what she knew.

Upstairs, Wright was working on the perfunctory parts of the warrant—his own experience, background on the case, and why the warrant was important. The harder part was explaining, in simple terms, how they'd gotten the DNA and what they expected to find should a warrant be issued.

"The affiant's training and experience includes the fact that serial killers often keep mementoes or trophies of their kill. The affiant therefore believes, based on training and experience, that there is probable cause to believe evidence of the crime of Murder in the First Degree will be located in the suspect's home, vehicle, outbuildings and/or real property," he typed.

Oliver was looking over his shoulder. "Nicely written. You don't want to say 'panties' in a search warrant?"

Oliver's Crime Scene Response Team had processed every scene for Wright. At none of them had they found that most intimate piece of women's garments. Since it was unlikely they'd all chosen to "go commando," it was presumed the killer had taken the underwear as trophies.

"The media will be all over this once the case is over and I'm trying to give them as little as possible to sensationalize. I'll tell the judge when we meet, but for now I'm just using the word 'trophies.'"

Wright went on to explain about the dirt, and Oliver coached him on why the delay in testing wouldn't have degraded the sample. Wright was typing as fast as he could to keep up with Oliver.

"Although not stored according to the regular process, the item was frozen within a very short time after being deposited on the ground. Had the sample simply degraded from incorrect storage, it would have been untestable. It would not have produced a sample at all, and there is zero chance it would have produced a false match."

Wright also went on to explain about good faith, and the fact that the dog handler who picked up the sample was simply trying to find out why his dog had apparently given a false alert. There was no effort to suppress or modify evidence, and Bryce's handling of the dirt had been scientifically appropriate.

Jones, meantime, had come back upstairs and asked Dana if he could see the sheriff. She didn't even check to see if he was busy, she simply walked over and opened his door.

"Hi, Sir," Jones said deferentially. "I hope I'm not interrupting anything."

"Not at all," was the response. "Good news from downstairs?"

"Well, if no news is good news then yes. His county card didn't show any charges, so at least it won't become an alibi. But there's some political news as well."

"OK...."

"Jenny said Garrison had come down asking about some things. I'm guessing it was after your meeting...where you got the DNA? At any rate, he wanted to know how much we'd spent on collisions and how much you'd spent on Wright and me for this case."

"What did she tell him?"

"All good, sir. All of us know the number of wrecks has plummeted. That guy from Seattle is a great instructor and we're all better drivers for it. She also backed you up on the special budget they passed for this case."

"What do you mean 'backed me up?'"

"The budget's in great shape. She told him you 'throw pennies around like they were manhole covers.'"

"Damn. Not good news."

"Sir...?"

"I was trying to see how he'd react if I wanted to ratchet up the case and needed more money. If he's our killer, I wanted to see if he'd try to cripple the investigation politically. I told him we were almost out of money."

"Ohhh. What'd he say?"

"He opposed it at first, just like I expected. But he eventually caved to some political maneuvering. I guess I overacted it… turned up the heat too much. My bad."

Wright and Oliver walked in at that moment, first draft of the warrant in hand.

"Wanna see this before I take it to the prosecutor, sir?"

"You're not taking it to any prosecutor. I know that's the normal protocol, but this isn't a normal case. You and I are going to see the judge directly. There's another bit of news—Garrison might have an inkling we're onto him. I screwed up."

"How so?"

"I was trying to test how much he'd try to shut down this investigation…if he was the killer. I lied to him about how much we've been spending on you and Davy. He apparently checked my numbers with Jenny downstairs and knows I lied."

"Wow. Well, we're breaking new ground here, boss. There have been lots of serial killers out there, but never a well-known elected official right under our same roof. We can be excused for a mistake or two."

"Excuse me, sheriff." It was Dana. "Jim Keiron is on the line. He's got his team en route. Line three."

The sheriff punched the button. "Jim…thanks for getting rolling so quickly. What have you got for a team?"

"Our best," the FBI man responded. "We've got the coldest of ratty vans with two people hidden in the back. It'll die on the road with a view of Garrison's house, and the driver will toddle off for help. We're also putting two guys into the woods out behind the house."

"That sounds perfect. We've just figured out Garrison might have an inkling he's under suspicion. Can you let me know for sure when you see that he's home? Then, if he goes anywhere, how will you follow?"

"We've got another very plain Honda that'll be a few blocks away. If either the front or back team see him leaving, we'll be on his tail. I have two more carloads on the way from Bellevue, but it'll take them longer to get in position. Once they're there, we'll be able to do a full three-car tail if it becomes necessary."

"Perfect. You don't know how much we appreciate this. I'm going to have Dana pick up and give you the cell numbers of everybody involved. I've got to go visit a judge for a search warrant."

"That works," Keiron replied. "I'll hold for Dana. She's a sweetie, by the way."

"She is indeed. Thanks." The sheriff hung up the phone, and turned to Wright.

"You said you had a judge who could keep her mouth shut. Barb Stanton?"

"Uh-huh. When we had the kerfuffle down at Banner Forest, she was really interested in getting this guy off the street."

"Well, I would hope any judge would have the same opinion, but if you think Barb is the right judge, then let's go see her."

The two men left the office, and Wright drove. The sheriff got on

286

his cell phone.

"Hey, Barb. It's Elroy. I need to come by and see you, if that's OK."

"It's always OK, Elroy. But it's a little unusual. Are you writing search warrants now?"

"No. Bob Wright...you know Bob...wrote the warrant. But I need to be there. It'll make sense when you see it."

"Well, now I can't wait. See you when you get here."

The twenty-minute trip went by like it was two minutes. Wright and the sheriff walked up to the front door to find Judge Stanton waiting on the other side.

"Always good to see you, Elroy...er, I suppose I should call you 'sheriff' if you're here officially."

"Your honor, you can call me whatever you'd like." He hardly paused before turning to the topic at hand. He sighed, and lowered his voice. "This is an ugly one, Barb. It's a political hot potato. I wouldn't be here if I wasn't sure of what we're doing, but nothing's ever 100 percent."

Wright handed the judge the warrant, and the two men saw the color drain from her face. "I was just at a community meeting with the guy," she said. "He walked me to my car, alone, in the back parking lot."

"Well, you're not exactly the type he kills. But, yeah, creepy," the sheriff said. "Look, I know this is really political. If you'd rather we went elsewhere I get it. But I really need somebody I trust. More importantly I need somebody who can keep us out of trouble with the Supremes. That's you."

The judge kept reading but said nothing until she had completed the task. Sheriff Elroy Patterson didn't get nervous about much, but her silence made him nervous.

Finally, a response. "I'm not the least worried about any political fallout, and this is a very good search warrant. I'm happy to sign with one exception."

Both the sheriff and Wright said "OK…." simultaneously.

"You've asked to search his county office and his personal residence, all very well done. What you haven't asked for is to search his county office for personal effects. He might claim an expectation of privacy if you find something personal in his office."

Wright thought the judge was being a little over-the-top careful, but he quickly made a pen and ink change to cover her concern. She signed the warrant and sent them off with a final comment.

"I hope you're right, and I hope you're wrong. Good luck."

"Thanks, Barb…your honor," the sheriff replied.

CHAPTER EIGHTEEN
First, One Shoe

The old Chevy van coughed to a stop at precisely the right spot. The kill switch didn't immediately shut down the engine. It closed an electric valve that starved the engine for fuel. Anyone watching would see a vehicle sputter, lurch and buck before breaking down beside the road.

The FBI agent driving was bundled up and wearing a hoodie, to hide both his face and his close-cropped federal-agent hair. He got out, raised the hood, pretended to look underneath, and then slammed the hood angrily. He reached in the driver's door and pulled a small gas can from behind the seat, striding off down the street and around the corner. The can was a total prop, having never contained so much as a drop of gas. Even when empty, used gas cans emit an odor, and who needs that inside a surveillance vehicle? After nearly a mile of walking, and making sure he wasn't followed, he "thumbed" a ride with fellow agents in a support car.

The two agents who remained hidden in back of the van had a

perfect view of the Garrison home. They could see the front door, the garage doors, and one whole side of the house. They also had communications with two agents in the woods behind the house who could see the rear of the home and the side not visible from the van.

"He's home. Second floor rear," radioed one of the two agents in the woods. They were both part of an FBI SWAT team but, tonight, were carrying spotter scopes instead of rifles. They had their standard issue side arms as always, but this was not a case when they'd need to take out a suspect with a precision shot to the head. They simply wanted to watch the house, and see what they could.

"Looks like he's sitting at a computer screen, probably surfing the internet. I can't see what he's looking at though..." the agent radioed.

"Let's be careful on that," the agent in the van radioed back. "The locals are getting a warrant but I'm not sure if they have it yet. We're here to keep tabs on his location, and follow him if he goes anywhere."

"Roger that," came the response from the woods. *"We don't care what he's doing, so long as he's doing it in the house. Out."*

Inside the home, Garrison was taking full advantage of his county's friendly attitude toward business and commerce. He'd long ago convinced his fellow county council members to offer free open Wi-Fi within the confines of the courthouse. Dubbed the "Universal Technology Initiative," they'd charge lawyers for access to an encrypted Wi-Fi system, but the public would have access to a free network throughout the building. The system was winning high accolades from everyone who did business with the county.

The county's Information Technology branch had gone to great lengths to make sure the encrypted system was truly secure, lest hackers delve into the private affairs of people and their attorneys. For the public system, signs promoting the network included ample warning that it was open and could be intercepted. One might look at Google Earth while seeking a building permit, but they probably didn't want to access their bank account to pay a tax bill.

For all the security, the IT folks missed one, single, all-important security step. They left themselves vulnerable in a way that none had expected, and which wasn't in any of the books on IT security.

They simply never bothered to turn the system off at night.

With the FBI staking out the Garrison home, the sheriff and Bob Wright returned to the courthouse. Warrant in hand, they quickly huddled with Davy Jones, who'd been teeing up everything they'd need to do in the next few hours.

Jones had contacted the cell phone companies to make sure security personnel would be ready for an evening call. In most cases, the companies' heads of security were former cops, and understood that something big was coming. Hanging around late made them feel like they were part of a big investigation. The result was that they'd generate their response in minutes, not hours or days. Not only would Wright and Jones know what numbers had been called or texted, but which cell towers the phone had been near. Jones didn't tip that they were hoping for a gap in coverage…the cellular company didn't need to know that.

Jones also double-checked phone numbers for the various credit card companies they'd be calling. They didn't have as tight a relationship with the card companies, but, at the very least, they wouldn't be slowed down by having to be referred here and there. He'd already pinned down *the* places to call, and *the* e-mail addresses to which they'd send copies of the warrant.

That legwork done, it didn't take long to get things rolling. Calls were made, and scanned copies of the warrant were sent to e-mail boxes at the cellular and credit card companies. While they waited for their answers, Wright and Jones decided to move ahead with the next step. They'd ride the elevator up and quietly serve the search warrant on Garrison's office.

Entry to the Garrison office was not difficult. As the sheriff's office provided security for the building, it had master keys to every floor. The sheriff had come along, and he carried the keys himself. "If this blows up in our faces, I want it clear that this was my call and you were acting at my direction."

Wright and Jones followed behind, turned on the lights, and began a systematic search of an office in which they really expected to find nothing. They all felt it unlikely that Garrison would hide evidence of his crimes there, but they had to rule that out for certain.

They began gathering personal mementos, ostensibly as evidence, but also to keep them from becoming collectors' items on the sicko internet market. Family pictures, sports trophies from college and a high school yearbook were among the things the two detectives boxed up for a later look. They also took Garrison's county computer, and would be running it over to the State Patrol's Computer Forensic Unit to see what might be there.

Miles away, at the Garrison house, an alarm sounded.

"MOTION...DETECTED" came the robotic female voice. Even though he was home to hear the announcement, Garrison's personal cell phone also vibrated with a similar text. *"MOTION... DETECTED."*

Kitsap County's IT department had every single county computer locked down so tightly you couldn't even connect a new printer without an administrator log-in. The IT security director had come from the military and knew his stuff. Not only did they want to keep out hackers, but they wanted to make sure employees didn't secretly add unlicensed programs to their network.

Garrison however, wanted a way to monitor his office at night. And while completely crazy, Garrison was not stupid. If he'd asked IT to set that up, somebody would have wondered why.

His solution was the twenty-four-hour-a-day Wi-Fi system that he'd pushed for in his role as the county's most business-friendly elected official. He didn't intend or insist that it operate twenty-four hours a day, but figured correctly that nobody would think to turn it off each night.

The councilman simply hid a Wi-Fi camera in his office, connected it to the system, encrypted the video, and let it run continuously. At the receiving end, he set up a motion alarm on his home computer. Two nights a week Garrison's alarm system was tested as the janitor cleaned his office. Otherwise the system had given him assurance that no one was sneaking and peeking. Until tonight.

"Somethings up!" called the FBI agent watching the house from behind. "Our target just got a lot more animated."

"Nastygram from a citizen?" replied one of the agents in the truck.

"Nope. Gotta be worse than that. He's really bouncin' off the walls…waving his arms…pacing around the room. Looks like he's sending a text."

He was.

"THE END TIME IS NEARING" was all it said. The recipient would know the meaning, and act accordingly.

Jones' phone rang while they were still in Garrison's office.

"Deputy…Jones, is it? It's Pete Davis, FBI. I'm out behind your target's house. About two minutes ago the guy went from calmly sitting at his computer to going completely ape."

"About two minutes ago, we walked into his office and started our search," was Jones' reply. "I don't believe in coincidences."

Jones started looking around as Wright and the sheriff continued what they thought was a simple search of an office. They eventually picked up that Jones was looking for something specific, but they couldn't tell what. Fearing that any hidden cameras also had hidden microphones, Jones had stopped talking.

On one shelf of his office Garrison had a collection of decorative birdhouses, in homage to his hobby of bird-watching. A careful look showed one with a power cord out the rear. Jones lifted the house to find the Wi-Fi camera underneath. The lens was pointed through the hole on the front. Jones gently pulled the power cord from its connector.

"I don't know what you just did," the Davis said, "but if it's possible to be even more amped up, he is. We're watching from the woods out back and he just ran downstairs at light speed. He's out of sight now…wait…a basement light just went on. He's down there now, screwing with a wood stove. Hang on a sec." The FBI agent switched from phone to radio.

"Hey…our guy is pretty lit up by something. The locals just hit his office and it's like he was watching or something. Can you see the light in his basement?"

"Got it," was the reply from the van. *"That's on your side, but we*

can tell there's a light on. It's confusing. With the slope of the property, what looks like a basement to us is probably a ground floor on your side."

"I'm on the phone with the locals. About two minutes ago our target started acting really strange. Turns out that was just as they went through his office door back at their courthouse."

Jones could hear both sides of the radio transmission over the phone.

"Hey...hey...you there?" He got the Davis' attention. "I just found a Wi-Fi camera hidden in his office. He was probably watching us. Do you guys have peace officer status?"

"I don't get what you mean 'peace officer status?'"

"Wait one," Jones said, still holding the phone to his mouth. He turned away from the now disconnected camera. "Sheriff...do FBI agents have peace officer status? They're federal agents but our warrant was issued by a state judge. Can FBI agents kick in Garrison's door based on a state warrant?"

"I think so. The sheriff's association went to the legislature after 9/11 to get them peace officer status." He walked over to the corner of the office where Jones was standing. "Why do they need to hit the house?"

Jones showed the sheriff the camera. "The agent out back says he's firing up a wood stove."

"God, yes. Have them get in there now. He's probably destroying evidence."

Jones went back to the phone. "FBI agents have peace officer status under Washington law. That means you can legally act on a state warrant. We think this guy's kept trophies from his kills and he's probably gonna burn them. You gotta get in there and freeze things. Don't search, just keep him from destroying evidence."

"No can do. I have to check with my SAC to make sure that's legal. I mean, I trust you, but I have to cover my butt."

"We really need you to get in there, man."

"I get it. I'll be quick, and call ya right back. Gotta go." The agent hung up and immediately re-dialed Jim Keiron.

"Sir, it's Davis, out behind that county guy's house. Yeah, something's gone sideways. The guy's gone ape and the locals think he's destroying evidence. They want us to hit the house... something about FBI agents having 'peace officer status' in Washington. I just transferred here. I don't even know what that means."

"It means their legislature passed a law that explicitly says FBI agents are the same as city or county cops. You're good to hit the house. My question is whether you can do so safely. What have you got for resources?"

"There's four of us here, and a couple more waiting in chase cars in case he split. Nobody's armored up. My partner and I are in camouflage and everybody else is in soft clothes. Is this high risk?"

"If you call arresting a serial killer high risk, then yes. You're not the type he kills, but nobody knows what he'll do if he's cornered," Keiron said.

"Boss, the smoke from the chimney just changed color. He was burning wood, but now the smoke's black and we're getting a plastic-y smell out back."

"The county's right, he'd destroying something. You're on the scene. If you think you can kick the door safely, I'll back you."

"We're on it…gotta go, sir." The agent hung up the phone and grabbed his radio. "All units, hit the house. The locals have a warrant and the target is destroying evidence. Chase units, converge on the house. I say again, hit the house. We need everybody."

The two agents hidden in the van were out like a shot, their pistols drawn. They'd shout "FBI, open the door," but a shoe would hit the lock just as the "r" in door was spoken.

The two agents in the woods, who were at least wearing military-style police uniforms, went directly to the ground floor back door. As they approached, they could see into the basement family room area of the house. Councilman James Garrison had a plastic bag of what looked like women's lingerie, and he was throwing items into a woodstove as fast as he could.

"FBI, search warrant!" the agents called. "Open the door…now." The nice thing about military-style uniforms is that they include heavy boots. As Davis said "now," his partner planted a size 11 boot next to the lock, and it immediately gave way. The two men went inside, just in time to see Garrison bolt through a door to another room.

The two heard a loud bang and only well-ingrained fire discipline kept them from squeezing off rounds. The two agents who'd been in the surveillance van had just kicked in the front door, one floor up. Knowing that Garrison had been in the basement, they hurried downstairs.

Once all four agents were together, they realized they'd made a huge tactical mistake. There was help on the way, but there were only four agents on the scene. All had been in such a rush to stop the destruction of evidence that all four were now clustered in the same room. A couple blasts from a shotgun could kill them all, and worse, there was no one holding a perimeter outside.

The next crash the agents heard was not a door being kicked in, but one being blown out. The door through which Garrison had fled led to the garage. He'd started his Mercedes SUV and simply driven it through the garage door. The chain from the door opener had fallen and wrapped itself around an axle. Garrison was rocking the car from drive to reverse, and the chain was reaching its breaking point.

"Chase units, how far out are you? The target's made it to his car and is in the driveway! I can hear him revving the engine."

The closest chase car, a non-descript older Honda, was half a block away, just as Garrison got the SUV loose. He punched it, and cornered wide getting out of his driveway.

The agent driving the much smaller Honda didn't try to ram Garrison, but also didn't try to avoid him. "This is gonna hurt," he said to his partner as the two vehicles collided nearly head on. The smaller Honda took the worst of it, and both agents got solid punches from their air bags. Stunned, they now lacked any ability to defend themselves as Garrison stepped uninjured from his larger vehicle.

The four agents who'd been inside the home had gone upstairs and through the shattered front door almost simultaneously. They saw Garrison, armed with a handgun, taking aim at their stunned and helpless fellow agents.

The two SWAT agents were the first to get off shots, and they could see Garrison stumble as their rounds hit home. But they were nearly one hundred feet away. Getting hits at all was masterful work. But handguns don't have the knockdown power of long rifles. Garrison, wounded multiple times but still standing, turned to face them.

"Drop it. Drop the gun. Do it now!" the agents yelled.

Garrison pointed the gun to the side, away from the agents. He was careful to avoid pointing it at them and giving them a reason to shoot again. He raised the gun quickly to his own head, and fired a single shot into his temple. His last act of defiance was to kill himself rather than letting a heathen do the job.

Davis went immediately to the body, and kicked Garrison's gun away from his lifeless hand. "Jesus...check on the guys," he shouted. "Are they OK?"

One of the surveillance agents ran to the small Honda, and saw his colleagues just beginning to regain their wits. "You back among the living?" he asked, trying to exude calm.

The driver, still groggy, was able to ask if he'd really heard gunfire.

"Yup. Davis and his partner saved your life. The dude you rammed was going to shoot, and they got him from over there," he said, pointing toward the porch. "They got good hits and distracted him enough that he decided to blow his own brains out."

"This was supposed to be just a sneak and peek," the driver said. "What the hell happened?"

"We don't know...we gotta make some notifications."

———————————

"911, what are you reporting?"

"Some guys just assassinated my neighbor," the caller yelled into the phone. "He's a county councilman and they just cornered him in the street and fired a bunch of shots."

"Wait...slow down...I need you to calm down and tell me where this is happening."

The caller provided his address and a brief description of the four men—two in sweatshirts and jeans and two "hit men" in military style uniforms. He was too panicked to notice or recognize the large "FBI" on the back of the camouflage uniforms. The call-taker hit "send," and the information was routed to a radio operator for dispatch.

"Information all on shots fired," the dispatcher began. She gave the address and other pertinent information. "Multiple shots fired...one subject down in the street. Caller says there are four suspects, two in battle fatigues...still on the scene. Caller described it as an 'assassination.' Victim is supposedly a county council member."

Every single on-duty deputy in Kitsap County heard that four men with guns had just assassinated an elected official. In a world of mass shootings and homegrown violent terrorists, they didn't know what to think. But they all knew they needed to be there, and nobody wanted to miss the action.

One thing that marked Elroy Patterson as a "cop's cop" was that even after being elected sheriff, he kept a police radio on his belt. Even when he was meeting about budgets or employee discipline or political issues, he kept one ear on his radio. Hearing the call go out, he grabbed the microphone clipped to the epaulet of his shirt.

"Car 1, WestCom. There is an FBI surveillance team at that location. Those individuals are likely agents. Broadcast that info and get an acknowledgement. We likely have friendlies on scene and armed."

The dispatcher swore under her breath. "Damned arrogant feds," she thought. "They're supposed to tell us when they do stuff, so this doesn't happen." Only then did she push the foot pedal that opened her microphone and she began to transmit.

"All units…Car 1 reports friendlies on scene. Armed individuals may be FBI agents. Use caution." She went on to confirm that each unit dispatched had gotten the word. She didn't want to trigger a friendly-fire tragedy because a deputy's siren had drowned out his radio.

As the sheriff was wrapping up that conversation, Jones was back on the phone with Agent Davis.

"What's going on out there? We're hearing you had shots fired. You guys all OK?"

"We've got two agents knocked around when the guy rammed their car. They'll be OK. The rest of us all got off rounds but the guy killed himself. He did his own coup de grâce. We wounded him but didn't…"

Jones interrupted the man, who was now acting on adrenaline left over from the shooting.

"Davis…stop. Don't say another word. I'm really glad you're OK, but there's a process to follow after a shooting. You shouldn't be telling me anything until you've talked to a lawyer."

"You're right. We're OK and your target is dead. We'll freeze our scene and hold everything for you."

"Our scene is inside, yours is out," Jones replied. "Do you have a couple people who weren't in on the shooting who can go in and clear the house?"

"Yeah…look…we can talk about the house, right? He was inside with this sack of ladies' underwear and was throwing them in a basement woodstove. I've seen some stuff in my day but that was weird. Were those the trophies you were talking about?"

"Yup. Sick, huh?"

The agent looked around. "One of your deputies just arrived. I'll let him know to go clear the house."

"Easy! He might not want to hear that from a suspect in a shooting. The 911 caller thought you were some kind of assassination team. You got badges and logos on?"

"Yeah, we're good."

Jones took two steps toward the sheriff and got his attention before speaking back into the phone. "I'll have the sheriff get on the radio to let them know you're cool."

The sheriff picked up the cue and got on his radio. "Car 1, WestCom. We've confirmed those are FBI agents on the scene. Have the first arriving deputy let me know everything is secure."

"57...I'm just arriving...these guys have badges on...I'll make contact and confirm."

"Car 1, 57. When you get a second deputy on scene go clear the house. We've got detectives en route."

It had only been five minutes since the sheriff, Wright and Jones had gone through the door of Garrison's office. Now, their suspect was dead and a very large cat was climbing out of its bag. Pretty soon everybody would know that James Garrison was, for reasons likely never to be clear, the killer he'd described as a chimera. The sheriff knew he'd be able to prove the "what," but doubted he'd ever know the "why."

As Jones and the sheriff had been working radios and phones, Wright had continued gathering and boxing items. He knew things were going to get busy, but he was disciplined enough to get key items in an evidence locker before heading out. They needed to get to Garrison's house, and soon.

"We can't just lock this door," Wright pointed out. "His staff has keys, and so do the janitors. Anyone could get in here,"

"We're flat out of road deputies," the sheriff responded. He got on the phone and reached a jail sergeant who was very surprised to be hearing directly from the sheriff himself. A very short conversation followed, and a corrections officer was soon standing in front of the door to Garrison's office.

The three men went downstairs to get organized before heading to the Garrison residence. Wright was hurriedly putting boxes in the evidence room and Jones took a moment to look at his computer. The retired cop at Garrison's cell phone company had turned the request in record time. Jones didn't have time to go through it all, but flipped through the texts to see if there was anything interesting.

There wasn't.

CHAPTER NINETEEN
And Then the Other

It was as if the entire community had exhaled at once. While it created quite the media frenzy and a huge black eye for the region, the revelation that James Garrison was the Chimera Killer had lifted a black cloud from over Kitsap County. Not lost on anyone was the fact that Garrison himself had given the killer his nickname.

Oh, there were recriminations. The sheriff was asked repeatedly "how could you have missed a killer in your own building?" The truly nutty suggested a conspiracy—that the sheriff was in on it. But the national news networks had finally left town, the county council had appointed a replacement for Garrison, and life was starting to get back to normal.

After so many horrific scenes, Bryce's mom had decided there needed to be a "family day," when Bryce wasn't training or running off to searches. A trip to downtown Seattle would be the perfect Saturday for her and her two men. They could park their car on the Bremerton side, and walk on the ferry. They'd arrive rested and refreshed, and ready for a walking tour of the Emerald City.

With gentle pressure from mom, a.k.a. "nagging," Bryce had agreed to skip his team's regular training day. Things had indeed calmed down since Garrison's death, though they knew it was possible more bodies could still turn up. The sheriff's office had far more missing reports than it had bodies.

Bryce agreed to visit Seattle without Katie, something that surprised his parents. Ever since that first meeting over a freshman's bloody gauze, the two had become inseparable. Well, except when Sierra separated them by nuzzling in between.

Katie had been visiting her father, but was expecting to return later in the day on Saturday. She and Bryce would be able to go out that night.

Bryce's interest in the day picked up immensely when he learned that all his favorite sellers of outdoor clothing and search gear had brick-and-mortar stores in downtown Seattle. He'd been used to ordering online, based on what other SAR members recommended. His folks didn't mind the expense, but suddenly realized that Bryce was shopping like a girl! They practically had to drag him out of the first store on a leash. Bryce's mom pointed out they were on foot, and would have to carry everything they bought.

"Well, we could buy that backpack and carry everything else in there." Bryce's seventeen-year-old sense of logic was in fine form.

"Um, that would be 'no," was his mother's firm reply as they left the store.

The day progressed to lunch at the Pike Place Market, and a short walk up to Westlake Mall. The Monorail would take them from there to Seattle Center, and the elevator at the Space Needle. The line was surprisingly short, and the ride up was accompanied by the operator's running commentary about the structure.

From the observation deck at the 500-foot level, one can see most of Seattle and across Puget Sound, back to Kitsap County. What the Finn family couldn't see was the sheriff's office kicking off a ground search around a newly discovered body. It was assumed to be a victim of Garrison's, and everyone expected there would be others. In this case, a mushroom picker had stumbled across the remains. Wright wanted to make sure there were no other bodies in the area.

The Finns, on their rare family day, were unaware of all that. They ooh'd and ahh'd at the views, looking through the telescopes and reading the various displays set up to explain the Seattle landmarks they were seeing. Not all the sights were outside the Needle.

"The people-watching here is fantastic," Bryce's dad whispered to his mom. "The girl over there has a piercing that's incorporated into her tattoo. I didn't know you could do that."

"I don't know why someone would, but I think I know why *you'd* find it interesting," was the cold, wifely reply.

The watching of scenery outside and people inside finally ran its course and the Finn family decided to head home. They were about halfway down the Space Needle elevator when Bryce's phone rang with the familiar "Rescue Me!" ringtone. He listened to the recorded message, with his parents scowling at him from each side.

"It's a 'Digger' search," he told his parents quietly, so as not to upset others on the elevator by using the word 'cadaver.' "They've apparently found another one and want the area checked. Any idea how long it'll take to get back?"

"Not a clue," Bryce's dad answered. "I guess it depends on the ferry schedule. We'll just have to see when we get there."

Bryce texted back that he'd be delayed by at least a couple of hours, but would be there for a later assignment if necessary. He almost never missed a mission, so nobody could give him any grief over being late.

He'd be later than he could have imagined.

The monorail to Westlake was quick, and the walk from Westlake to the ferry terminal took less than half an hour. But once there, Bryce was dismayed to learn they'd just missed a sailing. The next boat wouldn't leave for an hour and twenty-five minutes. Adding the one-hour crossing time, Bryce would be delayed by another two and a half hours on top of the time they'd already lost.

"I don't know whose body they found, but the funeral will be over before I get there," Bryce lamented. His head knew that he'd always been a diligent searcher, attending almost every training day and search. But Bryce's heart wanted to be there, and hearts aren't rational.

Katie, on the other hand, was already en route. She'd come home early from visiting her dad and was looking forward to her regular Saturday evening date with Bryce. She kept her SAR backpack always ready and her mother was available to drive her to search base. She was on-scene just thirty-five minutes from the time of the call.

The incident commander for the search was Deputy Jason Link. It would normally be Wright's to run, but he and Jones were still going through items they'd seized at Garrison's house and office. The "trophies" had all gone off to the Crime Lab. They hoped that DNA would help them identify the total number of victims, including any whose bodies hadn't yet been found.

At this same hour, Wright and Jones were back at the office, going through other evidence. Records from the cellular company confirmed that Garrison was indeed out of cell range when the trail runner saw Maria Santiago being led into the woods. There were no charges to any of his credit cards that would place him elsewhere at the time of the killing. At his autopsy, the Medical Examiner had identified a major cut on his arm that had mostly healed before his death. They checked with the trooper who'd arrested him for DUI, and he'd recalled Garrison's arm having a bandage.

Best of all, they'd found a single cufflink in the Garrison home that matched the one Sierra had found at the scene. Their best guess was that Santiago had fought back, scratching Garrison's arm and ripping the cuff link loose.

In other words, the pieces were falling into place. All of the evidence they had pointed to Garrison, and not one thing pointed elsewhere. Wright was somewhere between "comfortable" and "happy" about Garrison's death. He certainly thought Garrison got what he deserved, but would preferred to have taken a crack at him in an interview room.

After looking at so much evil, Jones needed a break. Something light. He began going through the souvenirs from Garrison's office. How could a guy who'd been a high school sports star, and a bird-watcher for God's sake, turn into a rabid serial killer?

Over at search base, Link saw Katie arrive and start to unload gear from her mother's truck. He was used to seeing her with Bryce.

"I got a text that Bryce and Sierra will be delayed," he called to Katie.

"I think they were doing a family day over in Seattle," she

responded. "I don't have to wait around for him…I can do whatever you need."

"OK, that works. I might have to put you in the field with someone else. Thanks for your flexibility."

"Sure. Let me know what you need." Katie stepped away from the command post and let Link get back to planning the search.

As Katie waited in base, she saw Alan Granger arrive, but paid little attention. He arrived alone, with no one from his team as his support person and navigator. His competitive drive to make finds was so annoying that even his own teammates didn't want to work with him.

The problem on this day was that Link had just been to a seminar. Regardless of one's field of endeavor, seminars are dangerous things. People assume that anything learned at a seminar must be better than the old way of doing things.

Link was no different. He'd gone to a SAR conference in neighboring Oregon, and come back with a laundry list of good ideas to "improve" search effectiveness in his county.

At the top of Link's list was that no K9 handler should ever go out alone. He'd heard the story of a police officer who'd drowned in less than six inches of water after slipping and hitting his head. Searchers walking through the woods are always at risk of tripping or slipping, and in western Washington, there's almost always six inches of water to land in.

Handlers have their dogs with them, but dogs don't have thumbs. If a handler falls and is knocked unconscious, their dog can't use the radio to call for help.

To Link, this search was a perfect time to try his idea. Katie was an experienced K9 support person, having worked with Bryce for many months. Granger arrived with no support, so it would be easy to pair up the two and get them in the field.

So Link thought.

"I've worked for twenty years without support and I have no interest in starting now," Granger argued. "I move fast, I go where I go, and it's not always the easiest way through the terrain. It won't work if I have to keep stopping and waiting for some teenager to catch up."

Katie didn't want to work with Granger either, except that his criticism pushed some buttons.

"I can keep up, sir. I've worked with Bryce, I know to keep my mouth shut and not bother your dog. If you fall down and hit your head, I'll get on the radio. That's it." She amazed herself by arguing for an opportunity she didn't really want.

Link finally ended the discussion.

"It's not a choice. Alan, you'll be taking Katie with you and you'll be reasonable in your expectations of her. Katie—you're young and fit and I expect you to keep up and not distract Alan's dog. I'll have an assignment for you in a moment, so I suggest you get acquainted."

Granger resigned himself to leaving base with "the girl," but the minute she fell more than forty feet behind he'd send her back to base. Katie, for her part, knew she'd have to find a balance between crowding Granger and falling too far behind.

"If you use the radio, use my call sign," was Granger's direction to his new K9 support person. "And if you use the radio, it better be because I'm dead."

"I'll just leave my radio off," she offered brightly. "You won't have to worry about it."

"Do what you want. I won't *worry* about it either way." Granger saw that Link was waving him over. "I'll be back," he said, and strode over to the command post.

Link was arranging search areas for the various dog teams that had showed up, but he'd forgotten that Granger liked to pick his own area.

"I was thinking of having you clear the area around our command post with your dog, and then take this area just to our south," he told Granger. "I think those are the high probability areas."

"I'd prefer to go long today. How about this area out west?" was Granger's reply.

"Well, I'd figured Bryce could handle that when he gets here," Link said. "It's low probability, and since he's going to be late, he can work that."

"I'd prefer to work it. Just a feeling."

"OK...I'm good with people having 'feelings.' You'll take the more distant area and I'll have somebody else clear what's closer in. I might put Bryce in next to you, a little east, if nobody's gotten to that when he gets here."

"Whatever."

Granger returned to his truck and jerked his head in Katie's direction. "Let's go."

"Where's my map?" was Katie's response. "Everybody on the team gets a map."

"You don't need one. I'll do the navigating and you're just along because that wet-nose deputy says you have to be."

Katie was not going to be intimidated. In fact, she'd asked for the map knowing the response she'd get. She had decided to put some limits on how she'd be treated.

"If you go over a cliff, how will I know where we are? Everybody on the team gets a map, that's fundamental. Link wants me with you, but I'm not leaving base until there's a map in my map case. I can go ask him if you're not comfortable..."

"Oh for God's sake..." Granger's voice trailed off as he turned on his heel and headed back to the command post. When he returned, he all but tossed the paper map at Katie.

"Thanks," was her only reply. She took a moment to put her name, date and time, and the state mission number in the margins. If they found anything, the map could be evidence in court and she wanted to be as complete as possible. Without another word, they set off down a logging road to their search area. The near-side boundary was a small stream. After crossing a small bridge, the area to be searched would be on their right.

As Katie and Granger were leaving base, Bryce and his family were in the middle of Puget Sound, making their way to the Bremerton ferry terminal. Bryce was at the very forward end of the passenger deck, outside the double doors, leaning over the rail looking into the wind.

"The back of the boat arrives the same time as the front," his father offered. "Standing out here won't get us there any faster."

"I know, but I'm worried. I know Katie's at the search, and I don't know who they're sending her out with."

"Young man, are you jealous? I think you can trust that she won't run off with some other searcher before you can get there."

"It's not that. But Alan Granger is probably there, and I don't want her going out with him. There's been talk of requiring every handler to have a support person. If I'm not there, she might get assigned to him."

"Is he that jerk that always has to outdo everybody? I don't see the problem."

"It's not the competition. There have just been some things happening that don't add up." Bryce lowered his voice, even though there was no one around. "He's finding people who've been murdered, but NOT finding missing people who should have been right under his nose. He tried to convince the deputy there was no blood at the Tiger Lake site, and we know there was. And last month he knew a body I'd found was face up with its arms folded across its chest. How could he have known that if he'd never seen it?"

"You're not suggesting...I mean, they found the killer. He's dead. He killed himself in the presence of six FBI agents."

"I know...it sounds as if I don't like the guy so I'm making him out to be...something. I just don't have a good feeling and I don't want Katie out with him."

"That's bizarre, but it'll be moot in another hour. We'll be ashore, get you home, and you and Sierra can head out."

"Not soon enough," was Bryce's response. He never stopped looking across Puget Sound, to the opposite shore. When they arrived, he was the first one to the family car. In the back seat with his mother driving, Bryce fidgeted the entire time.

It took them about twenty minutes to get home, and Bryce another ten to get the Suburban packed and Sierra loaded up. His worst fear came into play when he finally arrived at base and learned Katie was indeed out with Granger.

He asked to take Link aside, at the rear of the communications van.

"Look, Granger's been a little weird lately," Bryce offered. "Can we have our radio operator check on them?"

"He's not a 'little weird.' He's a temperamental ass." Link acknowledged. "But he's a competent searcher and there's no reason to pester him while he's in the field. You can ask the radio operator when they last heard from him if you want."

"It's not his temper I'm worried about." Bryce lowered his voice and Link could tell he was conflicted. "Didn't I hear in class that one of the ways you identify criminals is because they know something they're not supposed to know?"

"Yeah, but what's that got to do with..."

Bryce took a breath. If he was going to take the leap of saying such a horrible thing, he'd go in with both feet.

"It felt weird, but at that last search...Granger knew something. When we got back to base he said somebody my age 'shouldn't be seeing bodies face up with their arms across their chest.' He'd never been to the scene, I didn't tell him or anyone else, and I doubt the detectives told anybody."

"You're right." Link said. His voice started to reflect some real concern. "Posing of the body is usually kept pretty secret by the detectives. They don't even share that kind of info around the department. I hadn't heard it, that's for sure"

"My point. Here's what I've seen. The only bodies Alan Granger has found in the last year have been related to these murders. He's missed other bodies, like at Fragaria, that were right under his nose. Now that I think about it, it's all been happening since he got his latest dog. He retired his Shepherd and got that Malinois. That dog hasn't found squat except for dead murder victims..."

he's got no live finds."

"Wright and Jones already got their man and he's dead. This is a pretty serious allegation and one I think you should keep to yourself. I will *discreetly* mention this to Wright and Jones and they can take a look...but you'll get yourself in deep tapioca if you start..." Link's cell phone rang and he looked at the caller ID. "Well, speaking of Wright and Jones."

Link didn't say hello, he answered cold. "I wondered where you've been. We've got a little cadaver search going out here and you're usually involved. This is a pretty big show and I'm a little overwhelmed."

"Well stand by to go from a little overwhelmed to completely overwhelmed. Where's Mason 20?"

"Wait a minute? Granger? Bryce was just talking about him." Link turned away from Bryce, went into the command van and shut the door. "What's going on?"

"We're going through Garrison's stuff, and just got around to his high school yearbook. Guess who else's name starts with G?"

"Holy crap. Bryce was just telling me some stuff he'd noticed. This is too weird. You think they were buddies in high school?"

"We don't know yet. I haven't looked to see if they signed each other's book or anything. But it fits with lots of things, like the Santiago girl disappearing from her murder scene."

"I thought Garrison did that," Link responded.

"We assumed he did that, and then returned to get arrested. But what if he was there as a distraction..."

"...while somebody else was moving the body?" said Link, finishing Wright's sentence. "Dammit. I've got Granger out alone with Katie Lovering as support. Do you think he knows we're onto him?"

"You need to call them both back to base right now. Calmly. Have the radio operator do it so he doesn't pick up on any stress in your voice. We're on the way."

"We'll be waiting for you," Link said. "I'll make some excuse and keep him busy until you get here. I don't know enough about this case to start asking…um…wait, I do know something."

"What would that be?"

"Bryce Finn was just here. He shared that Granger knew something about a body he found that Granger shouldn't have known. Something about hands across the chest?"

"Oh, God. Maria Santiago had her hands folded across her chest. We haven't told anyone. Bryce and the coroner are the only ones who should know. And one gal from CSRT. You're saying Granger knew that?"

"According to Bryce, anyway. The kid really felt bad making the accusation but he had some other observations too."

"You can fill us in on that when we get there. Jones and I are thirty minutes out. Get Granger and that girl out of the field."

"On it. Bye." Link turned to the van's radio operator. "We need to get Mason 20 back to base. When was the last time you heard from them?"

"I was just coming to get you. There was some yelling on the radio—female—but they never gave a call sign. I checked status on every other team and the only one not answering is Mason 20."

"Crap." Link reached for his own radio, the one that talked to dispatch not SAR.

"137, WestCom. I need Code 3 backup here at search base. I need everybody you've got, including Bremerton and Port Orchard… and I need a sergeant to approve a SWAT activation. We have a missing SAR member who might have been abducted. Get on the horn to the State Patrol and get them ready to launch an AMBER Alert if we need one."

Link's next step was to leave the van and talk to Bryce. He wasn't sure what he was going to say, but in the end it didn't matter. Bryce was nowhere to be found. The back of his Suburban was open, as was the door of the kennel inside. Bryce and Sierra were both gone. Link went back in the comm van and told the radio operator, "Get Dog 44 on the radio and tell him to return to base. Now!"

Bryce heard the call, but paid it no attention. He wasn't sure what he'd do if he found Granger or even what might be necessary. He might be wrong about his suspicions and the garbled radio call might be merely the result of a dead battery. But he would go with his gut and worry about consequences later.

Bryce had told Sierra to "find Katie." Although Sierra wasn't a trailing dog, she had done some trailing as a puppy, before Bryce really knew what search and rescue was all about. She had certainly found Katie enough times to know what she smelled like, even without a scent article. Sierra was headed west, down the logging road where Katie and Granger had walked. She was running at top speed, her canine sense picking up on the tension in Bryce's voice.

After about three quarters of a mile, Sierra slammed to a complete halt, leaving skidmarks in the dirt. She looped back sniffing both sides of the road and finally went into a break in the roadside brush. Katie had turned off the road there. Sierra followed Katie

318

and Bryce followed Sierra. The path, through lighter portions of brush, made sense. It went where someone would have walked while searching the area.

About 200 feet off the road, Sierra broke into a small clearing, and stopped. She circled, sniffing first the air and then the ground. She eventually put her nose behind a small bush, turned to look at Bryce, and sat.

"Whatcha got, girl?" Years of training made Bryce put a happy lilt in his voice, to keep things positive for the dog. But he was clearly concerned that Sierra would be finding anything at all.

"A map? Good girrrllll. Somebody dropped a map," he said to Sierra. The map was partially ripped, but still appeared fresh enough to be from the day's search. Bryce aligned the torn sections and then noticed, in the margin, Katie's name and the date. They'd gone this way, but how did Katie's map get torn? And why was it on the ground?

Bryce had dashed out of base before being given his own map. He was simply following Sierra's nose. Having found Katie's map confirmed they were in the right area. Sierra continued to work due north, moving quickly, shifting from a trot to a full-on dead run. Bryce knew that if she found anything, she'd come get him. Eventually, Sierra was so far ahead that Bryce couldn't even hear her bell. Fortunately, he was making enough noise crushing brush that, if Sierra tried to return, she'd have no trouble finding him.

Bryce was beginning to tire, and had fallen a couple of times trying to run through the brush. As he picked himself up the third time he heard Sierra's bell returning, along with barking that he knew to be hers. Something had her especially excited.

Sierra raced up to Bryce, skidded to a halt with her butt on the ground, and never stopped barking. Before he could say, "Show me," Sierra had spun and begun running back where she'd come from. Bryce did his best to follow, falling once more before starting to catch up with Sierra.

Sierra's bell had stopped, but the barking didn't. It was a high pitched yelp that Bryce had never heard before. Sierra had clearly found something she didn't like, and was very worked up about it.

Bryce entered a clearing to find Sierra sitting next to Katie, who was face down on the ground. She was breathing, but barely.

"Katie...are you OK?"

"He was going to kill me," Katie muttered, "He told me I might be his last one, but that he'd send me to Hell with the others. He took off when he heard Sierra's bell."

"Don't move...let me get some help here." Bryce got on his radio, his voice breaking.

"B-b-base...Dog44Katiesbeenattackedweneedhelp."

"Dog 44 this is Base, we can't understand you. Who's been attacked?"

Bryce took a deep breath, and tried to calm himself. He couldn't help Katie if base couldn't find them.

"Base, Dog 44...I say again...Katie's...been...attacked. We need help."

"Attacked by what? Is there a bear out there?"

"Dog 44...it was Mason 20 and I don't know where he's gone. He's beaten Katie half to death and we need help."

Link stepped up behind the radio operator, and gently took the mic from her hands.

"We gotcha, Dog 44. You're doing fine and I've got the cavalry

coming. But we need to know exactly where you are."

"We're in the eastern half of Mason 20's area. Just come west out the road until you cross the little bridge over the stream. That's the eastern boundary of the area. Go another two or three hundred feet and turn north. Just keep coming and start yelling…we'll be able to hear each other."

"Dog 44, Base. Understood. Be sure to take some GPS coordinates when you can. Do you have a condition on Katie?"

"Dog 44, she's groggy but talking to me, there's blood all over and I need to get to work on her."

"Base understands. We've got help headed your way. If you spot Granger let us know. Did he have a weapon?"

Bryce turned to Katie, who was becoming more lucid. Sierra had not moved from her side.

"Did Granger have a weapon?"

"No, he just beat me and beat me. Why would he go off like that?"

"I don't know, but everything's going to be OK." Bryce keyed his microphone. "Base, 44, no weapon seen."

"Understood, thank you. Break…Base to all teams…return to Base immediately and stay together while you're getting here. Nobody goes anywhere alone."

Each of the other teams gave a quick acknowledgement. They'd all heard the radio traffic and although they didn't have the full picture, they knew something was drastically wrong.

Link got back on the radio. *"Mason 20…I know you're listening. Wanna talk to me?"*

Silence. Bryce continued listening as he tried to assess Katie's injuries. She'd been beaten horribly, but not stabbed or shot. Granger did all his work by hand.

"Mason 20, we've got it all figured out. I don't know why you and your buddy did all these things, but it's over. Let's get this resolved without anybody else getting hurt."

More silence. Bryce took a moment to get on the radio.

"ESAR 57, Dog 44…channel two." Dennis, ESAR 57, was back at base coordinating ground search teams.

"57 copies, switching to channel two."

"ESAR 57, Dog 44 on channel two."

"57."

"Katie's been beaten pretty badly. The only reason I think she's alive is that Sierra interrupted things. But she's not going to be able to walk out. I need you to arrange a pack-out whenever the deputy thinks it's safe to get out here."

"Understood. We'll have it all staged and ready to go the minute it's safe. I'll see if we can get an escort, in fact. I'm hearing a lot of sirens in the distance, so I assume we'll have lots of protection here soon."

"Soon as ya can. Back to one."

"57, back to one."

When Bryce turned the channel selector on his radio, he was surprised to hear Granger's voice, in full psychotic rant.

"…needed to be eliminated from the earth. We made a holy pact to rid this earth of the unwashed, the unwanted, and those who pollute their human temples with drugs."

322

Link had been trained as a hostage negotiator, but nothing could have prepared him for the stream of murderous nonsense he was hearing. In the woods, Bryce and Katie could only listen to their radio.

"OK, Alan, I get your concern," Link responded. *"But what about Katie? She didn't deserve what you did to her."*

"A small sacrifice…a final sacrifice before I go to my own judgment."

A final kill for your twisted mind, Bryce thought. This man just needed to kill, and his attempt to justify it through some fantasy cleansing of the earth was…well, fantasy. He'd become exactly the mythological fire-breathing monster his buddy had referenced. But this Chimera…these two Chimeras…were not myth.

Katie was starting to drift out of consciousness again. Bryce used his thumbs to gently lift her eyelids and saw her pupils were of unequal size.

"57, 44, back to two."

"57 copied."

"57's on channel two."

"44, Katie's out again, and her pupils don't match. She was awake for a while, but I think she's got a brain injury that's getting worse. I need to get her out of here right away."

"Understood, but we're being held in base. There are some cops with long guns getting ready to head out, but they've got to get a team together. Most of these guys aren't used to working in the woods."

"OK, I'm going to try to carry Katie your way. Tell them we'll be coming up the main road once we get out of this brush."

"Do you think that's safe? What if she's got a spinal injury?"

"I know, but if she dies because her brain swelled up, the spinal injury won't matter. I don't like it either, but if Granger comes back, I'm not sure I can protect her. It all adds up to us getting out of here."

"57 copies. I'll let 'em know you're coming. Back to one."

Bryce rolled Katie face down and then raised her waist by her belt. That allowed him to wriggle his head and shoulders under her torso. Katie was draped across the back of his neck and shoulders, much as a fireman or soldier might carry an injured colleague. Bryce was able to get first one knee, then the other, under him. He stood up, staggered in the brush, and realized that just getting her to the road would be difficult.

He'd go slow. He wanted to go fast, but dropping Katie on her head could be the end of it. One of three things would happen: They'd make it out, help would arrive, or Granger would return to finish his earlier work.

Using both hands to keep Katie draped across his shoulders meant that Bryce didn't have a free hand for his compass or GPS. He could easily be forced off course by heavy brush or the falling darkness. He could end up going parallel to the road, or even make a full turn and go completely the wrong way.

"C'mon, Sierra. Let's go back to the truck." Sierra had led him out of the woods before but never was the need so great. Sierra seemed to understand that there was big trouble afoot and bounded south with no hesitation.

The going was slow, with the unconscious Katie over his shoulders. Bryce had to look down for every step, lest he roll an ankle on a rock, or step in a hole. About halfway back to the road, something flashed in the corner of his eye. A Belgian Malinois in a search vest. It was Granger's dog.

324

"If his dog is here, Granger isn't far behind," Bryce thought. *"Nothing I can do but keep going."* Carrying Katie meant Bryce couldn't turn his head to look behind him. His footsteps made enough noise that he didn't hear the second set of boots coming up behind him.

The push from behind wasn't hard, but it didn't need to be. With so much weight on Bryce's shoulders, a gentle breeze could have blown him over. Alan Granger was not a gentle breeze. Bryce went down over a log, with Katie on top of him. He felt his left forearm snap, robbing him of half his ability to defend himself.

"You little twerp! You've interfered with my destiny for the last time," Granger screamed, continuing to spew nonsense. "You'll both be nothing but cobblestones on my path to heaven."

Bryce slid out from under Katie and rolled face up, to see Granger kneeling over him with a rock. He rolled to the side and the blow missed, and he tried punching Granger in the groin with his uninjured right hand. The blow was easily turned aside, as Granger had done so many times before.

A second time Granger raised the rock, but there was a bright flash and Granger was knocked to his right. The flash wasn't gunfire—there had been no sound. The flash was the reddish blonde hair of Sierra's coat as she body-slammed the huge man in the side of his chest. She now had the arm with the rock in her teeth.

"Good girl, Sierra. Get him!" Bryce cried. Granger screamed even louder, and tried using his other hand to pull Sierra off him. It didn't work, and his movements only sank Sierra's teeth deeper into his bicep.

Bryce tried to get up but was suddenly knocked down a second time. Granger's dog had shouldered him aside as it went to the defense of its master.

The Malinois tried to grab Sierra by the neck, but got only collar. It pulled and shook its head back and forth as dogs do when killing prey. Sierra was slowly being pulled off of Granger, who was now using his free hand to reach for the folding pocket knife that he carried in his chest pack.

Granger needed his other hand to actually open the knife, but Sierra still had that arm firmly in her teeth. She was losing her grip, tooth by tooth, as Granger's dog continued to pull at her neck. In a few seconds, the larger dog won and Granger's arm was free.

Sierra was now in a dogfight for her own life. The Mal's prey drive had kicked in, and he would not let the dog who'd attacked his master simply walk away. The two rolled through the brush, snarling and snapping, each trying to sink a fatal bite into the other's neck.

Granger, in the meantime, had used his injured arm to open the knife. Bryce could see the anger in his eyes as he raised himself, and Bryce tried to shield Katie as Granger stepped toward them.

This time the flash of light was accompanied by sound—a very loud sound. Two more flashes and two more sounds and Bryce could see three bloody dots start to soak through Granger's shirt. Granger went face down, his head at Bryce's feet.

Bryce turned to see Deputy Link with his gun drawn, a small wisp of smoke coming from the barrel. An entire team of officers was behind him, with guns drawn as well.

"Get the dog!" Bryce cried. "He's killing Sierra." The two dogs had continued to roll around, snarling and biting. Both were covered in blood, and it was impossible to tell which dog it had come from.

"Don't shoot!" Link told his team. "Pepper spray! Try to get the Mal, but if it gets on the Golden, we'll deal with it."

A Bremerton officer stepped from behind Link with his can of spray at the ready. As the dogs rolled, the Mal opened its mouth to grab Sierra and the officer shot a perfect stream right down its throat. The dog snorted, stepped back, and lunged forward a second time. A second blast, this time in the eyes, got the dog to back off. It moved away, eyeing the humans who had just inflicted such pain. The dog was clearly still in attack mode, and not just at Sierra. The humans involved were now in danger.

"OK, they're separated. Shoot if you have to," Link ordered. He got on his radio. "WestCom, 137. Shots fired, suspect down. We have multiple injuries. The scene is secure and EMS can come on out."

"Do you have officers shot?" came the dispatcher's reply.

"No, we have two searchers beaten and a K9 injured. Our suspect is deceased. And if somebody has a catchpole in the car, we need that for the suspect's dog. If not, get animal control started out here."

ESAR 57 heard that the scene was stable, and was moving his crew without needing to be told. He had a question though.

"Dog 44, ESAR 57, you copy?"

Bryce used his unbroken arm to reach for his microphone. A weak "Dog 44" was all he could muster.

"57 here. Sounds like you've got multiple injuries at your end. I've got one litter en route, but we have the old one in the back of the truck. Do you need a second?"

"44, I can walk out, but Sierra's pretty chewed up. She and Katie

327

are the two pack-outs. Can you also have somebody ready to get Sierra to the emergency vet?"

Link, standing near Bryce, heard the conversation and interrupted. "Tell him to get the second litter out here. We have a deal with the fire department that they'll transport one of our patrol dogs if they're injured. I'll ask 'em to do the same thing for Sierra. Katie has to go in the first one."

"57, 44. Get the second litter. The deputy will arrange transport if you can get Sierra out to base."

"57, on it!"

In the worlds of law enforcement and SAR, there's not much difference between people and their dogs. They're all loved, and when they're in trouble, everyone comes to their rescue. The teams got the second litter assembled and out of base in record time.

Katie was just being loaded into her litter as the second team arrived with the litter for Sierra. Both would be carried back to base.

Bryce's arm had been splinted, slung and swathed and he walked alongside the litter talking to Sierra. "Thank you, girl…you saved Katie and me both today." Sierra didn't know what the words meant, but all dogs recognize tone of voice. She was in shock, but looked at Bryce and panted slowly.

"Good girlllll," was all Bryce could add. He started to choke up. The two creatures he loved most in the world were now being carried out of the woods by his SAR buddies.

He tried to hurry ahead to the crew carrying Katie, but moving quickly jostled his arm which was now starting to really hurt. He finally caught up to see Katie still unconscious, and a look of concern on the face of the paramedic leading the operation.

"Katie, I don't know if you can hear me, but you're going to be OK. You're going to Harborview where they have the best docs on the planet. I'll be there as soon as I can."

The two litters arrived at base to find rescuers lined up along the road in. Those not needed for the operation were standing quietly and respectfully along the sides of the road. Spontaneously, applause broke out as the litters went by.

"We love you, Katie!" one older teen called as Katie's litter passed. "You're going to be fine!" another said.

As Sierra's litter passed, the clapping continued, and there were more words of encouragement. Virtually everyone had something to say for Sierra. "Good girl!" "Yay, Sierra!" Somebody squeaked a dog toy, and Sierra wagged her tail—about the only part of her that wasn't bandaged.

As it turned out, Katie was not transported by aid car. The paramedics had decided that unequal pupils equaled an airlift to Harborview. The helo was already on the ground as Katie was carried into base. The crew carrying her had set her litter on the ground, waiting for the flight nurse's direction to load. Bryce went up to the litter, and kneeled down beside it.

"I really *hope* you can hear me," Bryce said over the noise of the engine. "Almost losing you taught me that I never want to lose you...ever. I want you in my life for my whole life, if you know what I mean. I can't wait till we're old enough to make it official... but we'll know..." His voice trailed off as the engine got louder.

The flight nurse signaled that they were ready to load, and Katie was transferred from the Stokes to a more traditional gurney. Bryce wasn't finished but Katie needed to go. In what seemed like a flash, the 'copter was gone, headed east to Harborview.

Bryce turned to see Sierra being loaded in one of the aid cars for her trip to the vet. He tried to board, but was stopped by another paramedic.

"One of your other handlers...I think Maggie's her name...will ride with us and handle everything at the vet clinic. You need to go with these other medics. They'll get you down to the clinic at Harrison to get that arm x-rayed and properly splinted."

Bryce knew the medic was right, and Maggie was totally capable of advocating for Sierra at the vet. There would be decisions to be made, but Maggie would act in the best interest of the dog. Besides, the adrenaline was starting to wear off. He was suddenly exhausted and his arm hurt worse than ever.

"You're right. This really hurts," Bryce said as he walked toward the second aid car. "Can you give me some pain meds?"

"The hospital can and we're not that far away," said the medic, gently guiding Bryce in the right direction. As they walked, a familiar voice called to Bryce.

"Hey, Lefty, you trying to steal my nickname?" It was Lefty, who'd also been called to the search. He was pointing at Bryce's broken left arm.

"Hi, Lefty. They called you all the way here from Yakima?"

"Yeah, we pulled into base just as things were getting out of hand. The deputy told me what happened. Nice find, kid."

"Thanks..."

"That gal who hid for you...the one who was in the wrong place. Y'know, she was right."

"I'm not remembering...?"

"At your recert…what she said, after you found her in the wrong place. She was right. If anybody in MY family goes missing, I also want you and Sierra looking for them."

CHAPTER TWENTY
An Awakening

Bryce and Sierra strode into the lobby at Harborview Hospital as the very definition of "walking wounded." Bryce had a cast on his arm, and Sierra was sporting several bandages, a couple of shaved spots with stitches showing, and what most people call a "cone of shame" around her neck.

"That's a cone of heroism, now," the security guard at the front desk said. He'd been told to expect the little golden retriever and not to turn her away as he would most animals.

"She earned the right to wear that contraption, you know," he said to Bryce.

"Yes, sir," Bryce replied. "Can you tell us how to get to…I don't know what to call it…the head injury section?"

"Nope, not gonna tell you. I'm going to lead you there. It will be an honor to walk with you and that dog. Everybody's heard the story. I'll bet you're not getting much sympathy for the arm."

"Yes, sir. Everyone asks about Sierra and hardly mentions the arm. It's fine, anyway."

The guard had an assistant relieve him at the front desk, and very proudly led Bryce and Sierra to the elevator. "How's your girlfriend?" he asked.

"They told me she's awake and wanting to see both of us. That's why I brought Sierra."

Bryce wondered briefly what dogs think of elevators. They walk into a little room and the doors shut behind them. When they walk out of the little room, everything's different. To them, it must be as if they've been magically beamed to another place. Maybe there's a little Scottie dog at the controls of some machine....

A nurse was waiting as the three of them got off the elevator. She looked at the guard and said, "I'll take them from here," as if wanting her own moment with the two heroes. The guard took his cue to leave, but did so slowly.

"You be safe Sierra, and come back anytime you want." He kneeled down to Sierra's level. "Just see me at the front desk and you're in, OK?"

Once again Sierra couldn't comprehend the words, but reacted to the tone of voice. She nuzzled up to the guard and shed her reddish-golden hair all over his blue uniform pants.

"My own badge of honor," he said. "I'm never washing these pants."

"Katie's room is this way," the nurse said, trying to move things along. "She's awake, you know."

"Yes, ma'am. They said that. How's she...is she...does she know where she is?"

"She most certainly does. She also knows that you and Sierra aren't with her, and she's been crying for you both. It's a good thing you got to her when you did. I don't know all that happened, but the docs said one more knock on the head and she probably wouldn't have survived."

"Sierra did that, ma'am. She scared Granger off while he was beating her."

"I shouldn't tell you this, with all the privacy rules, but it was very close. The docs did a wonderful job, and got drugs in her to reduce the brain swelling. Stopping the attack was one thing, but if you'd taken any longer to get her out of the woods, it might have been too late. Her brain was really swelling up."

They arrived at Katie's room and the nurse stopped at the door, motioning Bryce inside. Katie was stable and the nurse knew there was no medical need to intrude on such a private moment.

Bryce and Katie looked at each other and simultaneously burst into tears.

"I'm sorry I wasn't there. If we hadn't been in Seattle…"

"Stop…this wasn't your fault. You and Sierra saved my life. I'm a big girl, and it made sense for Link to send me out with Granger."

"Link saved both our lives, you know," Bryce responded. "You were out of it, but Link showed up just as Granger pulled his knife…" Bryce couldn't continue with the description of what happened.

"My folks told me. My life was saved three times that day. Sierra scaring off Granger, you carrying me out of there, and then Link. I suppose you had to see Granger get shot."

"Uh-huh…"

The pause was long, and awkward. Katie spoke first.

"Why did he do this to me...and the other girls?"

"You realize it was 'them,' not 'him," right? There were two killers."

"*They* didn't attack me. Granger did, and I don't know why."

"I asked the sheriff, and he doubts any of us will ever know why. People go nuts all the time, and do horrible things. What's weird about this case is that they were both nuts, and both had the identical delusion. They wanted to rid the world of impure..." Bryce stopped himself.

"He said you were 'incidental,' and a small sacrifice," he rushed to say. "He didn't try to claim you were like the others they killed."

"I get it. And...?"

"Well, the cops say they took turns doing almost identical killings, so they could each have an alibi. They thought the cops would be looking for a single killer, so they'd keep each other off the hook."

"It almost worked." Katie looked down at Sierra and for the first time realized how seriously she was injured.

"What happened to you, girl?" Katie started crying again.

"Sierra knocked Granger off me, and grabbed his arm. Granger's Mal went to its master's defense. The cops had to use pepper spray to get him off Sierra."

"Oh girlllll...we're a pretty busted-up group, aren't we?" She turned to Bryce. "How's the arm."

"Fine. How's the head?"

"I still have a headache and a little double vision, but it's getting better."

"The nurse said it was close."

"Well, I was out for most of it, so I don't know. What I do know is I hope you'll do a little better when you propose to me for real."

"Wait...what?"

"It's like they say. Even though I was out, I could hear everything you said. I want you in *my* life too...for my *whole* life."

The only time Bryce had ever said that to Katie was while she was unconscious. He knew she must have been hearing him to know the words.

"I couldn't see anything, though," Katie added. "Were you at least on one knee?"

"Both knees, actually. I mean...you were on the ground, in a stretcher."

"Well, no matter. You got that part right. But the next time you say something like that to me there'd better be a ring involved. And with a rock on it, understand?"

"Yes, dear."

ABOUT THE AUTHOR

The author with his current search dog, K9 Ruger.

Robert "Bob" Calkins has been a search and rescue dog handler in Kitsap County, Washington, for more than a dozen years. He currently searches with Sierra's younger brother Magnum, a nine-year old Golden Retriever. He and his dogs have responded to everything from routine missing person cases, to homicides, to the horrific landslide that in 2014 swept over homes in the tiny community of Oso, Washington.

He is the author of the Sierra the Search Dog series of books for children and adults.

ABOUT THE REAL SIERRA

Sierra was Bob's first search dog, a Golden Retriever with the well-known "Golden smile" and a natural ability to find people who'd gotten lost. She liked nothing better than running through the woods hoping to pick up the scent of a missing person. Her paycheck was a simple tennis ball, and a scratch on the head. She worked with Bob for five years, responding to many missing person searches in and around western Washington.

Made in the USA
San Bernardino, CA
11 April 2017